REAPER

OF

SOULS

by Jo Harthan

*The entrance to Standedge Tunnel at Marsden
in West Yorkshire.*

1

Rye Top Farm was located at the end of a long gravelled drive on the edge of Saddleworth moor. It had long since passed out of use as a farm and was surrounded only by ramshackle outbuildings and bleak moorland.

The interior of the house was dark except for the light coming from the Ghost Hunting App on Sarah's phone, which she was holding out in the direction of the kitchen. The App was graphically displaying EVPs, or electronic voice phenomena to the uninitiated. The display, in the form of a histogram, showed the strength of electromagnetic anomalies and it was going crazy, flashing bright red and emitting a continuous clicking sound. It was telling them that a strong electromagnetic field had manifested by the kitchen door. In the background was the constant hiss and crackle of static.

"What's your name?" Stuart sounded too confident. They both understood what the colour red meant—an angry spirit that will do everything in its power to instil fear. This place was too remote to be taking chances. Sarah hadn't forgotten what had happened to Kylie.

"Tell us your name. You can talk to us."

There was an eerie glow shining through the doorway from the kitchen. It hadn't been that bright when they'd started. Stuart said it was just moonlight and told Sarah not to start freaking out on him.

"We mean you no harm...just want to talk." He was always so cock-sure, never had any patience for her misgivings.

The clicking intensified and was followed by a rasping voice that hissed from the phone. The name *McKenzie* flashed up in the text box on the App.

"Did Mr Waite tell you his mother's name?" Sarah asked Stuart, not taking her eyes off the phone.

Mr Waite was the owner of the property. He had told them that a stream of short stay tenants had talked of strange goings on and he had now decided to sell. Although he didn't think there were any such things as ghosts, which made a nice change as most of their clients were willing to believe anything, he said his mother, who had lived at the farm all her life, had been an avid believer.

"I'm curious," Mr Waite had said on the telephone. "If it is haunted, it is probably my mother and I'd be very interested to hear what she has to say before the sale goes through."

"No." Stuart replied in answer to Sarah's question, before adding with a hint of sarcasm. "But it wouldn't have been McKenzie would it?"

The phone was still flashing red and was now vibrating intermittently with such strength that Sarah had to use both hands to keep from dropping it.

"Did you die here McKenzie?" The tone of Stuart's voice betrayed his excitement. When Stuart got fired up, he took chances, pushed boundaries. Like he had done with Kylie that night in the tunnel.

Murder.

"You were murdered?"

Nothing.

"Please answer yes or no."

No.

"So you weren't murdered?"

Sarah interrupted, she knew exactly what this meant, "You mean *you* murdered someone?"

Yes.

This time the voice was clear, there was no need to look at the text.

"Who did you murder?"

The speakers hissed again but no text appeared. It sounded like laughter.

Stuart repeated Sarah's question. "Who did you murder?"

You. The voice was crystal clear. There was no doubt about what they had just heard.

"I'm switching it off," Sarah said. "There's something wrong here."

Stuart grabbed the phone from her, pushing her away.

"No way, this is mega. If you're freaking out, Sarah, you go and sit in the car. I'll handle this on my own."

Sarah hated him when he acted like this. He knew full well she wouldn't leave him on his own. That was their golden rule, a code of conduct drawn up when they started these psychic investigations.

"You don't scare me, mate." Stuart's voice was too loud against the backdrop of the empty room. "You can't harm us. Why don't you tell us who you murdered."

Nothing.

"You still here?"

Stuart motioned for Sarah to pick up the electro-magnetometer that was sitting on the only piece of furniture in the room—a Regency-style table that had seen better days. He motioned with his eyes for her to move the machine closer to the doorway that led through to the kitchen. There was still a faint light seeping through from there but it seemed to have dimmed a little. Perhaps the moon had gone back behind a cloud.

Sarah picked up the machine with trembling hands, feeling the tension rising. Her gut was telling her to think of Kylie. She could feel her body gearing up for fight or flight; a feeling that was happening too often lately. She hoped she could hold things together long enough to see this through.

She picked up the device and carried it across the room, placing it at the carpet edge that marked the boundary between the two rooms. Even before her fingers let go, the machine began to flash red and blue. That meant the energy was growing, spreading. This was not good. She turned to Stuart.

"I really think we should go. This feels like bad energy."

Perhaps he was too engrossed to hear her or perhaps he was choosing to ignore her.

"Can you give us more information, McKenzie? About who you are."

lee

"Do you mean Lees? Is that where you lived?"

dead

"You mean that's where you're buried?"

A barrage of incoherent voices, different from the first, came from the phone as the display began to flash up words in quick succession.

help . . . falling . . . damned . . . bad shore . . . more

"Sorry, we need more than random words."

The phone had started to vibrate again in Stuart's hand as the signal intensified. The rasping voice they had heard initially sounded loud and clear again.

Fear me.

"I'm not afraid of you, mate. You can't harm us."

1 . . . 8 . . . 4 . . . 9

"I don't understand. Is that a date? Explain please."

Sarah

"You want to talk to Sarah?" Stuart motioned for Sarah to approach but she shook her head.

"I'm not comfortable with this, Stuart."

"Just ask a question," he snapped. "For God's sake, Sarah, this is what we came here for."

not God

"What do you mean 'not God'." Even as Stuart spoke the words, Sarah wished he hadn't, for she knew the answer.

demon

The electromagnetic field detector in the doorway began to flash red, sending dancing shadows cavorting across the walls.

"Oh shit," Stuart exclaimed, his eyes fixed on the phone screen.

"What's wrong?" Sarah yelled, rushing over to where he was standing. He held the phone out so she could see.

The word *Appearing* was flashing in the text box.

2

Kylie was at home washing the dishes when she got the infernal whistling in her ears again. It had started that night in the tunnel and had never left her. She began to sing; it sometimes helped.

"Sssshh...." Josh, her boyfriend of six months, was lounging on the settee watching his favourite soap. She glanced over at him and began to sing louder. This was her flat. She could do as she pleased.

It had been Stuart's idea to go inside Standedge tunnel. There hadn't been any reports of anything untoward but he thought it might be a prime site for activity and suggested they check it out as he'd discovered there had been over fifty deaths recorded in there between 1811 and 1944. He said it would be a good training exercise as real hauntings had been a bit thin on the ground. Kylie wasn't blaming Stuart but, with him having more experience than any of them, he really should have been more prepared. Then again, he was so sceptical; always reminding them that ninety percent of all paranormal activity was nothing more than natural phenomena or the imaginings of an unbalanced mind. Kylie wasn't even sure that he believed that what had happened to her was real. He had accused her many times of being too irrational. 'Question, question, question' was his mantra. He was a science teacher, so she supposed he was worried about his credibility. But sometimes he went too far the other way.

She had heard the whistling just as they had entered the tunnel. She didn't know then what it was. She knew now. It was Ron, a benign spirit—irritating but harmless. He must have been warning her of the malevolent spirit inside the tunnel, the one that had attacked her; the one she had taken home with her. It had been an attachment that had made her life a misery—causing pictures to fall from walls, unexplained banging noises, slamming doors, making things disappear and then reappear somewhere else. More than once, she had rushed to answer the land telephone only to hear silence on the other end. Martyn, the fourth member of their paranormal investigating team, had said it was a poltergeist and he had exorcised it. The activity had reduced after that but it hadn't stopped completely and, in the end, she'd had to move house in the hope that it wouldn't follow.

So far, it seemed that it hadn't. But psychic attachments can be crafty. They know when to lie low.

She hadn't told the others about Ron. If Stuart knew about him, she'd get a lifetime ban; no more psychic investigations for her.

Despite her singing, the whistling seemed to be getting louder. The last time it had happened, the photograph of her mum, that hung on the wall in the lounge, had slipped to one side for no reason. She had rung her mum immediately to discover she had just scalded herself on a hot pan.

It was always something bad. The day she moved into her new flat, the whistling had been unusually loud. She received a phone call later that day to tell her that one of her uncle's had died of a heart attack.

Sometimes it alerted her to what seemed to be good things, like the time she heard the whistling as she thought about her sister. A phone call revealed that her sister had moved in with her boyfriend at exactly the same time that Ron had commandeered her ear canals. It hadn't taken much digging for Kylie to discover a history of abuse of former girlfriends. She'd got on the phone to her sister immediately but so far her warning had gone unheeded.

So what was it tonight? She looked around the kitchen wishing Ron would shut up. He'd got his message through, why carry on? She began to sing 'Yesterday' at the top of her voice. He didn't like that song, it seemed to make him morose, but it usually quietened him.

There was nothing out of place. She would finish the dishes and then make a tour of the flat. There would be a clue somewhere; there always was.

"Kylie, you really do have a shit voice."

"Cheers mate, love you too," she shouted over her shoulder. She'd given up caring what he thought. It was hard loving a man who never took you seriously.

"Load of bollocks," he had said when she first told him what she did for a hobby, though it was far more than a hobby to her. Kylie considered their investigations into the paranormal as semi-professional, after all they had been called upon before today to perform banishments for people who were convinced they had a haunting. One lady even paid them a hundred pounds because she was so pleased with the result.

She had told Josh about Ron weeks ago but he had just laughed. She'd not mentioned it since. He had never been very sympathetic of her 'irrational fear' as he called it and had dismissed most of the problems she'd had after that night in the tunnel. He didn't believe in the paranormal, so that didn't help. His mind was closed and he flatly refused to open it, even a chink. Give him his due though, he had been there for her on all those dark nights when she hadn't wanted to be alone because of the inexplicable, frightening things that were happening in her old flat.

She began to sing more loudly. Josh turned up the sound on the TV.

3

Stuart and Sarah looked from the phone to the doorway. The phone was still flashing but nothing was happening.

"If you're still here McKenzie...I'm closing this session down." Stuart didn't sound so confident anymore.

There was no response.

He looked at Sarah and she nodded her approval. They had never had an appearance before and this was something they hadn't prepared for, especially as there were only the two of them.

Martyn was supposed to have joined them with his PSB-7 spirit box but he hadn't turned up, despite having texted earlier to say he would be here. Martyn was the one who knew how best to deal with aggressive spirits—having been brought up in the Catholic faith he knew all about exorcisms and had even witnessed one as a boy, though every time he told that story it did change slightly with added embellishments each time so it was difficult to know what was actually true. But Martyn was never fazed by anything that happened and he had been the one to deal with Kylie's psychic intruder—though none of them really knew if he'd managed to get rid of it completely.

10

Stuart closed down the App as Sarah turned on the LED torch they always carried with them and made her way back to the doorway of the kitchen to switch off the EMF detector. It gave out a sudden burst of energy as she approached and then fell silent and dark. She picked it up.

"It's red hot, Stu. Do you think it's malfunctioned?"

"I'll check it when I get home. Maybe that's what the App was picking up."

They packed up quickly, in silence, only breathing more freely once they were outside and loading up the car.

"Check the phone," Stuart instructed. "See if anything's followed us."

Reluctantly Sarah pulled the phone from her pocket and tapped the Ghost Hunter App. Sweeping the phone around a full three hundred and sixty degrees, she noticed her hand was still trembling and wondered again if it was time to give all this stuff a rest.

"It's green and flat-lined," she said with relief.

Jumping into the passenger seat, she was already thinking about the hot mug of cocoa she'd have as soon as she got back to her warm, ghost-free pad.

She wondered whether Stuart was planning to spend the night at hers again. She hoped he wasn't; he'd kept her awake most of last night and she was in need of a good night's sleep. She used to be flattered by his insatiable appetite for sex but these days she didn't find it as alluring as she once did. It wasn't that she was going off him; that would never happen, at least she thought not, it was just that her priorities were shifting.

With her mind thus occupied, she hadn't noticed him struggling to start the car.

"What's wrong?"

"Sounds like the battery's flat...fuck me...I only had a new one put in last month."

Sarah's heart sank. She could feel the tension mounting again.

"Can you fix it?"

The scornful look Stuart gave her told her that he couldn't. There he was again, making her feel stupid. What did she know about cars anyway?

Without a word, he reached for his phone, tapping in a number.

"Who're you calling?"

No answer. That was her cue to keep quiet. She knew Stuart well enough not to piss him off further.

It was soon clear that he was calling a breakdown service and Sarah thanked God for his sensible side. If this had been Martyn's car they would have had to push it to the nearest garage. Martyn was a skin flint and a scatter brain most of the time and it would never occur to him to take out breakdown cover.

After a few automated messages and lots of tapping in numbers, a woman, with a cheerful voice, that was so loud Sarah could hear every word, said someone would be with them as soon as possible but it may be up to two hours.

"You should have let me call," Sarah said when the conversation was ended. She was trying hard not to sound reprimanding. "We're in the middle of nowhere and I could have said I was a woman on my own. They come out quicker then."

Stuart didn't answer. He had fallen into one of his moods, drumming his fingers on the steering wheel like an arsy teenager.

Sarah jumped as her phone announced the arrival of a text.

"It's Kylie...asking about Martyn."

She texted back. *Martyn hasn't turned up*.

Why not?

No idea don't care i'll ring you when i get home.

Sarah got out of the car. Out of all of them she was the one most susceptible to energy changes. People in a bad mood are like angry spirits, they give off bad energy that can spread like a virus, infecting everyone around them. Stuart should know better.

She walked over to the house, standing in front of the window of the lounge where they had set up their equipment.

Something was different, wrong. She took a step closer just to be sure. The moon had gone behind a cloud and it was difficult to see anything clearly but there was no question about it. She called out to Stuart but he didn't make any sign to show that he had heard. She walked back to the car and opened the passenger door.

"Stuart, you've got to see this."

13

4

As soon as Kylie walked back into the lounge she saw it, causing her heart to miss a beat.

Martyn had holidayed in Mexico last year and had brought back a figurine of an Aztec warrior for each of them. He said it could be the mascot for their psychic work, a sort of protective talisman. Stuart had told him that the Aztecs used to rip the heart out of their prisoners whilst they were still alive and he didn't want some blood-lusting native protecting him. He had refused to accept it, which Kylie thought was rather ungracious and very rude, but that was Stuart all over. When Kylie had moved into her new flat she had almost discarded hers, discreetly of course, she would never do anything to upset anyone on purpose, but at the last minute had felt uncharitable and changed her mind, placing it on top of the TV. It was now lying on the floor in two pieces next to a cushion that should have been on the settee.

"What happened?" she asked Josh who was still engrossed in his soap, feet stretched out on the settee.

"Dunno. Probably vibration. Perhaps a lorry went past."

"No it didn't," she yelled. "Is this your way of getting back at me for singing too loud?"

"Don't be stupid, Kylie. And shut up, I'm trying to watch Corrie."

Grabbing the remote, she turned off the TV.

"Go and watch it at your own place."

"What have I done?"

"I'm sorry Josh, but I won't be told to shut up in my own flat. And anyway, I want some peace and quiet."

Not much chance of that, she thought. Ron's whistling was getting louder.

Josh looked hurt. "You finishing with me?"

That made her feel bad. She shouldn't have spoken to him like that. But she felt anxious. She needed to think. "Of course not. I'm sorry. I just need some time on my own."

"Feels like you're throwing me out."

She felt like screaming at him to 'just go' but she didn't want to upset him any more than she already had. Instead, she handed him his jacket and forced a smile.

"Sorry, just feeling tetchy. I'll ring you later." As she steered him towards the door, her thoughts were with Martyn. Something was wrong.

As soon as Josh was gone, she grabbed the phone and dialled Martyn's mobile. It went to voicemail, prompting her to remember that there had been an investigation booked for tonight. She'd been excluded because Stuart had decided she needed a good three months off to recover from the trauma of Standedge tunnel. Her ex-communication was due to end next week.

No need to worry then. Martyn would be with Stu and Sarah. Whatever was happening, he was in good hands. But she texted Sarah anyway—just in case.

Sarah's reply wasn't reassuring. Something must have happened to Martyn. Despite what Stu and Sarah thought of him, he wouldn't let them down like that, not without telling them.

5

Stuart's arm was crooked on the door ridge and he was resting his head in his hand. He turned his head, "Just tell me...I'll decide whether it's worth seeing."

Sarah slammed the door and went round to the driver's side, yanking the door open, almost causing him to fall out.

"What's wrong with you?" he snapped. "For Christ's sake, I'm thinking."

"Well think about this," Sarah snapped back. "We closed the lounge curtains and now they're open."

Stuart grabbed the night vision camera that was lying on the back seat and leapt from the car, running over to the house with Sarah in tow.

"Turn the App on," he instructed, "and point it at the window."

As soon as the App loaded, the histogram was bright red and sounding angry with the clicks so close together that it was like one continuous scream. Meanwhile, Stuart had positioned the camera on the window ledge with the lens pressed up close to the window. A blinking red light showed it was recording in video mode.

"Can you see anything?" asked Sarah. "This App's going mad."

"I think we should go back inside," was Stuart's answer.

"We should ring Martyn," Sarah said. She didn't want to dismiss Stuart's idea out of hand, but there was no way she was going back in there without some protection.

"Martyn's a wanker. He's unreliable...hasn't even texted us with his latest excuse."

"Perhaps there's someone in there, Stuart. I've never heard of a ghost opening curtains before."

"Always a first time..."

Sarah decided it was time to disregard Stuart's lead on this. She closed the App and speed-dialled Martyn's phone.

"Fuck me," Stuart whispered. "Hear that?"

"It's me. I'm ringing Martyn."

"That's not you...listen."

Sarah cut the call and they both stood in silence. Nothing. Stuart looked at her with a quizzical expression. "Ring him again."

There was a delay of two or three seconds before they heard the tinny sound of the Star Wars theme tune coming from inside the house.

"Is he taking the piss?" Stuart had a right to be angry. If this was Martyn's idea of a joke he was for the high jump. Stuart fished around in his jacket pocket for the door key and stormed over to the front door. Sarah was behind him, torch in hand, flooding the area with light.

"He wouldn't do this, Stuart. He's not that stupid."

The lounge appeared to be empty. Sarah swept the torch light around but there was nothing and no one except the solitary table in the middle of the floor.

"The kitchen door's closed." Her voice was a little shaky. Stuart would normally reprimand her for that, tell her to pull herself together, but this time he didn't.

"You're sure you didn't close it before we left?"

"I'm sure."

"Ring Martyn again."

There it was again, the Star Wars tune, but this time it was louder and was accompanied by a bright light. Martyn's phone was lying on the floor underneath the table.

"Okay Martyn, you wanker...you can come out now." Stuart was livid. He kicked open the kitchen door. Martyn was in for a serious beating. Stuart wasn't known for his patience and wasn't one to back off from a fight. He had a brown belt in Taekwondo and wasn't a man to be messed with. Although he had never laid a finger on any of them, Sarah reckoned that might be about to change.

As Stuart entered the kitchen there was a terrific roar accompanied by a rush of freezing cold air that knocked Sarah to the floor. She could see Stuart leaning against the kitchen wall, making no attempt to help her. He wasn't even looking at her. And then suddenly he wasn't there anymore and she could feel someone pressing down on top of her. It wasn't Stuart; she was used to his weight. This guy was heavier and he didn't smell good. Whoever it was began to gyrate himself against her in a parody of love making.

"For God's sake, Martyn," she screamed. "Get off me."

Where was Stuart? What was he doing? She tried to struggle but found herself unable to move. She could hear laboured breathing and feel fetid breath on her cheek. Suddenly, a voice, husky and cruel, whispered in her ear, "I knew I'd get inside you." She thought again of Kylie in Standedge tunnel and then the world turned black.

6

Sarah came round with Stuart leaning over her, gently patting her face and calling her name. They were outside on a small patch of grass near the old barn with its creaking doors and dark shadows.

"Where's Martyn?" Sarah wanted to know. "Did you find him?"

Stuart was shaking his head. "He's not here."

"What happened, Stuart? What was that?"

"I honestly don't know, Sarah. Are you okay if I go and retrieve my camera...it's still on the window ledge...recording I hope."

Sarah grabbed his arm, holding on tight.

"Don't leave me."

"It's fine, Sarah. Whatever it was, has gone now. The camera's over there," he was pointing back towards the house. "You won't lose sight of me. I'll only be a minute."

With that he unclasped her hand and got to his feet. Sarah sat up, watching him and listening for any noise that might suggest they were not alone. There was nothing and Stuart was back at her side in no time.

"The breakdown guy is going to be here soon. So I suggest we go back to the car and wait. Okay?" He helped her to her feet. "By the way, your jeans are undone."

Sarah gasped and quickly zipped them back up, holding tight to Stuart as he supported her over the flagged yard back to the car. He eased her into the passenger seat with reassuring words. As soon as he slammed the door shut, she locked it. No protection against ghosts but what she'd just experienced had felt nauseatingly real.

She waited, expecting him to jump into the driver's seat at any moment. He didn't. He must have gone round the back of the car. She turned her head. There was no one there. Where was he?

She felt the panic rising, out of control, hyperventilating. Breathe deeply, she told herself, deep and slow. Keep it in check. Should she get out? Had something happened to him? She grabbed the door handle, fingers curling around the cold metal but then just as quickly withdrawing. Anything or anyone could be lurking in the disused barn or in the line of bushes that marked the boundary of the driveway. Fumbling in her handbag, she found her phone, but her trembling fingers couldn't manage the right pin number.

On her third attempt, the driver's door was suddenly snatched open letting in a blast of cold air.

Sarah screamed.

"What the fuck's wrong with you?" Stuart snapped as he slumped into the driver's seat.

Sarah was near to tears. "Where were you?"

"We left the front door open. I went to shut it. Mr Waite wouldn't thank us for leaving his property unsecured."

"You were gone ages."

"I thought I saw a light in the kitchen...I went in to check."

"What was it?"

Stuart was looking straight ahead, as if he didn't want to make eye contact with her. "It was the digital display on the cooker."

"But I thought the electricity was off."

"It is."

"So how can—"

"It can't. But it did. I pulled it out and checked the connections. When I switched off the socket, it flickered and went off."

"That can't happen, can it? If the power's off?"

Stuart shook his head. "No, unless it was a residual charge in the socket, but I can't see that. You were right...there's something bad here. And the car not starting, that's not right either."

21

"Is it worth giving it one more go?" Sarah said.

Stuart turned the ignition. The engine roared into life immediately.

"Seatbelt," Stuart said, releasing the hand brake. "Let's get the hell out of here."

Pressing his foot hard on the accelerator, the tyres threw up dust and gravel as they sped away, heading for the comforting lights of civilisation.

7

"I need a drink," Stuart said, pulling into the car park of The Waggon Inn. "You okay with that?"

"Sure." Sarah had long since forgotten about the hot cocoa, what she needed now was brandy and lots of it.

They saw Martyn as soon as they entered the pub. He was sitting with his back to the door, chatting to two uniformed Police Officers. Stuart motioned to Sarah to go to the bar and get the drinks. He walked over to Martyn's table.

"What's going on?"

"It's okay, he's a mate," Martyn said to the officer who had his hand on his radio about to respond to an in-coming alert. The officer got up and walked over to a quiet corner to take the call in private.

"My car was stolen," Martyn explained, "with me in it."

The remaining officer stood up in response to being called over to leave by his colleague.

"That's all we need for now, Mr. Curtis. We'll be in touch as soon as we have any news."

"That'll be never then," said Stuart. He didn't have much faith in the police since his Kawasaki 350 was stolen outside a burger bar three years ago and the thieves never caught despite being clearly visible on CCTV.

The officer ignored him and instead reached over to shake Martyn's hand. "We'll do our best."

Stuart sat down, looking long and hard at Martyn.

"Spill," he said as Sarah came over with the drinks.

"I was on my way home from work...stopped at the lights down Linney Lane when suddenly this guy jumps in the passenger seat and holds a knife to my throat...tells me to take a left...yelling and screaming at me...he must've been on something. Then he tells me to pull into the lay-by just before the turning for the M60. There's another guy waiting there. He yanks me out the car and shoves me in the back, holding a cloth to my face. Don't remember anything else until I came round a few hours later...lying in Taylor's field up on Church Road."

"So you never went to Rye Top Farm?"

"No, mate, why? What's wrong? Sarah? You look like you've seen a ghost."

"I tried ringing you...to see where you were..."

Stuart finished her sentence. "Your phone was inside Rye Top Farm, Mart."

"Hang on, let me get this straight. So my phone was where I was supposed to have been? That can't be coincidence. So the bastards must know me...must've known about our investigation."

"I texted you the address...they could have got it from your phone."

"We thought it was you messing about," Sarah said. "There were anomalies there..."

"Weird shit going down," Stuart interrupted, never one to mince his words. "We decided to call it a day when we started getting threatening EVPs on the App. We were ready to leave but the car wouldn't start. That's when Sarah noticed the curtains were open...they'd been closed before. We went back inside...that's when we found your phone."

"And then we were attacked," Sarah said. Speaking those words brought back the full recollection of what had happened to her. She felt she might burst into tears at any minute. "I felt like I was being raped," she said as a tear slipped from her eye.

She quickly brushed it away as Stuart took hold of her hand and squeezed it gently.

"She passed out," he said, "and we've come straight here, not had chance to talk about it yet."

"We need to get the police back," Martyn said. "They need to know about this."

"No!" Sarah jumped in, panicked by the suggestion. "We need to be sure about what happened first. There was no one there...it couldn't have been physical. I've got jeans on."

She glanced at Stuart, shaking her head. "The zip on these jeans is always coming down."

"You need to be checked out." Martyn was insistent, this was a side of him they'd never seen before. He was usually always joking, playing tricks, taking the piss.

Sarah got up to leave the table.

"Where you going?"

"To the toilet, where else? I'll be able to tell if anything happened. Won't be long."

"Want me to come with you?" Stuart had half risen from his seat.

"Don't be ridiculous."

He followed her anyway and waited by the door until she re-appeared.

"Nothing," she said.

Stuart grabbed her arm, whispering in her ear. "Are you sure...you know what it's like with me sometimes...in the middle of the night...you know...when you think you've dreamt it."

"I know when I've been fucked, Stuart, believe me. And anyway, where were you? What were you doing while I was being psychically humped?"

"Something had me pressed against the wall. I couldn't move. I could see you but I couldn't do anything."

Sarah could tell by the look on his face that he felt he had let her down. "So what did you see?"

"I saw something on top of you..."

"A man?"

He shook his head. "I don't know…a shadow. I felt odd, like I'd been drugged. I couldn't see properly, everything was dark...sort of blurry. And do you remember a weird smell?"

"It was from the thing that attacked me. It was vile."

"Didn't smell like a person to me, it was more chemical don't you think?"

"What, like some sort of gas?"

"Could've been but it smelled quite sweet...I'm thinking more like chloroform."

They returned to the table where more drinks were waiting for them. That was a first, usually Martyn was the last to buy a round and always needed reminding when it was his turn.

"Well?"

"The guys who abducted you, did they have a funny smell about them."

Martyn shook his head. "Faint smell of weed I suppose, but nearly everybody smells of that these days."

"What about the cloth they held to your face?"

Martyn shrugged. "Dunno..."

"They could have done the same to us, Sarah." Stuart was tapping into his phone as he spoke. "Look. I rang the AA at eight fifty. What time did we get here at the pub? Just before ten? So we must have left the house around nine forty five. That means we were back inside the house for well over half an hour. That doesn't add up."

He reached into his bag for the video camera. "Hopefully, this will have recorded everything."

"It was a psychic rape," Sarah said. "I don't know how or why but it definitely wasn't real."

"Depends how you define 'real', Sarah. You should know that."

Sarah knew Martyn was right. 'Real' was not necessarily just those things experienced by the five senses.

"Shit," Stuart had opened the camcorder screen. "It was only recording for a few minutes...and it's all black. Doesn't look like it picked anything up."

"This is what happened to Kylie isn't it?" Sarah was reluctant to admit what she had heard before she passed out, but recognised that it may be the most important clue they had to help them unravel the events of the night. "Whoever, or whatever, did this to me, said while it was happening, 'I knew I'd get inside you.'"

"We all need to write down everything we remember about tonight," Stuart said. He had his teacher's head back on. "Every little detail, independently, then we need to get together, without any alcohol, and sort this out. I think we may have stumbled on something we're not equipped to handle and we need to get our facts straight before we involve anybody else."

"But it doesn't make any sense," Martyn quizzed. "The guys who jumped me were bloody real, believe me. And they must have gone to Rye Top Farm after they took my car. Why did they go there? And why leave my phone there? I really think you should go to the police, Sarah. Whether it felt real or not, you were attacked and the guys who stole my car are implicated."

"I'm not going to the police, Martyn. They'll put me through an invasive medical examination and take swabs which will turn out to be Stuart, so they'll either arrest him for raping me or, if they find no evidence of rape, which they won't, I'll be accused of wasting police time. No thank you."

Martyn threw up his arms, "Okay...your call."

"Dead right." Sarah snapped before adding, more gently, "I know you mean well Martyn...thanks for your concern but let's just do what Stu said."

They quickly finished their drinks and left. Martyn declined a lift home, said he needed the fresh air. Stuart and Sarah watched him go, both of them concerned that they hadn't really asked him how he felt. He must have been terrified having a knife held at his throat. It must have crossed his mind that he wouldn't survive it.

"I'll ring him later," Stuart said, "make sure he gets home okay."

8

It was 3am and Kylie was sitting up in bed trying her best to make sense of the nightmare that had just woken her.

Why hadn't Sarah rung her back? Something was wrong, she knew it. She wanted to ring Josh, wanted reassurance that everything was alright. He was good at that, but after asking him to leave last night she wasn't sure she would be hearing from him again. Besides, he had to be up for work in three hours. She couldn't do that to him.

The bedside lamp was casting shadows on the wall that were scaring her, seeming to move when she wasn't looking at them.

Steeling all her nerve, she leapt out of bed and switched on the main light. Then she went out into the hallway, then the bathroom and the spare bedroom, switching on all the lights. From there to the lounge and the kitchen area, switching on wall lights and lamps until the whole flat was as bright as day.

She made herself a cup of tea and switched on the TV. The Full Monty was on a Freeview channel—that would take her mind off it. There was no way she was going to go back to bed.

It wasn't long before she realised she was watching and listening but not hearing or seeing anything of the movie. The nightmare would not leave her thoughts and the memory of what had happened in the tunnel was crowding in with such force that she found it impossible to stop it.

It was while she was making a second cup of tea that the thought occurred to her that she should write the nightmare down in as much detail as she could remember. Ron was whistling in her ear again, trying to tell her that it was important and she needed to tell the others. After all, they had all featured in her dream, one way or another.

Taking pen and paper from the drawer she settled herself down at the dining table and began to write.

'I was in a car with Martyn. We were stopped at traffic lights and when the lights turned green Martyn said the car had broken down and we'd have to walk. Then I was in a bathroom, not my bathroom, it was a house I don't recognise though in the dream I seemed to know every inch of it. Don't know what I was doing there but I suddenly noticed a flickering light coming from the lounge downstairs and there was a sound like static. I turned round just as a man lunged through the doorway. He put a knife in my hand and kept hold of it while he stabbed me, over and over again. I felt like I'd experienced my own death. I remember seeing my blood spreading over the tiled floor. But I didn't die because next thing I know I'm in a bedroom, in bed. I think it's the same house. I can hear Sarah. She's shouting up the stairs to me, telling me to get out of the house. Then Stuart's there, in bed with me. He's talking but I can't tell what he's saying. But then he changes and is not Stuart any more. He has a bushy black beard and horrible black eyes with no light in them. I want to scream but nothing comes out. He's laughing at a little girl who has just come into the room. Her eyes are lit up inside, as if she's got a torch inside her head. She's crying that she's lost and wants her

mummy. Then Sarah comes into the room and says that Lee is on her way. She puts her arms around the girl to comfort her. I try and get out of the bed but I can't, my legs don't seem to work. I'm lying on my back, can't move. Suddenly, the man with the beard is above me, near the ceiling, and he zooms down towards me as if he's come from a long way away. I wake up screaming.'

Writing the nightmare down seemed to make it more real somehow and Kylie felt even more un-nerved. It was as if the attachment she'd had before was back. Had it done something to Martyn? Had it hurt him? The black eyes gave it away. She had never seen the thing that had attached itself to her but, in her imagination, that was how she had always pictured it. Black, dead eyes that could suck you in and never let you go. Those eyes were like the entrance to a tunnel into Hell. Perhaps it had regained its strength and was seeking her out again. Perhaps tonight it had found her.

She put the kettle on again. She was shaking and nauseas, sweating profusely even though there was no central heating on and the room thermometer was only reading seventeen degrees. At least that meant there was nothing here.

She decided on coffee this time. She wouldn't be going back to sleep tonight.

Kylie's fears were confirmed the following morning when she rang Sarah to find out what was going on.

Sarah told her of Martyn's abduction but wouldn't be drawn on the details, saying they would discuss it at the meeting.

Their fortnightly meeting was scheduled for this evening and it had already been agreed that it would be held at Kylie's new flat.

They took turns to host and tonight's meeting had been ear-marked as a sort of welcome back into the fold after the suspension Stuart had imposed on her.

The reason he gave for her temporary banishment was that he had to be sure she had got over what had happened in the tunnel. Until then, he said she may be vulnerable to another attack and that could put them all at risk. He seemed to think she was the weak link in the chain, a magnet for anomalous activity, whether real or imagined.

Of course, he had never voiced that opinion, but it wasn't just her that knew what he thought. She could tell that the others did too by the way they looked at her sometimes.

She wondered if they talked about her behind her back; wondering if the haunting of her old flat had unhinged her; made her weird.

It had been tough being excluded from their investigations. It made her feel like an outsider. But all that was behind her now—at least it was providing she didn't mention Ron.

She cast her eye over her flat. Everything was prepared, the room tidied and dusted ready for the meeting. She had made a special effort by buying nibbles and two bottles of Pinot Grigio which she placed on the coffee table. This meeting would not only be to welcome her back but she also wanted it to be a celebration for Martyn's safe return after his terrifying ordeal. She imagined sympathy for him from Stuart and Sarah would have been in short supply last night. They didn't seem to realise that Martyn's happy-go-lucky persona was only a front to hide his true feelings.

As she plumped up the cushions on the corner sofa for the umpteenth time, she became aware that she was feeling anxious. She was relieved that Martyn was unharmed but the things Sarah had hinted at had brought back her own experience in Standedge tunnel, and the memory of that night had come flooding back in vivid Technicolor. She couldn't get it out of her head. Her heart was racing again, making her feel dizzy, the way it had done then.

She stood up and took a deep breath. It usually helped.

When it had happened before, she'd gone to the doctor's, frightened there was something wrong with her heart, thinking she might die at any moment.

"They're panic attacks," the doctor had told her, wanting to know why she was anxious. She hadn't told him the reason. If she'd told him what had happened that night, and all the weird and scary

33

stuff in her flat afterwards, he'd have been another one to think her crazy.

She'd left the surgery with a prescription for pills she had no intention of ever taking. And she never had despite the bangs in the night and lights being switched on and off. She hadn't been seeing Josh long then but she encouraged him to start staying over two or three times a week. She wouldn't be so forward normally but those were difficult weeks. Nothing ever happened when he was there. She tried to talk to him about it once but he just dismissed it, said it was her imagination. Said he didn't believe in 'all that crap' as he put it.

She never mentioned it to Josh again but their relationship, despite him staying over regularly, didn't seem as close after that. Kylie knew only too well that non-believers come across weird phenomena all the time but, because they don't believe, they are unaffected, explaining it away as something mundane, something to be misinterpreted by the gullible. Stuart, Sarah and Martyn were the only ones who understood but she hadn't told them everything. She didn't want Stuart putting doubt in her mind about the authenticity of her experiences.

The doorbell rang. She jumped.

It was Sarah and Stuart. They always arrived together despite maintaining they were not a couple and there was nothing going on between them. They looked like two bookends in their 'His and Hers' paranormal sweatshirts, which they always wore for the meetings. The slogan on the back pronounced

'Spirits are not just in bottles'. Kylie thought the shirts a bit tacky and refused to have one. Martyn was just a cheapskate; he didn't see why he should buy another t-shirt when he already had a *Jasper* one that he'd bought off ebay years ago.

"Martyn will be along later," Stuart said as he closed the door and removed his shoes—a ritual they all adhered to whether or not it was asked of them.

"You were at Rye Top Farm just off Knowl Top Lane last night?" Kylie said in greeting. "I don't know why you wouldn't let me go on that investigation."

Stuart looked at her with that hound dog, patronising look she knew so well and hated.

"You weren't ready, Kylie, not for a suspected haunting. It was too soon."

"I should have been the judge of that," she retorted angrily. "Who are you to say I'm not ready?"

"We all agreed at the very start that we wouldn't take any risks." Stuart's voice was marginally softer now and his tone a little more considered. "And you've been through enough lately. Unsettled spirits are attracted to vulnerable states of mind, you know that. And this is a big one."

"I'm not vulnerable," Kylie was beginning to feel cross at having to defend herself like this. It just wasn't fair. If they knew what she'd had to deal with and how she'd pulled herself through it all, he wouldn't talk like that.

"Believe me, it's a good job you didn't come," Sarah chirped in.

They were both wearing a stern expression that told Kylie immediately that something serious had gone down. "Why? What happened? Tell me—"

"Let's wait for Martyn," Stuart interrupted, reaching for the empty wine glass that was sitting on the table by his chair.

Kylie filled his glass and then handed one to Sarah. The one she poured for herself was noticeably larger. Stuart began to rifle through a pile of papers he had brought with him.

Just then the door bell rang.

It was Martyn with his usual greeting. "Hi, all you freakin' ghost busters. How you doin'?"

10

"What we're gonna tell you, Kylie, is going to freak you out," Stuart began. "I personally don't think you should hear it, but Sarah thinks you should. So I give you fair warning. You can stop us anytime you like, we won't think any less of you."

"Don't be so patronising, Stuart! I've been excluded long enough. So come on...what happened?"

They took it in turns to tell their story. Martyn first, then Stuart. They had already agreed that Sarah should go last, her version being the one that would impact Kylie most of all.

Sarah needed to know if what had happened to her was the same as what had happened to Kylie in the tunnel. Although nothing untoward had happened since last night, she had a sense of it playing a waiting game...planning a big entrance. Like it was watching, waiting.

When Sarah had finished her story, all eyes turned to Kylie, waiting for her response.

She looked stunned but said nothing. Instead she reached underneath the coffee table and pulled out the transcript of the nightmare she'd had last night.

"You all know that I take dreams seriously?" They all nodded. "And that I've experimented many times with psychic dreaming—mutual and telepathic dreaming?"

"You gonna tell us all this was a dream?" Stuart's tone was scornful as it always was when she ventured into the territory of sleep.

"It's real, it happens. I know you don't believe in it Stuart, but you really need to put your scepticism aside for this. Agreed?"

Stuart shrugged as he stuffed his mouth with more cheese and onion crisps.

"I had the most horrible nightmare last night and I think I picked up what you went through. It woke me at 3am. Shall I read it out?"

Stuart nodded, casting a sideways glance at Sarah.

When she had finished, Martyn was the first to speak.

"Whatever it was...is...seems to have involved you as well, Kylie. There are striking similarities between what happened and your dream."

"Tenuous," Stuart chirped in.

"Dreams are never a blow by blow account of the facts, Stuart. How can they be when it's our conscious mind trying to verbalise an experience that's beyond language?"

"It's interesting you were in a car with Martyn at the beginning," Sarah offered. "And that morphed into the car not starting. Just like what happened to us. Can't place the bathroom though...we didn't go upstairs. I guess that could just be metaphorical? A psychic cleansing perhaps? Though Martyn was threatened with a knife, weren't you Mart?"

"What about the lost child and someone called Lee?" Kylie asked. "Did you pick anything like that up on the EVP?"

"Actually we did," it was Stuart who spoke, sounding a little less incredulous now. "The entity mentioned Lee. We took it to be where he was buried. Lees is only four or five miles away from Rye Top Farm, so it was a natural assumption to make."

"Do you think it could be a person, maybe a boy? Perhaps a name on a gravestone? Could it be the person he murdered?"

"Okay, let's make some notes, see if we can qualify any connections. Kylie, do you have pen and paper?"

Kylie pulled out a huge pad of white paper that she kept slotted behind her bookcase. She'd bought it for a dream workshop she had run in the local church a couple of years ago. She laid it flat on the floor. There was a thick red felt pen clipped onto the top and with it, in huge red writing, she wrote:

'FACTS'.

"Right," Stuart had his teacher head on again. "Come on, just the bare bones. Kylie you be scribe. Let's make some sense out of this. Everyone check their call logs for times of phone calls."

They all pitched in with Stuart assembling their input in time order.

1. Martyn abducted by two thugs 6.10pm. Car and phone stolen.
2. At some point thugs must have gone to Rye Top Farm.
3. 7.30pm Stu/Sarah arrive at Rye Top Farm. Contact McKenzie who threatens them. They leave 8.45pm.
4. 8.50pm Car won't start.
5. Notice anomalies in house. Martyn's phone ringing inside. Go back inside 9pm. Martyn's phone couldn't have been there before because it went to voicemail when Kylie rang him around 8.40pm.
6. Stu and Sarah attacked by unknown entity. Seems to last only minutes but must have been about twenty five minutes. Sarah thinks her attack is same as Kylie's.

7. 9.45pm Car suddenly starts.

8. 3am Kylie has nightmare that includes similar events.

Taking the pen from Kylie without asking, Stuart wrote the next heading on a new sheet.

'INFORMATION FROM ENTITY AT
RYE TOP FARM'.

1. Name of McKenzie – a murderer.

2. He mentions Lee.

3. help – falling – damned – bad shore — more (this sounded like a few voices and different to McKenzie. Could this have been a different entity?)

4. McKenzie threatens us.

5. Gives the numbers 1849 – is that a year?

6. Says he's a demon

7. Says he's 'Appearing'.

"In my nightmare Sarah said that Lee was on her way. This suggests to me that whatever Lee is, may become apparent to us in the future."

"Do you think the entity that attacked me is the same one that attacked you?" Sarah was looking intently at Kylie, almost pleading for her to say no.

"I don't know, Sarah. There are similarities but that's all."

"Did you keep a detailed record of what happened in your old flat, Kylie? If it is the same entity, there may be something there."

"Sorry, no. I was in too much of a state."

"Perhaps if you jot down everything you remember," Stuart said, handing her a clean sheet of paper. "There may be something important."

It was clear he was irritated; the first rule of paranormal investigation is record, record, record. He'd spent hours drumming that into them over the years.

Kylie hesitated before speaking. "I do remember one evening...I was in the bath at my old flat. I had candles lit but the door was ajar and the hall light was on. I thought I saw a woman walk past the door. Josh was in the kitchen making dinner, so I shouted him...I was spooked, you know. I was hoping it had been him, but it wasn't. When he came to see what I wanted, the landline started ringing. It was a man asking for Hannah Bradshaw. Josh said the line was crackly and then went dead. I'd been having loads of weird stuff like that happening so I put it down to the haunting. Josh said it was just a wrong number."

"We got the words 'bad shore' at Rye Top Farm, Stuart." It was Sarah, her eyes glinting with excitement. "We assumed they were just random words but what if the voice recognition interpreted the EVP wrongly? It won't have 'Bradshaw' in its dictionary and 'bad shore' could have been its nearest match."

"I think that might be stretching it a bit far," Stuart said.

"I don't," Kylie chirped in. "That sounds quite plausible to me." She was thinking about Ron, about how he sometimes made verbal contact, telling her

41

things she wouldn't otherwise know. Perhaps that call hadn't been anything to do with the entity, perhaps it had been him?

"Okay," Stuart conceded. "We'll run with it for the time being. We need to find out if anyone called Bradshaw or Lee had any connection to this McKenzie."

Stuart proceeded to write a list of action points on the paper.

1st AP – check out name Lee or Lea and also Bradshaw (murder victims?)

2nd AP – check out name McKenzie – convicted of murder

3rd AP – check if date 1849 had any significant events (including murder).

"Anything else?" he asked.

"Here," said Kylie handing him a sheet of paper. "It's a sketch I made of the house in my dream last night."

The colour momentarily drained from Stuart's face as he stared at the drawing.

"It's the same layout as Rye Top Farm," he said, handing it to Sarah.

Martyn leaned over her shoulder to get a closer look. "This is where we found your phone," Sarah said, pointing to the room at the front that Kylie had marked *parlour*.

"What does this mean?" she asked, now pointing to the words *stay out* that Kylie had scribbled next to an arrow that seemed to denote a flight of stairs.

"I can't really remember. I'm sure it was something to do with the man with the beard. Everything was a bit blurred at the end."

"Can you remember if the stairs you've indicated went up or down?"

"Definitely up. I'm sure about that. I remember walking up them at some point."

"And is it relevant that you wrote those words there?"

"Yes, I think so. The words were definitely to do with the stairs. Something up the stairs—perhaps a room. I don't know."

"Okay, let's crack on." Stuart said, having regained his composure and adopted his official voice once more. "Martyn, you take the first action point. Sarah the second and Kylie...you okay doing the third?"

"What will you be doing?" Martyn asked, never one to let anyone shirk their share of the library work.

"I need to work more on the video footage; it was almost totally black. I've played around with it, brightened it and increased the contrast but it's hard to make anything out. I've had a quick look but it's only a few minutes long."

"Can we see it? Have you brought it with you?"

"Actually, yes I have...and my projector. We can give it a go on the big screen."

He took his projector out of the black case he'd brought with him and proceeded to set it up on the dining table.

Once everything was connected he switched off the lights, projecting the footage onto the blank wall above the TV.

It took a few seconds for the camera to focus and when it did, it appeared to be focussing on the dirt on the window rather than the room inside. Stuart's voice was loud and clear, saying they should go back inside, and after that there was silence.

A grey, hesitant shadow passed across the screen.

"That's a moth," Stuart said. "But see, beyond that, movement inside the room. That's me and Sarah checking things out. But look what happens next."

There seemed to be a figure reflected in the window. It was approaching the house from behind the camera. As it got nearer, the figure seemed to stoop as if it were looking inside. Stuart paused the video.

"What's he got on his face?" Kylie was peering at the screen, her face only inches away.

Stuart zoomed in but the picture became grainy and it was hard to make anything out. The face, if that's what it was, seemed to have a long black nose, rounded at the end rather like a pig's snout. And glasses, thick and round.

"It's wearing goggles," Sarah said. "See...here and here."

"Not goggles, Sarah." Martyn was on his feet also wanting a closer look. "That's no ghost. That's a gas mask."

Stuart pressed play again. The reflection of the man disappeared when the torchlight inside the house was directed onto the floor.

"That's when we found Martyn's phone," Stuart said.

"Do you think he was the one tampered with your car...so it wouldn't start?"

"Could be," Stuart said. "But then why hang around and chance being seen. And if he did tamper with the car, why would he then fix it?"

"For a laugh? To freak you out? Sick bastards like that get off on frightening folk."

"No, it can't be that simple," Kylie said. "There must have been a reason for planting the phone there. Didn't you say this was just before the attack on Sarah? Could the phone have been a beacon for some malicious entity? I know you're all assuming that the figure outside was the man who attacked Sarah. But you can't be sure about that. What if, like Sarah has always said, that it was a psychic attack and this person, and don't assume it's a man as you all seem to be doing, was the one who summoned the entity McKenzie?"

"Did the entity that attached itself to you in the tunnel have a name?" Sarah asked. "I don't remember you saying."

Kylie shook her head. "It only communicated by speech once and that was in the tunnel. All I know is that it was a man."

"I'll check all this out," said Stuart, "try and find out who these fuckers are. I'll need a detailed description of them from you, Martyn."

Stuart pressed the play button again. The video continued until there was a sudden flash of light, prompting him to press the pause button again.

"This is when Sarah was attacked. You can't see me...I was pinned up against the kitchen door...and see here...this is Sarah...she's been pushed to the floor...but look what's on top of her..."

There was a dark shadow covering most of Sarah's body though it was difficult to see exactly what it was because of the darkness and the mist caused by the window. Kylie looked at Sarah. This is how it had happened to her; she knew what this was like. She rushed over and flung her arms around her, hugging her, trying to stop her looking at the screen.

"Oh my God," Martyn said. "If this was a psychic attack, it's a real manifestation."

"Wait until you see this," Stuart said, as he set the video rolling again, stopping it moments later when the shadowy form on top of Sarah raised its head, seeming to look directly at the camera. They all gasped.

"That's the man from my dream," Kylie said. "That's him."

"I think it's safe to assume, that that's McKenzie," pronounced Stuart.

11

The following evening Martyn was standing outside Rye Top Farm just as it was going dark. He couldn't afford to lose his iPhone and anyway the police might want to see it; it might help them catch the bastards who had car-jacked him.

He was on foot, having convinced himself that a brisk walk up the steep lane from Greenfield village would do him good and help alleviate the tension of his abduction. He had been careful to choose a pair of leather gloves to wear—if his phone was still here, he didn't want to smudge the fingerprints that were likely all over it. As for McKenzie, he was well aware that such entities are all around, all the time, but because their vibrational energy is higher than gross matter they are, essentially, existing in an entirely different universe. It was only the changes in electrical and magnetic fields detected by ghost hunting equipment that signalled their presence. That being the case, he wasn't overly concerned about meeting McKenzie and, even if he did, he had the means to defend himself. He was made of stronger stuff than Sarah or Kylie.

He stood by the front door, trying to figure out how to get into the house. Stuart had the only key. Perhaps he should wait, come back tomorrow with the others? This had been an impromptu decision. He felt ostracised from the world without his phone. But he was here now and wasn't about to leave without it. The thieves must have got inside somehow. Perhaps they got in through a window. Closer inspection confirmed this wasn't an option, at least not through the front windows as they were all secure. Perhaps they got in around the back.

Getting to the back of the house was no easy matter. The ground was overgrown with stinging nettles and wild sapling. Martyn ploughed his way through, looking all the time for evidence of someone having been here before him.

There was a broken fence at the rear of the house, opening onto fields that he guessed stretched all the way over to Running Hill quarries at Diggle. The undergrowth was flattened where the fence was broken down completely. That must be how they had got in. Turning to the house, he inspected the ground floor windows. The smallest window had been smashed and all shards of glass removed. He peered inside. There was a toilet directly under the window and a small hand basin on the left hand wall. The door appeared to lead into a small hallway.

Martyn eased himself inside. He was slim but it was a tight squeeze and he only just managed it. He had given descriptions of his assailants to the police but he hadn't described any of them as slim. He wondered whether kids were involved, he'd heard about county gangs recruiting kids to ferry drugs around the country.

It was dark inside the house, darker than it was outside. Until he found his phone he had no way of bringing in light, always assuming of course that the battery hadn't died, which actually seemed quite likely. Going through the door, he stepped into a hallway with a stone flag floor. Another door led into the kitchen.

The house was silent with no evidence of the horror that had unfolded there for Stuart and Sarah only two nights before. After a cursory glance round, Martyn walked through into the lounge. Just as Sarah had said, there was nothing but an old table placed in the centre of the room. He bent down and reached underneath it, breathing a sigh of relief when his fingers homed in on the phone. But what was that? There was something else under the table. It was black and the size of a cat.

He tapped the Flashlight App on his phone and directed the beam at the shape. Two large round eyes peered back at him with shapes moving inside them. He jumped backwards, startled, falling against the kitchen door and causing it to slam shut. The sound of it echoed around the room, causing the house to tremble. The flashlight dimmed. There was only fifteen percent charge left on his phone. The black lump wasn't moving.

This wasn't like him and he chastised himself for freaking out. He stepped closer, bending down to get a closer look. He laughed when he recognised it. It was the gas mask the reflection in the window had been wearing. So this wasn't a haunting. This was someone, probably a gang, screwing with them. Trying to frighten them.

He turned off the flashlight and brought up the list of contacts on his phone. He tapped Stuart's name. He should let him know where he was and what he'd found. His call went to voicemail. Stu was probably still at school. Out of the four of them, he was the only one who was seriously committed to his job, working long hours. Martyn had often wished he had such a vocational commitment. His job as a Tesco delivery driver didn't inspire anyone to be conscientious. It was just a job to pay the bills.

"Hi Stu, Mart here. I'm currently inside Rye Top Farm collecting my phone. Give me a bell back when you pick this up."

As he cut the call it occurred to him why it was darker in this room than the kitchen. The curtains were closed. Didn't Sarah say they'd been alerted because someone had opened them? He tapped the Flashlight App again and directed the beam towards the window. The curtains were moving as if they were being blown by a breeze. He strode over to them and yanked them open, checking the windows. They were all secured and there didn't seem to be a draught strong enough to cause the movement. Just then there was what sounded like a footfall on the stairs, followed by a creaking floorboard.

The door to the front hallway was open. Those were human footsteps and, by the sound of it, they were going up the stairs, not coming down. Someone must be squatting here, probably the same bastards who had stolen his car. He stepped towards the doorway and then into the hall, shining the torchlight from his phone up the stairs. There was no one there.

"Come on you fuckers, show yourself. I know you're up there."

Silence. Should he venture up the stairs? Not such a good idea, they might still be wielding the knives they had threatened him with before. He turned to check the front door and was relieved to see it could be opened from the inside without a key. Suddenly, the Star Wars theme tune began belting out its tinny melody, making him jump. It was Stuart returning his call.

"Stu, yeh, I'm still here. The fuckers are living here. Hang on. Just seen some movement. There's someone standing at the top of the stairs...fuck me...oh shit..."

12

Stuart was shouting Martyn's name down the phone, over and over again, but the connection had been lost. There had been a loud bang making him think Martyn had dropped his phone and probably smashed it. He needed to get over there right away.

Alone? He couldn't ask Sarah to come, not after what happened before, and Kylie wasn't up to it yet despite what she said. Perhaps it was time to call in help.

He checked his watch. It was almost five thirty. The kids he'd had in detention were long since gone and he could finish his prep for tomorrow at home later. He had the phone number of the guy in charge of the Waterford Paranormal Society somewhere, Kevin Venkman. He had been called Smith but changed his name by deed poll a few years ago, describing himself as The Tameside Ghost Buster. Everyone thought that was a bit over the top, but at least he had a good handle on dangerous hauntings and wasn't afraid of anything or anyone. He was also well known for separating real paranormal phenomena from the sort of stuff they show for entertainment on popular TV. Somehow the guys who had stolen Martyn's car were involved in this and there was always a chance that they had set it all up—the EVPs, the manifestation, even the attack on him and Sarah. Kevin would at least know if all that was possible. Kev worked from home as a freelance reporter so providing he wasn't on a job, he would be available at a moment's notice.

The others wouldn't like it. They had all voted at the last meeting against involving anyone else at this stage, but it was a chance he had to take. There was no way he was going back to that house on his own, not knowing what might be waiting there.

"Sir?" Haskin, a Year 4 who had caused more trouble than all the other kids put together in the short time he had been at the school, was standing in the doorway.

"I thought I told you to go home half an hour ago. What are you still doing here?"

"Been in the library, sir."

Well that was a first!

"And?"

"I want to report something, sir."

"Can't it wait? I'm just about to leave. See me about it tomorrow."

"But sir," the boy looked close to tears but Stuart was not in the mood to be emotionally coerced.

"Tomorrow, Haskin. Now beat it."

The lad dropped his eyes to the floor and disappeared back into the corridor. Afterwards, Stuart was to wonder why he hadn't realised something was seriously wrong with the boy, but there really hadn't been anything untoward about him apart from the fact that he was usually intolerably rude and insolent but that afternoon he had been polite and softly spoken. It was an oversight Stuart would later regret.

Stuart rang Kevin Venkman from his car. He had been unable to find the number in his contacts and had to go on the group's website for contact details. He hoped the number he was ringing was Venkman. He didn't want a gullible rookie accompanying him.

It went to voicemail. "Kevin, Stuart Ryder here. I've got a paranormal emergency. I need your help...like now. Can you meet me at Rye Top Farm on Knowl Top Lane a.s.a.p. I'm on my way there now, be there in ten. Cheers mate."

He hoped his message had enough urgency to make Kevin understand the seriousness. The last time they had spoken, Stuart had joked about him being a Ghost Busting travesty who had been dismembered by a poltergeist and jumbled back together in totally the wrong way. As he jolted to a halt at yet another set of road works, he was hoping Kevin wouldn't hold that against him.

As he reached the top of the drive at Rye Top Farm he could see that the front door was wide open. He parked up and pulled the torch from the fascia, checking his phone for battery charge. Almost full. That was a relief.

Stepping out into the chill November air he wondered if he should ring Kevin again before venturing inside. Or maybe the police? He had been assuming that what Martyn had seen at the top of the stairs was an apparition, probably McKenzie, but what if it was the guys who had held a knife at Martyn's throat? He decided against phoning anyone. He'd wasted enough time already. Reaching back into the car he pulled out the cricket bat that had been lying on the floor since school sport's day. No use against an angry ghost but a damned good weapon against violent thugs.

His palms were sweating against the smooth wood of the bat as he inched his way towards the house. He wiped each one in turn on his trousers. The house loomed before him, silent and dark, threatening, like a monster waiting for its next victim. Stepping over the threshold, he was expecting to see Martyn's phone in the hallway where he must have dropped it. A good few minutes passed before he realised it was nowhere to be seen. He called out Martyn's name. No answer.

He needed a plan. He would check downstairs first, make sure there was no one and nothing hiding, and he would make sure he closed the door of each room after he had searched it. That way, if he missed anything he might be alerted by the sound of a door opening. He kept his phone live all the while with the dial pad displayed and his thumb hovering over the number nine, just in case.

He walked through the lounge and into the kitchen. Everything was just as he remembered it from two nights ago. There was a door on his right, leading into a small hall. A downstairs toilet led off the hall and ahead of him was the back door, presumably leading out to the garden. The window above the toilet was broken giving easy access for the thugs and probably Martyn too.

Closing all the doors behind him, Stuart walked back into the lounge. There was no sign of Martyn ever having been here and he was relieved that there was no evidence of a struggle—the solitary table was still dead centre. But what was that underneath it? Reaching down he pulled out the gas mask they had seen reflected in the window. Turning it over, he shone the light from his torch inside it. There was a familiar tag that he recognised, the lab technician attached those tags to all school property. So was this someone from school trying to frighten him? One of his students?

Closing the lounge door, he returned to the bottom of the stairs and steeled himself before going up, concerned of what he might find. This must have been where Martyn was standing when he rang. He reassured himself with the fact that he had found the front door wide open. Maybe, having been startled, Martyn had accidentally bashed his phone against the door post and run away. Then again, he could be lying upstairs, bleeding to death.

The first step is always the hardest, Stuart told himself. Just do it, come on. Slowly he climbed the stairs, each footfall filled with trepidation. Taking a deep breath, he began to shout Martyn's name. If there was anyone waiting up there for him, they'd already know he was here so there was little point hiding the fact. There was no response. The light from his torch illuminated the landing at the top of the stairs before he got there. There didn't seem to be anything untoward.

Four doors were evenly spaced across the landing and they were all shut. Kicking against the first one to his left, it didn't yield. He reached out and turned the handle, letting it swing open.

The unmistakable rancid smell of death filled his nostrils. Sweeping the torchlight around, he could see the room was empty except for a stained mattress under the window and bedding in a heap on the floor at the side, not big enough to hide a body.

The thugs must be squatting here but there didn't appear to be anyone home. A weak shaft of moonlight was shining in through the curtain-less window, illuminating the floorboards where it fell and on which he could now make out the putrid remains of a large rat.

Walking over to the heap of bedding, he used his foot to flatten the pile and reassure himself that there were no human remains hidden there. Satisfied, he closed the door and moved to the next room. Something was stopping this door from swinging all the way back. There was a toilet in front of him and a strong smell of damp mixed with a disgusting hint of sewage. He ventured inside. The toilet seat was raised and he could see shit in the bowl. Someone hadn't flushed. He turned to inspect the bath. It was full of water and the surface was littered with dead flies. He took a step closer but had trouble lifting his foot from the sticky floor. Shining the torchlight downwards he could see that he was standing in the middle of a dark red pool of gunge. It could only be blood, not yet dried.

Just at that moment there was the sound of tyres screeching to a halt outside and moments later Kevin was shouting his name.

"Up here Kev," Stuart called, his voice raspy and hoarse.

Kevin bounded up the stairs two at a time and burst into the bathroom. A look of shock spread over his face as he recognised what was on the floor.

"That ain't fuckin' paranormal," he said, pointing to a large, bloodied knife that was sticking out from under the bath. "You need to ring the police, mate."

13

"Kylie? Sarah here."

"Hi. What can I do for you?"

"I need to talk to you...in person."

Kylie had just flicked on the TV and was watching the evening news. She muted the volume.

"Okay. Do you want to come round here?"

"I'd rather you came to me...if that's alright. Do you mind?"

The familiar whistling began to sound loud and clear in Kylie's head.

"Are you all right, Sarah?"

"Not really."

"Just let me grab some food and I'll be straight round."

"I can make you something if you like."

"It's that urgent?"

"Yep."

"I'll be right over."

Sarah had already prepared a huge pan of chilli. She hadn't been to work today, first day sick in almost five years. She wasn't sure she would be able to go tomorrow either.

It had started with throwing up in the middle of the night. Fortunately she managed to get to the bathroom. After that came expulsion from the other end. She was telling herself it must have been something she had eaten but at the back of her mind there was always McKenzie and the things the entity had threatened. She needed to know exactly what Kylie had gone through when this had happened to her. She was praying she wouldn't have to go through the same trauma but it was starting to look that way. She didn't remember Kylie reporting sickness though.

Kylie arrived less than fifteen minutes later and the girls had a big hug on the doorstep. It brought tears to Sarah's eyes—she had never been very resilient and any kindness shown to her when she was upset always made her cry.

"Here, I've brought a bag of salad."

Sarah laughed, "I'm all out. How did you know?"

Kylie touched the side of her nose and smiled. Taking a pair of travel slippers out of her bag, she removed her shoes and followed Sarah into the living area. Sarah had wished so many times she was more like Kylie. Caring and thoughtful and gentle in her ways. Not like herself, often out spoken and too loud. Not known for her nurturing skills, she did care about other people, of course she did, but she just didn't show it in the same way Kylie did.

Sarah took down a bottle of wine from the shelf in the kitchen area but Kylie shook her head.

"That's probably not a good idea, Sarah."

"Can't eat chilli without a glass of wine, it aids digestion."

Kylie laid her hand over Sarah's as she was about to unscrew the cap.

"No...really, Sarah. I know why you've asked me over and believe me, alcohol is the last thing you need."

Sarah removed her hand, allowing Kylie to place the bottle back on the shelf.

"Okay," she sounded exasperated, which made her feel slightly ashamed. Kylie had dropped everything to come over and help her; it wasn't fair to be cross with her.

As Sarah was shaking the salad into a large bowl, Kylie ventured to ask, "So what's happening to you, Sarah?"

"I've been sick. I mean physically sick like I've eaten something. But I don't think it is that...I'm frightened, Kylie."

"Could be shock...what you went through must have been awful."

"But that was two days ago...how long does it take to get delayed shock?"

"What's Stuart said?"

"I haven't told him."

"So you're worried that this is to do with what happened at Rye Top Farm?"

Sarah nodded. "I keep thinking it's the same entity that attached itself to you in the tunnel."

"I suppose it could be, though this seems different."

"But you recognised this McKenzie from your dream."

"That can't be taken as fact...yes, dreams are important, they aren't JUST dreams...but it's difficult sometimes to tease out where the different elements have come from. The man I saw in my dream may well be a real person, maybe it was McKenzie, but I don't know that it was the entity that attached itself to me. The thing that infected me wasn't a person, it had no identity. Though I think that's what it was looking for; a full blown possession. I was lucky, it didn't get in. I think Martyn stopped it."

"Why do you think this is different?"

"Because it looked like a man attacking you. Did you see anything like that attacking me in the tunnel?"

Sarah shook her head, though was still not convinced.

"Apart from this sickness...are you okay?"

"I don't know. I haven't been sleeping. I feel tense all the time."

"That's probably just worry...and some post trauma anxiety too. What you went through was awful, especially seeing the video footage afterwards...that was probably worse than the actual event."

Sarah was nodding, tears filling her eyes again.

"What do you make of it, Kylie. Do you think this...this McKenzie has attached itself to me?"

"No Sarah, I don't."

"You sound very sure."

"Believe me, if it had you wouldn't have needed to ask that question."

"So how is this different?"

"The energy's not the same, Whatever attacked me in the tunnel was more amorphous. It had no identity, no purpose other than attaching itself to a living person. It wanted to experience what that was like and it got hooked on the fear it was causing, as though the fear was feeding it somehow, making it stronger."

"It didn't cause physical symptoms then...like nausea?"

Kylie shook her head. "At first I wasn't sure what was my own body reacting to the fear and what was the entity. I remember that first night, when I got home, I sat up all night with all the lights on. I was terrified. I rang Josh. He came round and gave me a good old dressing down. You know what he's like...doesn't believe any of this stuff. That helped to be honest...put me into denial and the symptoms subsided. I even went in to work the day after."

Kylie paused to take a mouthful of chilli but never took her eyes off Sarah.

"But very quickly I realised that something was wrong and had to go home. I felt like something was on my back, clinging to me. I could feel it there all the time. It remained stuck to me for weeks."

"I've always had the impression you never told us everything, Kylie. Did you keep stuff from us?"

Kylie was silent for a moment, thoughtful. "With Josh telling me it was all in my head and Stuart spouting off about psychic trauma causing long-term mental health issues, I got to the stage where I didn't know what was real and what wasn't. I went to the doctor. I didn't want you all to know that in case you excluded me forever."

"You can tell me, Kylie. I won't breathe a word to Stuart. But I need to know. Really...everything."

"Okay," Kylie sighed, "from the beginning?"

Sarah nodded.

"You remember when we entered the tunnel...in that small row boat? And I said I felt weird?"

Sarah shook her head. "No, I don't remember that."

"Well I did. I felt like there was an electrical charge buzzing through my head. The EVPs were picking up nothing much...just the usual stuff of discarnate entities drifting in and out of the radar and not saying anything in particular."

"I remember that. We were thinking of calling it a day and going home. It was freezing cold wasn't it?"

"It hadn't been so cold when we first went in. Do you remember that?"

"I just remember being really cold and Stuart noticing a rapid drop in the temperature from fifteen to five degrees."

"And he insisted on rowing further into the tunnel to check it out."

"Yes, I remember that because you and I wanted to go home and he wouldn't."

"That's right. And as we went deeper into the tunnel the EMF detector began to register a startling anomaly. Whatever it had picked up was approaching from the inside of the tunnel. Do you remember seeing a passageway a bit further on? Didn't Stuart say we should go and check that out before turning back? And do you remember Martyn saying he wished he'd brought some of his mother's holy water? That it was a really angry spirit?"

Sarah shook her head. "It all happened so fast. I don't remember much."

"Well he did and it was then that I felt hands on my shoulders, they were shaking me."

"That was Stuart. We were frightened you were going to fall out of the boat."

"That's what it wanted. It wanted me in the water. And then I banged my head...I thought Stuart had pushed me."

"He didn't push you, Kylie. He grabbed you and pulled you back. You were slumped over the side. Perhaps you banged your head on the wall?"

"Well anyway, it felt like the bang on the head was the thing latching onto me. It felt like a cat or something with sharp claws, clinging onto the back of my head."

"I know there were sexual threats coming up on the EVP screen and the static was echoing off the walls of the tunnel. We were all horrified."

"Do you remember hearing the voice?"

Sarah shook her head. "No, but you told us at the time what you heard...and that was what I heard at Rye Top Farm."

"You know Marshmallow Man from the Ghost Buster film, that's how I felt; huge and spreading. Can't explain it any other way. I knew him, it, whatever it was...it was male and familiar. And it was sordid and perverse. It was evil. And then it moved down my body and I could feel it around my hips, writhing about, biting. And then it spoke...in my head. It said it was a demon. It said its name was Stuart."

Sarah gasped. "You can't think...demons do that. They're deceivers."

"Yes well...you know the rest. After that I felt there was someone standing behind me all the time. I kept looking round...no one there."

"I've been feeling that. Like I'm being watched."

"That progressed into feeling breath on my neck...something brushing past. And I had no energy. I was so tired all the time. Never been like that before."

"So that feeling that it was inside you, like it had threatened in the tunnel, you never felt that?"

"No. It was like it wanted to get in but couldn't."

"You never told us this."

"Yeh, well...Josh kept telling me I was just imagining it."

"So that's why you ended up at the docs?"

"Uhu...he prescribed anti-anxiety pills and gave me a sick note for four weeks. I didn't take the meds but it meant I was at home full-time and that's when stuff really started to happen. At first it was harmless, phones disappearing and re-appearing somewhere else, knives appearing on my bedside table, lights switching off and on by themselves. I'd set the table and turn round to find the cutlery all over the floor. Josh was there one time but he still wouldn't believe it. Said I'd probably left them on the edge of the table. It nearly split us up to be honest. I felt he was accusing me of doing all the weird stuff myself.

I ended up going back to the docs and he prescribed sleeping tablets so at least I was able to sleep through the worst of the night time psychokinetic goings on. You remember Martyn did an exorcism of the flat; well in a fashion, anyway. I don't think that's quite how it's supposed to be done but at least he had some holy water that he'd half-inched from the local church. After that, the entity seemed to lose a lot of its power but it still appeared to be hanging around, like a big lump of amorphous negative energy that drained me and made me feel ill all the time. I knew I had to get out of there, find somewhere else to live."

"But it stopped when you moved out? That's what you said."

"Yep. Not been troubled since. Have to say though, I was a bit cross with Stuart telling me to contact the new tenants to ask whether they were experiencing anything untoward. What did he say? It's unethical to leave behind an unresolved haunting and I had a duty to ensure the new tenants were okay."

"I had a go at him for that. Told him to go round himself if he was that concerned."

"Did he?"

"Actually he sent Martyn round on the pretence of asking if the flat was still up for rent. The new tenant said she might not be staying long and did he want to look round."

"So he went inside?"

Sarah nodded. "She made him a cup of tea, even offered to cut his hair—she works at that new salon in the village. He said there didn't seem to be anything weird going on there, and she never mentioned anything. Though he did say he felt drained when he got back. I know we all tried to get to the bottom of what it was that had attached itself to you. Why didn't you tell us it gave you a name?"

Sarah noticed that for the first time that evening Kylie broke eye contact and looked away, as if trying to find the right words for what she was about to divulge.

"You know why? It would have been like accusing Stuart," she said at last.

"You can't think it was anything to do with him, Kylie. For heaven's sake!"

Sarah's reaction was the reason Kylie hadn't breathed a word of this before.

"No of course not. And anyway, there was something else. Something else followed me out of the tunnel that night. Something much more benign...it's given me an extra sense...how can I put this...I sort of know things...heightened intuition if you like...but it's more than that."

"Like the salad?"

Kylie laughed, "Yeh...like the salad but more like a full blown banquet."

"I can feel something, Kylie. Something physical, inside me, that won't let go."

Kylie reached over the table, taking Sarah's hand in hers.

"I don't have any sense of anything attached to you, Sarah."

"I can feel it."

"Sometimes, the monsters are in our mind."

"That's Stuart talking, Kylie. Don't patronise me."

"I'm sorry...I didn't mean to. What happened at Rye Top Farm must have been terrifying but this entity, this McKenzie, could just have been a projection."

"From who? Me?"

"No, Sarah, not you."

"Then who? Stuart?"

"I really don't know. All I know is that when I saw the video, that's what I thought."

"But you weren't there, were you? So how can you know?"

"Like I said...it's just a feeling. I can't explain it."

"So why didn't you mention this at the meeting?"

Kylie shrugged, "Stuart seemed so sure...I didn't want to contradict him."

Sarah stared long and hard at Kylie, trying to figure her out. There had been so many instances lately of Kylie knowing stuff without having been told. Yet she had never mentioned that she had any sort of psychic gift.

"What else do you know, Kylie?" Sarah was hoping that didn't sound in any way confrontational, as if she was interrogating her friend, but her emphatic denial of it being the same entity seemed odd.

"I know that you and Stuart are an item."

"Okay. Guilty."

"Nothing to be ashamed of, Sarah. I just don't know why you've tried to keep it a secret."

"We didn't want to change the dynamics of our little group."

Kylie took hold of Sarah's hand across the table. "We need to be strong together, the four of us, if we're to carry on with what we're doing. We can't afford to have secrets."

"You're right. But that applies to you as well, Kylie. You need to come clean with Stuart. He's talking about bringing in the Waterford group by the way. You need to discuss this with him before he does that."

"Yes, you're right. I will. And can I suggest that you go to the doctors, Sarah...get checked out, just in case this sickness is something else."

"What do you mean, something else?"

"Suddenly throwing up, feeling there's something inside you..."

"You think I might be pregnant?"

Kylie hesitated a long time before answering.

"I don't think so, Sarah. I know so."

14

By the time the police arrived at Rye Top Farm, Stuart had told Kevin the whole story. Neither of them could make any sense out of this new development. A bloodied kitchen knife under the bath didn't bode well and Stuart was beside himself imagining the blood was Martyn's. Kevin's assurances that it couldn't be, did nothing to calm him.

"It's not that long since you spoke to him on the phone. This blood has been here a long time, maybe even days."

"We'll need statements from you both," a tall, burley police inspector told them. "Probably best to get that over with down at the station."

"What about Martyn?" Stuart asked. "I can't leave until I know he's safe."

"We'll check the grounds, sir. Try not to worry. I believe a Mr. Waite owns this property? As soon as he arrives we'll get the power back on but from what you've said and what I've seen, I think we can afford to be optimistic about your friend. From what you've told me, it seems likely that the same men who threatened him and stole his car, are behind this latest incident. Just one thing, sir...what were you and your friend doing here?"

"We're paranormal investigators," Kevin jumped in before Stuart had time to think of a plausible lie. In Kevin's world, it was always better to tell the truth, especially to the police.

The D.I. raised his eyebrows, "Nothing paranormal about this," he said, "it's a crime scene now."

It was the early hours of the morning before Stuart and Kevin had finished giving their statements. There had been no word about Martyn.

"Look, mate, try not to worry," Kevin's voice didn't sound as reassuring as it had done earlier. "We both need to get some sleep. How's about I come round to your place tomorrow night, about seven? We'll talk it all through then."

Stuart was shaking his head, "I need to know where he is."

"There's nothing you can do that the police aren't already doing, mate. The best thing for you to do is to get some rest. Ditch off school tomorrow if you have to."

"I need to go back there."

Kevin took hold of his arm. "No you don't, Stu. Besides, it'll all be cordoned off. Like the police said, it's a crime scene."

"We could drive round the villages. If he ran off, he might be lying somewhere, injured."

"Okay," said Kevin, caving in, "But I'll need to drop my car home first...pick me up there?"

Kevin's house was a short drive away from the station and so they were soon on their way in Stuart's car, heading back towards Greenfield.

They hadn't been driving long when Stuart's phone rang.

"Forgot to put the bloody Bluetooth on again," he said, exasperated.

Screeching to a halt on double yellows, he fumbled it out of his jean's pocket, checking who it was before answering. He half expected it to be Sarah. He always rang or texted her if they weren't seeing each other that day. But this was late even for her. But no, it wasn't Sarah. There was no name, just an out of town telephone number.

He put the phone on speaker so Kevin could hear.

"Stu, it's Martyn." He sounded odd, not his usual cheerful self.

"What's wrong? What happened? Are you okay?"

"No, I'm not okay..."

"Where are you? I'll come and get you."

"No. I need to think."

"The police are looking for you. Do you want me to call them, tell them you're safe?"

There was silence on the other end of the phone.

"You still there, Martyn?"

"Yeh, still here. Don't call the police. I'll be in deep shit if you do. I'll come to yours tomorrow if that's okay. We'll talk then."

Kevin was shaking his head. That was clearly not okay with him.

"Yeh mate, that's fine. I'll ring you when I'm home. See you tomorrow." Stuart cut the call before Kevin had time to object.

15

The following day was not a good day for Stuart. He only just managed to struggle into work on time, barely having slept, only to be summoned immediately to the Principal's office.

"Sit down, Stuart."

"Oh dear...that bad, eh?" Stuart said, laughing as he slumped down into the low leather office chair, set low enough to intimidate the occupier.

"I'm afraid it is," the Principal replied, his dour expression unchanged. "There's been an incident. I believe Haskins approached you yesterday after classes ended. Is that correct?"

"Yes. It was late, around five thirty. He said he wanted to report something."

"And?"

"I was about to leave...I'd been called out to a personal emergency. I asked if it could wait until today."

"That isn't what Haskin's is saying. He says you didn't ask...you told him."

"Okay, I told him. Why am I in the firing line for that?"

"Haskin's was found by the cleaners this morning in the boys' toilets. He'd been threatened with a knife and sexually assaulted."

It took a while for the horror of this pronouncement to sink in. Stuart had been leaning forward in his seat, eager to look attentive, but now he slumped back, rubbing his forehead.

"I don't understand," he said at last. "Are you saying that that's what he wanted to report...that he'd been assaulted, here in school?"

"No, at that point nothing had happened. He wanted to report the boys who had been threatening him. He was still in school because he was too afraid to leave. And I'm sorry to say, that if you had listened to him and brought it immediately to my attention, the lad would probably have been spared this dreadful ordeal."

Stuart was on his feet immediately. "I'm not a social worker for God's sake. I shouldn't even have still been in school. I'd stayed behind to do some marking and—"

"But you were in school...and while you're on these premises, you are expected to carry out all your professional duties...and that includes looking after the welfare of your pupils."

"And whose responsibility is it to make sure school premises are secure against intruders? How could somebody just walk in with a knife?"

"We are all culpable, Stuart. And I promise you there will be a full investigation but, for now, this is about a pupil asking for help and being refused it by his form tutor."

"Are the police involved?"

"They're at Haskin's home now, talking to him and his parents."

"Do they know who it was?" Stuart asked, slumping back down in the chair.

"The CCTV on the ground floor corridor picked them up. Looked like Phillip McKenzie and Tommy Thompson...you remember them? They were both in your tutor group four years ago before they got expelled."

Stuart felt a cold shiver running down his back. This couldn't be coincidence. Yes, he remembered McKenzie and Thompson—two thugs off the Halten Estate. They were bullies who terrorised younger pupils. Always in detention. Always having their parents summoned into school. Not that their parents were any different—they made it clear they had brought their sons up to be the top dogs in a dog eat dog world. Things came to a head when the two lads drew a knife on him during a morning tutorial. The police were involved and they weren't just expelled—they were put on remand in a correction institution. They must have just come out.

What McKenzie had said to him before being taken away flashed into Stuart's mind. *I'll be coming back for you*, he had hissed between clenched teeth so the arresting officer wouldn't hear. Stuart had dismissed it as an idle threat at the time, but had never really forgotten it. His thoughts now went into over drive, considering all the possibilities of how this could be connected to what he and Sarah had experienced at Rye Top Farm.

McKenzie wasn't a common name round here. Why hadn't he made the connection when the name first came through on the Ghost Hunting App? But if it was the same McKenzie, how could he possibly have appeared to be a ghost three days ago? And how did he get his hands on that gas mask? It had been part of a world war two display in the school library, locked up in a secure cabinet. It didn't make sense. Unless Haskin was involved and it was him who had stolen it.

"What's going to happen?" he asked, rubbing his forehead again.

"I'm afraid Haskin's parents are calling for your suspension. I'm very sorry but I have no choice but to comply, at least until we have more information."

"Will I lose my job?" Stuart knew if he was found to have disregarded a pupil's welfare, he would never work in a school again.

"Let's not get ahead of ourselves, Stuart. The Board of Governors will, of course, want to hear your side of the story. You say you had a personal emergency, I suggest you go home and write a detailed account of it. If you let me have it before five o'clock tonight, I'll make sure it's on the table in time for the meeting."

Stuart rose from his chair wondering how much detail they would need about his personal emergency. Paranormal investigations were probably not on their list of emergency call outs.

"Oh...and Stuart..." the Principal called as he was leaving. "McKenzie is still at large, so I'd keep your doors locked if I were you."

"Cheers for that inappropriate parting shot," Stuart said as he left, slamming the door behind him.

16

Martyn turned up at Stuart's house in a taxi later that day. He looked tired and dishevelled like he hadn't slept in a week.

"I'm glad you're safe Martyn but, honestly, I can't talk right now."

"I'm in deep shit man."

"So am I. I'm being hauled over the coals at school for abdicating my responsibilities," Stuart explained without being asked. "I rushed off to find you instead of taking care of a pupil. Claims he was sexually assaulted by a lad who got expelled years ago. McKenzie. Ring any bells?"

Martyn looked shocked. "You think it's the same guy? So you don't think it was a ghost?"

"Haven't got a clue...I don't know what's going on. I suppose you'd better come in. But I warn you, I've a report to write in my defence, so I ain't got that long."

"I think you'll find this is more important than your fuckin' report, Stuart!"

Stuart was taken aback. This wasn't like Martyn. Something serious must have happened.

"I'm listening," he said when they were both sat down with coffee that had been percolating for over an hour in the kitchen.

"I told you on the phone there was somebody standing at the top of the stairs last night?"

Stuart nodded.

"He had crazy eyes, black as coal, no whites. And a big black bushy beard, wild hair. It looked to me like the guy you caught on video—the one that attacked Sarah."

Stuart shuffled in his chair. "Don't suppose you took a photo?"

"He threw a fucking knife down the stairs at me...taking a souvenir photo was the last thing on my mind...besides I dropped my phone. Fortunately the knife missed me 'cause I lunged to one side, nearly knocked myself out on the wall. Next news, whatever it was, is flying down the fuckin' stairs. It didn't move like a regular guy that's for sure. I picked the knife up and stabbed out but there was nothing there. Honest to God, Stuart, whatever it was had just disappeared. Then I made a really bad mistake...wasn't thinking straight. Never been that frightened. I took my gloves off to try and phone you back. I had 'em on so as not to spoil the fingerprints on my phone, but obviously I still had the knife in my hand. And my phone was broken anyway. I opened the front door to get the hell out of there and the fuckin' weirdo was standing right there, outside, waiting for me. And then someone came up behind me and shoved something in my face. I must've blacked out."

"I went round there to look for you with Kevin Venkman. We saw blood in the bathroom and a knife."

"And I suppose you called the police?"

Stuart nodded again. He wasn't about to apologise for that. "We had to. What would you have done? That blood could've been yours."

"So the police have the knife now?" Martyn's face was ashen. "With my fingerprints all over it?"

Stuart nodded. "I don't know. Is it the same knife? The one we found was in the bathroom. So go on...what happened next?"

"Oh it gets worse! I don't know what happened between then and coming round about two hours later. Perhaps I got chloroformed again. I woke up in the driver's seat of my own car, the one that was stolen. I was in the car park at Hartshead Moor services on the M62. Not a clue how I got there. I got out, was thinking to get a coffee and ring the police from a pay phone when I noticed something dripping down the back bumper. It was coming from the boot. When I opened the trunk, there was a fuckin' dead body in there. I've been framed, Stu."

Stuart couldn't speak, the shock had silenced him. A hundred and one different scenarios were playing out in his head, none of them ending well.

"I need to tell the police you're safe," he managed eventually. "They're out looking for you."

"Fuckin' hell, Stuart. It's this McKenzie guy that's behind all this...not a fuckin' ghost at all...a fuckin' psycho. And I'm in it up to my neck."

"Where's the car now?"

"I dumped it."

"You did what! You should have phoned the police."

"I panicked."

"You should ring them now."

"What? And tell them I dumped a car with a dead body in it? What do you think they'll do? Say 'well done lad, thanks for ringing us'. They'll assume I'm a murderer who's given himself up. I can't do that. If they ask, I'll say I haven't seen my car since it was stolen...and I want you to back me up on this Stuart."

"When they find your car, which they will, they'll sweep it for fingerprints, including yours...it's routine—"

"—and they'll match the prints on the knife. I'm fucked, Stu, without them knowing I dumped the car with a dead body in it as well."

"I really wish you hadn't told me this, Martyn. I'm in enough trouble as it is without lying to the police."

"You won't have to lie. They're not gonna ask the question are they? They'll find the car and the prime suspects will be the bastards that stole it. When...if...they find my fingerprints on the knife, I'll tell them what happened in the house...there'll be no need to mention that I woke up in my car. I'll tell them I got dumped in a wood somewhere."

"They're not stupid, Martyn. They know when folk are lying."

"Well then, whichever way this goes, I'm well and truly fucked."

<hr>

17

Stuart emailed his report to the Principal with only five minutes to spare. He hoped it was enough to get him off the hook. He didn't mention his hobby or the connection to Rye Top Farm, simply reporting that a good friend whose car had been stolen at knife point had called him in distress after another assault, asking for his help.

He wasn't sure it sounded plausible and could guess what sort of questions the Board of Governors would be asking. 'Why didn't his friend call the police instead of Stuart? Why didn't Stuart call the police? Why did Stuart appear calm enough to pack his books away and have a conversation with Haskin before leaving?' Stuart knew he was in deep shit, but not as deep as Martyn, who was up to his neck in it.

After dealing with the report, he rang round everyone, calling for an extra special meeting that evening—and invited Kevin along to meet the rest of the team. The agenda was to try and sort out what exactly had happened at Rye Top Farm on the night he and Sarah were there and for them all to listen to what had happened to Martyn. That was, of course, providing Martyn wasn't arrested before then.

He had agreed that Martyn should lie low for a few more hours before Stuart rang the police to tell them he had turned up at his place in great distress. Worryingly for Stuart though, he was now harbouring the man who would be the main suspect in a murder case—assuming, of course, that the police had found Martyn's car with the body in the boot. It didn't seem likely they would have overlooked that.

Kevin was the first to arrive and was horrified to hear Martyn's story.

"For God's sake man...think this through...you need to ring the police immediately. There's a chance they haven't yet found the car...if you tell them about it, they're more likely to believe your story. Hiding away like this, you're acting like you're guilty...and implicating the rest of us."

Martyn shrugged. "They're not going to know I was in the car. Nobody saw me."

"Ever heard of CCTV? First thing they'll do is check all the cameras around where you dumped the car. Where did you dump it...no, don't tell me...I don't want to know."

Stuart went over to where Martyn was sitting and put his arm around his shoulders. "Kev's right," he said. "If you tell them the truth, they can check the CCTV at the service station. They'll see that you weren't driving the car."

"And what if it's not on CCTV? What then?"

Kevin picked up his phone.

"No, mate, please don't." Stuart had never heard Martyn so scared.

He laid a hand on Martyn's arm. "We have to, Martyn. It really is the only option."

Without any further discussion, Kev rang the police. They were round at the house within fifteen minutes and were leaving with Martyn just as Sarah and Kylie were arriving.

"What's going on?" Sarah exclaimed. "Why are they taking Martyn away?"

"There's been some developments," Stuart answered, handing both girls a mug of coffee before sitting himself down at the dining table opposite them.

"This is Kevin, from the Waterford group." And turning to Sarah, "I think you've met each other before? At the Mind, Body, Spirit conference last year?"

Sarah nodded. Yes, she had met Kevin before and she didn't like him very much. He had been the one to debunk her report of strange lights on Saddleworth moor. The equipment she had used had gone berserk up there that night and she concluded they were the spirits of people who had died up there, may be even with a connection to Brady and Hindley. Mr. 'High and mighty' from the Waterford Paranormal Society had said that the cause was nothing but methane gas seeping up through the peat bogs—a natural and very common phenomena, he had said, making reference to the public house that used to be there. The Floating Light was now sadly a private residence, another casualty of the modern way of socialising. He had made her look stupid and less than professional. And to make it worse, Stuart had agreed with him even though Stuart had never mentioned anything like that to her, and he had been the one to look through her report before she'd submitted it.

"Before we start," she said, her tone less than friendly, "can I just say that I don't agree with Kevin's way of doing things."

"Sarah...please don't." Stuart knew exactly where she was coming from but he wasn't about to let her cause ructions that would affect them all. "We've got enough shit going on, without you adding to it."

Sarah was about to retaliate as Stuart reached over the table and touched her hand.

"There have been some developments that you girls don't know about...serious developments that are calling into question what happened that night at Rye Top Farm."

It didn't take long to bring the two girls up to speed.

"Let's go over again what happened that first night there, Sarah, but this time, let's think in terms of it having been McKenzie, the real guy, not an entity."

Sarah was shaking her head. "It's just not possible. There was no one there—we'd have seen him if he'd been in the room with us...and I certainly would have known if it was a real person that threw me to the floor and jumped on top of me."

"But it all happened so fast, didn't it. I'm not sure I remembered it properly at the time anyway."

"But what about the instruments...they went crazy...and the EVPs—"

"Any electrical source will emit electromagnetic radiation that can affect the sort of instruments you were using..." Kevin butted in. "And didn't Stuart find an electrical fault in the kitchen. As for the EVPs, the Apps have a voice recognition system built into them, and a very limited dictionary. They pick up static that's all and if they recognise a random pattern that could be speech they match it up with a word in their database. You know yourself, sometimes it just throws up random words that don't make any sense."

"And what about the video..." Stuart must agree with her about that.

"It was dark," Stuart said, "shot through a dirty window. I've gone through it with Kev and we can't be absolutely sure it wasn't just shadows inside the house."

"You'll be telling me next, there's no such thing as the spirit world," Sarah yelled.

No one answered, not even Kylie who Sarah had hoped would back her up.

At last Stuart spoke. "Both Martyn and I are in deep shit. It wasn't ghosts that assaulted one of my pupils. It wasn't ghosts that killed somebody in that house, it wasn't a ghost in that gas mask and it isn't ghosts who are trying to frame Martyn. To be honest, Sarah, those are my only concerns at the moment."

"Okay," Kevin said. "We've got McKenzie, the real McKenzie who promised to get his own back on Stuart, and his accomplice, Tommy Thompson. And you're saying they were both caught on CCTV at the school around the time that lad was assaulted? Presumably that attack was to get back at you, Stuart. They're probably hoping you'll lose your job over it. Right?"

Stuart nodded.

"Okay. That part's pretty well cut and dried. Next. They were in school around the same time that Martyn says he saw this McKenzie entity at Rye Top Farm. Does the real McKenzie know Martyn?"

"Not as far as I know. But it's not beyond the bounds of possibility that they've been watching me for the past few weeks. They've been out of remand about eight weeks according to my boss."

"Okay. So going back to how this all started. Let's assume it was McKenzie and Thompson who car-jacked Martyn. What time was he abducted?"

"He was on his way home from work, so it must have been sometime after six."

"And what time did the name McKenzie appear on the phone App?"

Stuart and Sarah looked at each other. Sarah spoke first, "We waited a good fifteen minutes for Martyn, didn't we? And I guess we were at least half an hour into the session when the name flashed up?"

Stuart agreed.

"So it must have been round about eight fifteen...ample time for them to have dumped Martyn and driven round to Rye Top Farm to set things up. Does that make sense so far?"

They all nodded.

"Just bringing in the question of the body for a minute. I reckon that body was already in the house the night you were there...the blood in the bathroom had been there a while. And when we checked the bedrooms there was evidence of squatters...that would account for the strange noises the owner reported."

"So they were probably upstairs the whole time we were there," agreed Stuart.

"Exactly. It wouldn't have been difficult for them to affect your equipment...all they would have to do would be to switch on a source of electromagnetic radiation and the App would do the rest. You said you actually heard a voice though, didn't you. Was the name McKenzie a voice or did it come through on the App."

"It came though on the App," Sarah confirmed. "I remember it flashing up in the text box."

"Can you remember what came through as an actual voice?"

Sarah took a notepad out of her handbag and proceeded to flick through the pages.

"There was hardly anything came through on voice," she said, running her finger down the page. "The word 'Yes' in answer to my question, 'Did you kill someone?' Then Stuart asked who he had killed, and a voice said 'you'. The most frightening was the voice that whispered in my ear when I was being attacked."

"What did it say?"

Sarah's eyes filled up, it was clear she was trying hard not to break down again.

"It said, 'I knew I'd get inside you'."

"Okay. Let's go back to when you were first in the house. How long after the word 'Appearing' flashed up did the entity McKenzie manifest?" Sarah thought how she may as well have just made a comment about the weather for all the compassion Kevin was showing.

"We had wrapped it up for the night," Stuart said, "Sarah wasn't comfortable and we decided to call it a day."

"So you left the house?"

"Yep...that would have been about eight forty five, but then the car wouldn't start. Sarah noticed the lounge curtains were open. They had been closed. Then she tried to ring Martyn...that's when we heard his phone inside."

"Chances are then, that they tampered with your car whilst you were inside. Do you think Martyn's phone was in the lounge the whole time?"

"No. We've already established that Kylie rang Martyn at 8.40 and it went straight to voicemail without ringing. When we tried around ten past nine, it was inside the house and ringing out."

"So it looks like they planted it there while you were outside trying to start the car...maybe to entice you back in?"

"But it doesn't explain why the name McKenzie came up on the App does it?" Sarah interjected.

"No it doesn't," Kevin said, "and having looked at the rest of what came through on the App before the...let's call it a manifestation for the time being, even though I doubt it was...what you picked up obviously still needs investigation, but I'm thinking the name coming up was just coincidence."

Sarah immediately looked agitated. "Coincidence? What sort of paranormal investigator are you if you believe in random coincidences?"

"A thorough one," Kevin batted back, "and not one that is easily duped."

Sarah was about to respond in kind when Kylie interjected. "There's far more going on here than any of you realise."

All eyes turned in her direction.

"What do you mean?" Stuart asked.

"Think about it. It's not possible for McKenzie to have been in school and at Rye Top Farm at the same time. The thing you're calling a manifestation, and Kevin seems to believe was the real live McKenzie, was probably nothing but a projection."

"What?" Stuart sounded incredulous.

"You're talking about some sort of hologram?" Kevin asked, obviously taking Kylie's input seriously.

"May be," Kylie answered, "though I was thinking more of a psychic projection from someone well practised in the art."

"McKenzie?"

"I really don't know. But whoever sent it may not be consciously aware of what they're doing."

She was looking directly at Stuart when she said that.

18

The following day was Saturday and Stuart was in a foul mood. What was it about Kylie? What had happened to her to make her suddenly so objectionable? He had enough on his plate with his suspension from school without her insinuating that he had somehow manifested a projection that attacked Sarah. She had said it may have been unconscious but for heaven's sake, Sarah was his girlfriend why would he do that to her, unconsciously or not?

It was true, he had experimented in the past with manifesting thought forms; and Kylie knew that. He'd studied the Toltec traditions as a hobby when he was at University, it had fascinated him after reading all the Castaneda books. Don Juan Matus claimed to be able to be in two places at the same time, whilst appearing completely physical and real in both locations. His experiments had come to nothing and so he'd concluded the books were works of fiction. But what if it was true. What if people really could do that—at will? What if McKenzie could do it?

No, Kylie was talking nonsense—her experiences since the tunnel must have messed with her head, affected her sanity. And yet such an explanation would fit the facts and Stuart was very aware that Kevin hadn't dismissed her claim out of hand. He said he would investigate the possibility, said he had no experience of psychic projection and would seek the advice of someone more knowledgeable in that area. Stuart knew who he was talking about— Gaynor. She was a member of the Waterford group and one of his ex-girlfriends before he'd met Sarah. She was the last person he wanted to meet up with again. They hadn't parted on particularly good terms and he was still convinced she'd tried to put a hex on him, even though he didn't believe that such things were possible. She had a long history of shamanic involvement with a later boyfriend to the extent that an obscure indigenous Amazonian tribe had made her an honorary shaman. At least, so she said. As far as he knew, she now ran courses up on Ilkely Moor, convincing gullible westerners that they too can be shamans and charging them a fortune for the privilege of proving her wrong.

And on top of all that, Martyn had been detained by the police and it looked likely that he would be charged with murder. The body found in the boot of his car had been identified.

Stuart had suggested to the police that they check school records, as he suspected the dead man may have been one of the lads that gave evidence against McKenzie at the time he was expelled. And there was still the question of the school gas mask. The police hadn't been able to explain that yet.

It turned out that the dead man was a would-be priest who had been a member of a spiritualist church in Dewsbury—a church that was only down the road from where Martyn used to live. That connection, along with all the forensic evidence, pointed to Martyn being the murderer. It all hinged on whether the police believed Martyn's story or not and currently it wasn't looking good. And that didn't help his own case. Despite the evidence of the gas mask found at Rye Top Farm, the police were not connecting the murder with the assault on Haskin. But there must be a connection, Stuart was sure of it. And he was starting to worry that McKenzie might decide that losing him his job was not enough revenge.

The morning was dragging and his brain was going into overdrive, mulling over the whys and wherefores of the last few days. He had to do something and remembered the action points he had allocated at their meeting on Tuesday. It had been Martyn's job to check out the names of Lee and Bradshaw but he obviously couldn't do that now. Even though Stuart had delegated the action points, he'd already done numerous internet searches for the names and the year 1849 but had pulled up nothing at all. He decided to go down to the library in town and see what he could dig out of their archives.

Maybe he could ring Sarah; they could meet for lunch in her favourite café. She'd been so tetchy at the meeting last night. He had the impression he'd done something wrong, again, but had no idea what—unless it was bringing Kevin in. She definitely didn't like Kevin.

The library was unusually quiet for a Saturday morning and Stuart was allocated an assistant to advise him on what records may help him in his research. He was amazed at the amount of archival material available and wondered why he had never investigated this resource before. He asked about parish records, having heard from a work colleague that they were crucial in researching genealogy, but the assistant advised him that Parish records only went up to 1837.

"What you need," she patiently explained, "is the census and official records of births, marriages and deaths for Saddleworth and Oldham. She duly produced both and helped him sift through them, making a list of all relevant entries. He soon discovered that Bradshaw was a common name, particularly in the old Saddleworth parishes of Grasmere and Lordsmere. He was looking for the death of a woman with the surname Bradshaw in 1849 and maybe for someone called Lee. It was a long shot, especially as the name Bradshaw was nothing more than something conjured up by Kylie from a wrong number. He didn't tell the library assistant that, though she did ask why he was interested to find those names.

"I'm trying to find a branch of my family that appeared to have split from the main tree. I'm particularly interested in the years around 1849."

He felt bad lying to her, but it was only a little white lie and it was enough of an explanation. She was called away by a more pressing enquiry and didn't ask any more questions.

It was a time-consuming task but he stuck at it until two o'clock when he had arranged to meet Sarah in The Green Fig on Market Street—a cosy little tea shop that they often frequented on their trips to town. He had managed to track down three Bradshaw's that he thought might be relevant to their search—all had died in the nineteenth century. All three had lived in the Delph area before the reservoirs had been built there. It was, therefore, probable that they were all buried in the graveyard at St. Thomas's, Heights. He had found no record of a Lea, Lee or Leigh but had discovered that the name Lee meant a clearing in a wood and it wasn't very popular as a Christian name in the nineteenth century, which made him wonder if the information they had got from Kylie's dream was even more unreliable than they thought. He had jotted it all down in his notes anyway—aware that any snippet of information could prove crucial.

Sarah was already at The Green Fig by the time he arrived. She was sitting in a quiet corner by the window, looking pensive.

"Hi, babe," he said, leaning over to kiss her on the forehead. "You okay?"

"Not really...babe," she added the last word with a flavour of sarcasm, which Stuart found confusing. It made him wonder what he had done this time to upset her.

He didn't respond and instead walked over to the counter to order two coffees and request a menu.

"What's up?" he said as he sat down beside her, taking her hand in his. For the first time, he noticed her eyes. It looked like she'd been crying.

Sarah reached inside her bag, pulling out a long white tube. She passed it to him. "See the blue line?"

He nodded.

"That means I'm pregnant...and this is no freakin' ghost done this, Stuart."

"But...you're on the pill...did you forget to take one?"

"No I didn't," she said, snatching it back off him.

"Then how?"

"How the hell should I know?" she snapped back. "But it's an un-nerving coincidence, don't you think? I feel I was raped by a ghost and next news I find out I'm pregnant...but only because Kylie made me check...she knew I was pregnant...this is the same Kylie who reckons the entity that attached itself to her in the tunnel gave her some sort of weird second sight or something."

Stuart took a deep breath. This needed careful handling and he wasn't sure what to say. He wanted to ask if it was his but then thought better of it. Was it possible that it was something to do with the entity that had manifested at Rye Top Farm—the entity that had appeared on top of her on the video. The entity that Kylie had dreamed she was in bed with?

"Well?" Sarah wanted some comment from him, something, anything.

"How far gone are you?"

"How the hell should I know? My last period was only two weeks ago."

"I didn't know pregnancy tests were that sensitive." It sounded lame but it was all he could think of to say.

The coffee arrived and they both waited in silence until the girl had gone.

"What are we going to do Stuart?" Sarah's voice was softer now. He was worried she was going to cry.

"What do you want to do? I'll do whatever you want?"

"Do you want it?"

"Do you?"

"I don't know. It's so sudden."

"I don't know either, Sarah. We need time to digest this...fuck...what a weekend this is turning out to be."

"Oh, that's charming." Sarah was on the offensive again. "This is just another fuck up is it?"

"You know I didn't mean it like that—"

Sarah stood up, slinging her handbag over her shoulder, preparing to leave.

"Menus..." the waitress had come over to their table, waving two sheets of paper at them. "Can I get you some more drinks?"

"Sorry," Stuart said, reaching in his pocket for his wallet, "we've changed our minds."

19

Stuart and Sarah had a difficult evening, talking through the pros and cons of having a baby together. They both agreed that an immediate termination didn't feel as bad as an abortion later on.

Sarah was adamant that she couldn't kill a child that was growing inside her, but a foetus, probably only a couple of weeks old at most, was a different matter.

They both agreed on that.

But then she got upset. This was a new life, a new human being, what right did they have to end its life. They weren't gods. When Stuart agreed with that as well, Sarah got the impression he was just agreeing with everything she was saying to avoid upsetting her. All she wanted was for him to tell the truth, to be open and honest about how he felt about her and about the prospect of being a father. Why couldn't he do that?

In the end they settled down to watch an upbeat movie, agreeing not to discuss it further until they both had time to get their head round it and decide what they wanted to do without being influenced by the other. They hadn't been an item for that long and neither of them had ever had thoughts of marriage, or even living together. That just hadn't been on the agenda.

Although they had agreed to shelve the discussion for the time being, they were both very much aware that if the outcome was a termination, it would be better to make that decision sooner rather than later.

When they'd eventually gone to bed, Stuart had refrained from his usual foreplay. Sarah was glad about that because she would have found it hard to ask him to stop, it would just have caused more tension between them. As he lay down beside her, he gently wrapped his arms around her, holding her close. It made her feel safe and more optimistic about the future.

She woke at 3am from a bad dream to find Stuart was not lying beside her. He had probably gone to the bathroom and she thought no more of it as she snuggled back down to sleep. But then she heard him walking around the bed. He stopped at her side, standing over her, looking down at her. She could feel his eyes on her. She tried to open her eyes but couldn't. Tried to move, but couldn't. Tried to speak, ask him what he was doing, but although she could feel her mouth moving, nothing but garbled words were coming out.

And then she felt his breath on her cheek—he must be bending down over her, his face close to hers. Was he sleep walking? What the hell was he doing?

The panic she felt released the paralysis in her body and she sat bolt upright. Stuart wasn't bending over her, he was standing in front of the window, naked except for a sheet draped over his shoulders.

He was perfectly still, motionless, but looking straight at her.

"What are you doing?" she screamed. "Stop it...what..."

"Sarah! What the fuck..." Her screams had woken Stuart.

He wasn't standing by the window, he was lying in bed beside her. The apparition was nothing but the faint light seeping in around the blackout blind and filtering in through the lacy curtains.

"Are you okay?" he asked, putting his arm around her and pulling her gently down so that her head was resting on the pillow. "Bad dream?"

"I woke up...it seemed so real...I couldn't move."

Stuart switched on the bedside lamp. "It was probably sleep paralysis," he said. "It can happen if you're stressed. You partly wake up but your body's still asleep. It's quite common. It happened to me once."

"But it was so real, Stuart. I was awake."

"No, you were asleep, still dreaming. It's what's called a false awakening, that's what happens with sleep paralysis. I know it can be terrifying but it's nothing to be frightened of."

"Honestly?"

"Honestly. It's well documented. I'll show you some research papers tomorrow." He wrapped both his arms around her to warm her. "You're shivering."

"I felt someone breathing on me...I thought it was you. Kylie said she felt that too. And then I saw you standing in front of the window."

"It was just a bad dream, Sarah. Come on now, go back to sleep. We've a busy day tomorrow."

"Tomorrow? What's happening tomorrow?"

"You remember. We're meeting the others up at Heights, checking out the gravestones."

Yes, she remembered now. The library research that Stuart had done had seemed to corroborate some of the stuff they'd got through the Electronic Voice App on their phones. So although Stuart and Kevin had disregarded most of the stuff they'd experienced as not being paranormal, they had all agreed there was still stuff to be investigated.

"Okay if I switch the lamp off?"

Sarah nodded and cuddled up closer to him. She was thinking of what Kylie had said at their last meeting about unconscious projections. Was what she had just seen really from her own imagination? A bad dream? Or had it come from Stuart? And if so, was the man who attacked her at Rye Top Farm, Stuart as well? They had assumed it was the entity that had come through on the EVP, but McKenzie was a real person and seemingly hell bent on revenge, so maybe it wasn't McKenzie at all. Perhaps they had jumped to the wrong conclusion.

Perhaps the messages coming through the EVP App had not been threats. Perhaps they had been warnings.

20

Stuart pulled up behind the Toyota truck that he knew belonged to Kevin.

Heights Church, perched on top of a windswept hill, looked cold and bleak even in daylight. And it had started to rain, making it look even more eerie. Built in 1765, the austere Georgian chapel with its 19th century bellcote surmounted by a cross, looked intimidating and less than inviting.

The graveyard, bounded by blackened dry stone walls, was sprouting old gravestones, many leaning at jaunty angles. The whole scene was more gothic than the scariest horror movies.

"Recognise it?" Stuart asked the girls.

"Should we?"

"They shot a movie here in 2014, with Liam Neeson. In fact, it's been used a few times. Remember 'In the Flesh'? That was filmed here. So was a BBC adaptation of Daphne du Maurier's 'Jamaica Inn'."

"Doesn't seem right somehow," chirped in Kylie. "To use a sacred site for entertainment."

"It's not used as a church now," Stuart said.

"Still disturbing the dead though."

"What are we looking for?" Sarah asked, admiring the views from the car.

"The name Bradshaw, specifically Joseph or Elisa Bradshaw, but we need to get a feel for the entire family so we know who we're dealing with if anything else comes through."

"And don't forget, Hannah Bradshaw." Kylie chirped in from the back seat, still remembering the ghostly visitation at her old flat.

"It's a common name round here...there might be loads of them." Sarah didn't sound too enthusiastic at the prospect of wandering round an old graveyard in the rain.

"That's okay...they'll all be related in one way or another."

Switching off the engine Stuart reached into the fascia compartment, pulling out sheets of paper and handing one sheet to each of them.

"This is a rough plan of the graveyard. If you find a Bradshaw, note down the details, the name and the position of the grave on the plan. Clear?"

Sarah and Kylie both nodded. Stuart could be bossy at times, to the point of being irritating, but they knew without him their little band of paranormal investigators would have floundered long ago.

"And no EVPs today," he added. "We need to focus all our attention on finding these graves. Where's Kevin?"

Kylie pointed over to the lytch gate where Kevin was bending over something on the ground.

102

"Hey Kev," Stuart called. "What you doing?"

Kevin raised an arm, beckoning them over. He was standing by a gravestone that was forming part of the path that led to the church. He read out the inscription.

"Alice, daughter of Joseph and Elisa Bradshaw. Departed this life 31st March 1849 aged six years. Resting in the arms of Jesus."

"Bingo, well done," said Kylie, giving Kevin a beaming smile.

"It's a bit sacrilegious to have people walking over a grave," Sarah exclaimed.

"The grave may be somewhere else," Stuart said, busily noting down the details on his plan. "If the memorial stone was unsafe, they could have moved it here."

"What's that little motif?" Kylie asked. "Can you see it...just there under her name?"

They all peered at the stone where she was pointing. There was something there but it was mostly worn away by the hundreds of footsteps that must have walked over it.

Kevin took a thick leaded pencil out of his jacket and laid his copy of the graveyard plan over the motif.

"Good idea," Stuart said. And then added, "It seems a bit odd that Alice's name didn't come up in my search of the records. I got Joseph...he died in...let me see...1898. And I got Elisa. I also got Hannah, daughter of Edward Bradshaw who was Joseph's son and of course that was the name that

103

Kylie gave us...from the supposedly wrong number."

"Perhaps they didn't record children?"

"It would be very unusual if they didn't. Why wouldn't they?"

"Perhaps she hadn't been christened, or baptised, whatever it is you say?"

"She's buried on consecrated ground," Kylie pointed out, "and her headstone mentions Jesus."

Stuart was getting exasperated again. "Just because we have a headstone here, doesn't mean she's underneath it. And just because it mentions Jesus, you can't conclude she'd been christened. It's all conjecture."

Kylie made a face at him, which he ignored.

The rubbing done, Kevin held it up for all to see."

"What is it?" Sarah asked. "A star of David."

"That's no Star of David," Kevin pronounced. "That's a pentagram...in a graveyard on consecrated ground...that's pretty weird."

"At least it's the right way up," said Kylie. "means it's there for protection. It would be really weird if it was upside down."

A short discussion followed about the possibility of black magic rituals being conducted on sacred ground.

"You know what's just occurred to me?" Kylie added, interrupting their thoughts about the pentagram. "The name Alice...it sort of ends in Lee doesn't it? Maybe the phone App got that wrong too?"

There were quiet mutterings though no one ventured to comment that that was an interesting point. They were all a little wary about encouraging Kylie since she had announced she had been blessed with second sight. They didn't want her seeing herself more as their oracle than a team member.

"We still need to sweep the entire graveyard." Stuart broke the silence as he ushered them all into line. "So, come on, let's get to it. It'll be dark in a couple of hours and believe me, we don't want to be up here then. Kylie you take the Eastern quarter, Kev you okay with the North? Sarah and I will do this half. Try and make sure you don't miss any out."

An hour's search pulled up more Bradshaws, six of whom could be discounted because of the dates. One of those was Hannah, daughter of Edward and Elizabeth, and mother of Frank. She had died in 1995, too recent to be relevant to their search though Kylie had misgivings about that seeing as that was the name given in the spooky phone call that Josh had answered.

"It leaves us with Alice, Elisa, Joseph, Mary and George." Stuart explained as he spread the plans out on the ground, pointing to the position of each grave in turn. "George was Joseph's brother and Mary was his wife. And although we have a mention of Alice as the daughter of Elisa and Joseph, there is no grave for Elisa. Yet the record I pulled up clearly stated that Elisa, apparently like her daughter Alice, died in 1849. She must be buried somewhere else. As for

Joseph, the gravestone agrees with the records, he died in 1898."

"Doesn't it seem a bit odd that there's no grave for Elisa?" Kylie asked.

"Not really. The headstone could have long since been destroyed," Kevin explained. "She may not even have had one. Perhaps the family couldn't afford two in the same year."

Stuart now asked in his authoritative tone of voice. "Who did I assign to check if there'd been any murders around that time?"

They all looked at each other.

"I think that was you, Kylie. Wasn't it?" Sarah said with an accusatory look.

"I thought I just had to check events occurring in 1849?"

"Yes...durr... a murder perhaps?"

"I made a list. Didn't find any murders though."

"How did you search?" asked Stuart.

"I Googled...actually tried Microsoft Edge as well but they pulled up more or less the same stuff. There was nothing local."

"Do you not think it would have been a good idea to go to the library or the local newspaper and check their microfiche?" Stuart sounded irritable.

"I don't know what that is! You should have been more specific if that's what you wanted me to do."

Stuart glowered at Kylie for making their group look less than professional.

"I'll do it," Kevin interjected. "If not me then someone in my group. It's fine. We're used to doing proper research."

"You told me to check the name McKenzie," Sarah butted in, easing the tension, "but it was like setting off on a tour of the world with no map. And anyway, Stuart, I'm beginning to think the name McKenzie was not the name of the entity we contacted. I think it may have been a warning about your ex-pupil and what he was going to do."

"Do?"

"Or should I say, had done...murdered someone at Rye Top Farm."

"We don't know it was him. The police think it was Martyn."

"Come on Stuart, you can't believe for one minute it was Martyn."

Stuart shrugged. Truth was, he didn't know what to think. None of them did.

"Have you seen McKenzie lately?" Kylie was directing her question at Stuart.

"No."

"Seen a photo of him?"

"No."

"We could do with seeing one, don't you think? Martyn gave you a description of the two men that dragged him off the other night, and framed him for the murder. We could compare his description...then we'd know."

"The police will already have done that," Stuart said defensively.

"Have you asked them?"

"No."

"Well then. We could also see if the entity that attacked Sarah matches the same description. That would tell us whether or not it was a projection from McKenzie."

Stuart saw the glance that Sarah threw over at Kylie when Kylie said that. He knew full well what Kylie thought and it wasn't anything to do with McKenzie. Perhaps Sarah thought the same.

21

First thing on Monday morning, Kevin rang Gaynor to ask if she had time to wade through the microfiche at the local newspaper archives for the year 1849. He seemed surprised that she already knew about the investigation at Rye Top Farm. He didn't ask how or why and she was glad about that. That was her private research, nothing to do with anyone else.

Gaynor ran a Tarot Reading Group and all members took turns to man the small shop they rented in Uppermill. She was down to take the evening session and so she had the whole day to devote to the research. She told Kevin she was happy to do the work since their own patch had been a bit quiet lately.

Being a seasoned hand at researching by means of microfiche in the dusty archives of the local town's paper, she was always well received there and made to feel welcome. They even kept her fed and watered with plenty of fruit teas and gluten-free biscuits, though she usually carried a good supply of those things in her over-sized hippie handbag.

The problem with microfiche is that it has to be turned manually and there is no search function to aid the process. But Gaynor had a keen eye and despite the tediousness of the task she very soon located a relevant article. It was dated the 2nd April 1849 and had made front page news.

It was about Alice Bradshaw. The little girl had been found dead on the side of the turnpike road that led over to Holmfirth. The report said there was evidence of her having been 'interfered with' and it was assumed she had died from her injuries. The report said an inquest would follow.

Gaynor marked the page for printing out and continued with her search. The next thing she pulled up was about Elisa, Alice's mother. Distraught over the death of her daughter she had taken to standing in the market square at Delph, accosting passersby and warning them that a devil was on the loose and they should leave the area or their children would be next.

A 'clean and wholesome woman' from Denshaw said she had seen Elisa foraging for wild plants up on the moor 'for which to make her unholy potions.' There was mention of a cockerel being sacrificed, as witnessed by Widow Mary, 'a God-fearing woman from Diggle'. As if that wasn't enough, Elisa's husband, Joseph, had given evidence of her performing strange rituals in the shed that housed the cows.

To avoid a charge of witchcraft, Joseph had arranged for her to be incarcerated in a mental institution in Wakefield on the grounds that she was suffering from lunacy, caused by the tragic death of their only daughter. That article was dated the 20th August 1849.

That prompted Gaynor to remember Kevin saying that Stuart had discovered a record of her death in 1849—the same year as her daughter's.

Gaynor made a note in her writing pad to check Elisa's fate in the mental institution as she knew it was unlikely she would ever have been released. The West Riding Pauper Lunatic Asylum was familiar to Gaynor. She had been one of the investigators there when the Waterford group had conducted an overnight investigation.

Continuing with her search, she nearly missed a small piece tucked away in the middle of the Saturday edition dated only a week after Elisa's incarceration. It was reporting on the inquest into the murder of Alice. Joseph Bradshaw was present at the inquest but there was no mention of Elisa. The report said that Alice, who her father reported as being a precocious child, older than her age in many ways, had left home on the morning of that fateful day to dig out potatoes for a stew that evening. Joseph reported seeing her on the hillside around noon just as some of the gypsy platters were returning from the moors after picking rushes for their basket making. He said she was first missed in the late afternoon as it wasn't unusual for her to stay out the whole day. When he realised she was missing, he called on his brother George and they began to search the area. It was George who discovered the body. The inquest concluded that death had occurred due to assault by person or persons unknown.

Rolling the microfiche on, it was November 1849 before anything else of interest jumped out at her. It was the front page of the Late Edition for November 16th. That was creepy because today was the 16th November. This one was the biggest story of all. It was the murder of two young girls, found in similar circumstances to Alice. The girls had been helping out on Joseph Bradshaw's farm, digging out the last of the potato crop, but Joseph Bradshaw said he hadn't seen them since they left his property around noon on the 10th November. The article went on to say that Mr. George Bradshaw, brother of Joseph Bradshaw, had discovered the bodies near the Running Hill quarries, only a stone's throw from his brother's farm, known locally as Hobhole Farm. It was noted that the bodies were found in very close proximity to where the platters had been camped before they moved on and out of the area. The girls, Ashlee Grimshaw, aged ten, known as Lee to her friends, and Mary Buxton aged 12, had not been seen since leaving home to help out on the Bradshaw's farm two days earlier.

Gaynor added the article to her list of requested print outs. It was a good afternoon's work and by four o'clock she set off home with a wad of notes under her arm, looking forward to seeing Stuart that evening and presenting him with her findings. She was hoping this might entice him to work more closely with her. They'd been a good team way back and could be again. After all, she would be a great asset to his investigations at Rye Top Farm and, although he didn't know it, he was essential to furthering her own theories about how all this was fitting together. They might even get their names in the annals of proven paranormal phenomenon.

Visions of chat shows and Channel 4 documentaries crowded her mind. Fame was a measure of success—why shouldn't she have a piece of that?

22

"Do we have any news on Martyn?" Kevin asked when he arrived at Stuart's house that evening. It was late, having had to arrange the meeting for ten o'clock to fit in with Gaynor's Tarot card reading commitments.

"Sort of...I rang his mum this morning. She said they'd got a solicitor on the job and she's hoping he'll be released on bail in the next few days. From what she said, despite all the incriminating evidence, the police don't believe he did it. Mainly because there's no motive and there was something about the body that doesn't add up."

"Like what?"

"They wouldn't say. They often keep stuff like that quiet don't they...anyway he was up front about our paranormal investigation and, it seems, he's also told them about my suspension."

"Have they been in touch with your school?"

"God, I hope not."

"Have you heard anything?"

"No. I was going to ring the Principal this afternoon but thought better of it. I'm on full pay so, to be honest, I'm not complaining at the moment. Anyway, I'm confident they'll accept the grounds I gave for not listening to Haskin. Murder, after all, must be the best reason anybody could come up with."

"Going back to Martyn, do they know who it was in the boot of his car?"

"A guy called David Gray. He was something to do with a spiritualist church in Dewsbury. He was training to be a vicar or something."

"I'm surprised it's not been on the news."

Just then the doorbell sounded.

"Before you answer that," Kevin said, "what's going on with you and Sarah?"

"None of your business, mate."

"Fair enough...just to let you know, if you need to talk...I'm here."

Stuart shrugged as he got up to answer the door. "There's nothing to talk about."

This would be Gaynor arriving. He didn't want to be talking about Sarah's condition in front of her.

"Wait until you see what I've got," Gaynor exploded into the house, pushing past him in her eagerness to reveal what she was carrying. Within seconds she had removed her jacket and had spread reams of paper out on the table. "You making coffee, Stu?"

Stuart dutifully retired to the kitchen to produce the goods. It reminded him of how their relationship had panned out before. This was one of the things about her that irritated the hell out of him. She was one of the few people who were more bossy than him and they had spent two years in a power struggle. Not that she had ever seemed to recognise that. When he'd brought it up she had accused him of being too controlling. His response on the lines of, 'that's the pot calling the kettle' signalled the end of their not so beautiful relationship.

He had only ever seen her once since then and that was at one of the Waterford meetings. He'd made a quick exit when he saw her heading his way looking like a ballistic missile homing in on its target. She'd always been built for speed.

Coffee made, which she didn't drink nor thank him for, they gathered round the papers to hear what she had to say. Stuart had to admit it was damned impressive.

Alice had clearly been sexually assaulted, probably raped, and had died of her injuries. It made Stuart sick to think of it. Her mother, Elisa, had gone mad with the grief and had been incarcerated in a lunatic asylum in Wakefield and, according to the reports at the time, that was at her husband's instigation. There was clearly a connection between Elisa publically spouting off about a devil in the village and the pentagram on her daughter's grave. The dates suggested that the daughter was buried before Elisa went mad, yet the presence of the pentagram would suggest that she had these beliefs before the madness took hold.

"We need to dig more into Elisa's life," Gaynor said. "I did a Tarot card reading for her when I got home and the cards clearly showed that she was into the occult before her daughter's death. I hesitate to say witchcraft but that is actually what the cards showed—though I'm guessing she was a white witch because of the presence of the High Priestess."

"You can't believe what Tarot cards say, Gaynor." Stuart wondered if she remembered how many times he had said that to her before.

"And the other two girls that were murdered...are these reports saying it was the same as Alice?" asked Kevin.

"Seems so," replied Gaynor, flashing Stuart a seductive smile. "I did a reading for Joseph as well and I'm telling you, he was one bad dude."

"You think he might have been responsible for all the deaths?" Kevin sounded intrigued, this was probably more than he had hoped for.

"I do."

"Surely if it had been him, the police at the time would have known. These paper clippings don't even mention him as a suspect." Stuart loved playing devil's advocate where Gaynor was concerned.

"It was a close community, and a small one. They mustn't have had any reason to suspect him. And there were platters up on the moors. They were like gypsies; no one trusted them. Some people thought it was them that murdered the two men up at Bill o'Jack's in 1832. Don't forget, they didn't know then that most murders are committed by people who are close to the victims. They would have understandably blamed strangers."

"You're honestly telling me that Joseph wasn't questioned at the time, when he was the last person to see all three of them."

"He was questioned for sure, but only to give evidence of when the girls had last been seen. He doesn't seem to have been a suspect."

Kevin had picked up some of the photocopies and was scrutinising the one about the inquest on Alice. "When did Joseph die?"

"1898 according to the county records. Aged eighty two."

"So he survived his daughter by...what...forty nine years. Lived to a ripe old age."

"He remarried after getting rid of Elisa, to a woman much younger than himself," Gaynor added. "He already had a son, Edward, but he went on to have another three children with his second wife. But that's another story."

"How's this for a scenario," Kevin was looking thoughtful. "Joseph Bradshaw was a paedophile and his wife, Elisa, knew it. When he killed their daughter, Alice, she completely lost the plot but women in those days had no power did they? They were totally at the mercy of their husbands. When she started to go public, Joseph must have decided that the best way to silence her was to have her certified insane and have her put away somewhere she would never escape. How did she die? Do we know?"

"No, but we can soon find out. She was incarcerated in the West Riding Pauper Lunatic Asylum at Stanley Royd."

Stuart was laughing. "That's the name of a Kasabian album."

Gaynor threw him a scornful glance. She hated being interrupted.

"We did a lock-in there a couple of years ago, didn't we Kevin? It was only closed in 1995. I rang them to check if they still hold the old records and they do."

"The West Riding Pauper Lunatic Asylum. Came out in 2009. Best album ever...must dig it out, haven't played it for ages."

Kevin, like Gaynor, was totally ignoring Stuart's digression. "We got a lot of suicides. Didn't you say she died the same year as her daughter, Stu?"

"Yep, about six months later I think."

"Bet that's it then...and that's probably why she's not buried up at Heights. Apart from dying in an institution, suicides couldn't be buried in consecrated ground."

"Do you still have the transcripts of your investigation there?" asked Stuart.

"Of course we do." What Kevin's somewhat curt reply was really saying was, 'our outfit's professional, Stuart, unlike yours'.

"The other interesting thing," Stuart decided to disregard the inference and picked up his own notes from his investigation at the farm, "is that Rye Top Farm belonged to George Bradshaw, Joseph's brother. I'm wondering if there's a connection there with McKenzie...only because of the EVPs Sarah and I recorded there. And another thing, the name of one of the murdered girls...look...it says here, Ashlee known to her friends as Lee. That's the name we got on the EVP and it's also the name Kylie came up with in her dream."

Kevin was leaning over Stuart's shoulder, looking where he was pointing.

"We should call a meeting tomorrow night," he said, "and have another look at the transcripts you and Sarah made that night. See if we can make any sense out of it."

"Okay by me," Gaynor chirped in, smiling at Stuart. "That okay with you, Stu?"

Martyn was released the following day. His mum, a kindly-looking woman in her mid-sixties, had put up the bail by re-mortgaging a huge chunk of her little terraced house in Dewsbury.

She was to be his keeper for the foreseeable future, at least until this mess was sorted out.

"I don't want you going back to Saddleworth. You're in enough trouble without getting yourself into more."

"Have to," he argued. "I need to see Stuart."

"Then I'll come with you," she insisted, "no argument."

Martyn couldn't refuse and he certainly didn't want to upset her after all she had done for him. She'd bailed him out of a few scrapes over the years. He wasn't known for being her most responsible offspring. How often had she said to him, "Why can't you be more like Michael?"

His brother Michael was in Dubai working for a large telecommunications company, happily married with two perfect children. It didn't take a genius to figure out why they didn't get on. Not that he resented Michael his wealth and status, he just didn't want to be like that—all white teeth and designer chinos.

Stuart picked them up from the railway station in Stalybridge—the TransPennine Express didn't stop at Greenfield because the platform wasn't long enough.

"You're very welcome," Stuart said to Martyn's mum when Martyn explained why she was with him. "It's a very worrying time for you."

Martyn put his arm around Stuart's shoulders. "I knew you wouldn't mind, Stu. God, you're so polite."

He watched in admiration as Stuart did all the right things, escorting his mum out of the station and along the side streets to where he had parked the car, always making sure she was on the side of the pavement farthest away from the road. He even opened the front passenger door for her, making Martyn take the back seat. His mum would be saying next, "Why can't you be more like Stuart. He's so kind and considerate."

Once inside Stuart's house, his mum insisted on having a guided tour full of 'ohs' and 'ahs' and 'oh how lovely.'

It had been late afternoon when they had arrived and the light was already starting to fade.

"You're both very welcome to stay the night," Stuart announced when they re-joined Martyn in the lounge. "There's plenty of room. You could have the spare room, Mrs Curtis. Martyn will be okay on the bed settee down here."

"That's very kind of you, Stuart. Martyn's very lucky to have such a considerate friend."

Here we go again, thought Martyn. Not that he could argue with her sentiment.

"What's happened with you and the school?" he asked.

"I have to attend a Board of Governors meeting tomorrow, one o'clock."

"Want me to come with you?"

"Never thought about that...but yes, it might help. I'll ring the Principal later and make sure it's okay. They did say I could take someone with me, but just for support, not to speak on my behalf."

"Martyn can give evidence though can't he?" chirped in Mrs Curtis. "To back up your story. Surely they can't deny you that."

"We'll see. School Boards are quite Dickensian affairs, Mrs Curtis."

"I'll speak up anyway," Martyn was not one to be silenced. "What's the worst they can do, throw me out?"

"The worst they can do is fire me," Stuart retorted. "I don't want you there if you're going to be disruptive."

Mrs Curtis patted her son's knee. "You listen to Stuart, Martyn. You're far too hot headed sometimes. Don't want to make things worse."

"Anyway, Martyn," Stuart said, forever the diplomat and changing the subject. "What about you? Banged up since Friday night."

"Bit of a bummer," Martyn always liked to make a joke out of everything. "I had a great weekend planned as well...I'd set up a Tinder date...she'll think I stood her up."

Mrs C made a very loud tutting sound. "Arrested for murder and that's all you can think about."

'Here we go again,' thought Martyn. "Mum, please stop it. If you're gonna keep having a go at me, we're going home."

Stuart was laughing. "Mrs Curtis, Martyn is the life and soul of our little group. We wouldn't have him any other way."

She smiled at that and gave Martyn a little wink. "He's a good boy really. I know that."

"We've arranged a meeting tonight, Mrs C." Stuart said, changing the subject again. "Not sure how much Martyn has told you, but we're paranormal investigators, semi-professional of course. We need to discuss the research surrounding what's been happening. You're welcome to sit in if you like. Or there's a TV in my room. You can make yourself comfortable up there until we're done."

"How interesting, dear. I'm a bit of a psychic myself."

"What!" Martyn couldn't help blurting out. His mum had never, in his entire life, given any indication that she was that way inclined.

"Oh yes, Martyn. There are quite a few things about me that you don't know. Where do you think I've been going every Monday night for the past twenty years?"

Martyn couldn't speak but felt his eyes widen with the shock. This was a revelation he had never expected.

"The Spiritualist Church on the corner of Forest Road. I'm rather well regarded for my mediumship, even though I say so myself."

Stuart gasped. "Then you must have known David Gray—the man that was murdered?"

"Yes dear, I'm afraid I did. He was such an amiable young man though we didn't see much of him. He was training to be a priest or something. I don't think the Catholic church would have condoned him dabbling in spiritualism but I always had the impression he was doing it more for research than belief, if you know what I mean."

"No, not really." It was Martyn's turn to look aghast. "Why didn't you tell me you knew him?"

"I didn't want to worry you," Mrs C. answered, patting his hand. "The police seemed to think it was an important connection. It was best you didn't know."

"Well you're very welcome to join us," Stuart was grinning from ear to ear. "It will be a great help to have another head on the case."

24

The meeting had been arranged for eight. Stuart pulled out the extensions on the dining table and arranged the chairs neatly around it, bringing extra ones in from the spare room that doubled as his office. There would be seven of them and they would need lots of table space for the paperwork they had so far accumulated.

Sarah was first to arrive. Stuart thought how tired she looked and gave her a hug and a kiss in the hallway. He whispered to her that Martyn and his mum would be staying the night but assuring her they would get together tomorrow night to discuss what they were going to do about their predicament.

Next came Kevin with Gaynor in tow, fluttering her false eyelashes in Stuart's direction and giving him a peck on the cheek in front of Sarah. Stuart had no idea whether Gaynor knew he and Sarah were an item but somehow he didn't think she would change her behaviour even if she did.

Kylie was last to arrive, seeming a bit more subdued than usual.

Introductions over, they all settled themselves down to look over the evidence they had before them. As usual, there was no agenda, which Kevin commented on, suggesting they rectify that for their next meeting. He was the first one to take the floor.

"I've brought along the transcripts of the Waterford group's investigation at the West Yorkshire asylum. You're going to find this interesting."

"Hang on," Stuart interjected, "Let's begin by bringing everyone up to speed. Don't forget Martyn, Sarah and Kylie weren't here last night so they're not privy to what Gaynor uncovered from the microfiche. And also you Mrs C. We need to put you in the picture."

Questioning glances were exchanged round the table.

"Turns out," Martyn muttered, almost under his breath, "my mother is a spiritualist."

"Wow!" Gaynor's exclamation sounded a little too enthusiastic. "That's fantastic."

Martyn grimaced, causing his mum to playfully smack his hand.

"Thank you, Gaynor. You see, Martyn, not everyone thinks like you."

The next hour was spent going through Gaynor's findings and the photocopies of the newspaper articles, with everyone pitching in to draw conclusions and to suggest possible connections.

"So, that's what we have, but there are some unknowns." Stuart began to go through his listed gaps in their knowledge. "Firstly, the Bradshaws. Did Joseph kill those children, including his own daughter? Was Elisa into the occult before her daughter died, and how did she herself die? Kevin, I'm hoping you'll be able to help us find the answers."

Kevin nodded. Stuart continued, relieved that Kevin hadn't tried to ambush his little prep talk.

"Secondly, we need to investigate the history of Rye Top Farm and maybe do some more EVPs there. If George Bradshaw lived there, what Sarah and I got that night could well have come from him trying to warn us."

"It's a crime scene," Kevin pointed out. "You won't be going back there for a while."

"We could do card readings...and maybe hold a séance now we have a spiritualist amongst us." Gaynor was glowing with enthusiasm, undeterred by the fact that no one responded to her suggestion.

"What about the entity, the one who gave his name as McKenzie?" It was Martyn's turn to ask for an explanation.

"Can't say. We know what Kylie thinks...that it was a projection possibly from someone living. I've never come across anything like that before, have you Kevin?"

"I haven't but I think Gaynor has. Gaynor?"

For the first time Stuart had known Gaynor, she looked uncomfortable and hesitant. She seemed to be trying to find the right words.

"I did know someone once who could do that. It's actually a well known Shamanic...process...I was going to say trick, but it's not a trick...it's real enough and there are Shamans trained in it, but it can also happen spontaneously. When that occurs the person doing the projecting usually doesn't even know they're doing it."

"That's what I said," Kylie butted in, looking straight at Stuart. "Didn't I Stuart?"

Stuart looked away, disregarding her question, "Mrs C. Do you have any experience of this?"

"Well, I wouldn't really know. I have been known to see apparitions, ghosts if you like," she cast a glance over at Kylie, "but I've never wondered whether they were anything but what they appeared to be. Perhaps if you show me the video

126

you took, I'll be able to tell you if it's the sort of thing I sometimes see. Would that help?"

"I'm sure it would," Stuart had his diplomatic persona on display again. "We'll all watch it again later. Gaynor hasn't seen it either, see if we can pick anything else out of it. Where was I?"

"You were up to number three," Sarah offered. Stuart shuffled his notes.

"Ah yes. It's possible, nay probable, that one of my pupils was assaulted by McKenzie, for which I may be for the high jump. There's definitely a link with Martyn being set up for murder and the name McKenzie coming through on the EVP that Sarah and I got. Now I don't know what the connection is, but the entity we saw on the video is definitely not the real live McKenzie."

"But how long is it since you saw him?"

"Four or five years but he can't have changed that much. And anyway, Martyn didn't you ID McKenzie as your attacker from photos at the station? You also gave me a detailed description. McKenzie has a very distinctive crooked nose. Broke it in a fight in Year 4, so I don't think there's any doubt that the real events are all linked to him. I'm honestly coming to the conclusion that the EVPs Sarah and I got were from a friendly spirit, warning us about McKenzie."

"But Stuart," Sarah looked agitated, " I know what happened to me, and it felt real. And another thing, the entity we contacted clearly said it had murdered someone, and gave the name Lee, which

127

we now know is one of the murdered children. What if we picked up EVPs from Joseph Bradshaw himself? And could he be working through McKenzie? Could all of this somehow be related?"

"She's got a point there," Kevin said, shuffling onto the edge of his seat. "That would make sense wouldn't it? I wonder if it might be useful to look further into Joseph Bradshaw's family tree; see if there's a family connection?"

"I'll do that," Gaynor offered.

"Great stuff. Anything else, Stuart? Or shall I launch into what I've found out about Elisa?"

"Go ahead," Stuart said sitting back down, "unless anyone else has anything to add before we move on?"

"Just one thing," Kylie said, raising her hand. "Do we have the name of the person killed at Rye Top Farm yet?"

"His name was David Gray," it was Martyn who answered. "Twenty six years old and training to be a priest...and believe it or not, my mother knew him. He was a member of her spiritualist church. The police said he'd been missing for quite a few days before turning up in the boot of my car. They've still got my car by the way...not that I'm gonna want it back."

"So is it safe to say he was killed before Sarah and I went to Rye Top Farm?"

"Probably. I'm surprised you haven't been pulled in for questioning."

"Isn't it a bit odd then that we didn't pick up any EVPs from the dead guy?" It was Sarah asking but no one seemed to be offering any comment. At last Martyn's mum spoke up.

"Not all spirits hang about dear. They usually accept they are dead very quickly and make their way to the other side. It's only those who are confused or have a strong earthly link that stay around in the earth plane. Usually it's a strong bond to a person or a place that keeps them tethered." She was looking directly at Kylie now. "Like the gentleman who's here with us tonight."

All eyes turned to Kylie. She said nothing.

"He's telling me he worked on the barges. He was one of the leggers. Part of the tunnel collapsed on him and he fell into the freezing water."

"He's called Ron," Kylie said at last. "He whistles, drives me mad."

Mrs C laughed. "He's telling me it's the only way he can get your attention. He was a good man, a caring man. I'm asking why he's here but he's not answering."

"What's going on, Kylie?" It was Stuart asking. "Why haven't you mentioned this before?"

Kylie shrugged but didn't answer.

"She didn't want you banning her forever," Sarah spoke up for her. "We all know how you rubbish people who claim to have spirit guides."

Mrs C was still staring intently at Kylie. "He warns you about things, doesn't he?"

Kylie nodded.

"He may prove useful. Be nice to him."

Kylie's eyes lit up and she broke into a smile.

"Okay," interjected Stuart, "we'll talk about this later, let's move on to Elisa. Kevin?"

Kevin stood up, a wad of papers in his hand.

"These papers are the result of the Waterford Paranormal Society's investigation at The West Riding Pauper Lunatic Asylum at Stanley Royd, Wakefield on the 28th August 1998. The asylum was opened in 1818 and closed down in 1995. According to a local news report at the time, Elisa was incarcerated there in August 1849 with Chronic Melancholia. The asylum was what's known as a panopticon design, which meant that all the inmates could be observed at all times, twenty four seven." He was holding up a drawing of the plan so they could all see it. "It was a system of total control that must have been unbearable for the inmates...though this institution was the first to actually offer treatment and treat the inmates with at least some humanity. The design consisted of a circular structure with an inspection house at the centre from which staff could watch all the inmates, who were housed around the perimeter in partially open fronted cells. The design was used for prisons in some countries, Cuba and the Netherlands for example."

"Is this relevant?" Stuart didn't really like the way Kevin was holding the attention of the group, many of whom seemed to be hanging on his every word.

"I mention the design, Stuart, so you can all understand where we positioned ourselves for the investigation. Two set up in the observation room at the centre, here, and the other four were deployed in four cells in each of the cardinal directions. I was in the observation room at the centre, sweeping round the full three hundred and sixty degrees. As I mentioned to Stuart yesterday, we picked up many suicides in addition to demonic elements, clearly attracted to the place because of the things that had gone on there and the type of person the institution housed. If anyone wants to see the full transcripts, you're very welcome to send in a request to our secretary...just ask me for contact details. We picked up some amazing stuff but the only one we're interested in tonight was one of the suicide victims. I could hardly believe it when I spotted it going through the transcript last night. She came through very early on in the proceedings and identified herself immediately as Elisa. She was distraught and repeated the name Joe several times...which we now know must have been her husband, Joseph. We also picked up the name Allie or Alice who she appeared to be saying she was trying to find. When we checked the records of the institution, we discovered that Elisa hung herself in her cell on the 10th December 1849."

Stuart nodded his agreement; that was the date he had got from the county records.

"We went into the archives after the investigation, checking all the stuff we'd picked up.

The records they hold are very detailed because the asylum was one of the best of its kind in the day and was a model for other institutions so the inmates and the procedures were well documented. I have a copy of a photograph of Elisa here that we pulled out at the time."

They all gasped. This was far more than any of them could ever have hoped for.

Kevin held up the picture for them all to see. It was a woman with a haunted look in her eyes set into sepia toned skin. It was passed round the table, each person hesitating to pass it on to the next, as if somehow they could heal her pain by holding onto it.

"And that's not all," Kevin pronounced with the authority of a champion poker player. "We have here a copy of her patient records...they're incredibly detailed...and, believe it or not, they allude to her interest in the occult before her incarceration. I would add, that she made it known to us that she would not have hung herself had she known her torment would continue."

It was decided they would break for coffee to give themselves a chance to browse the records that Kevin had brought along. Elisa, it seems, had been well practised in the craft and, as well as dabbling in herbal remedies from foraged vegetation, she had often held séances at her brother-in-law's house. The reason she gave to her nurse at the asylum was that her husband, Joseph, had forbidden her to practise the ancient art and had threatened her more than once with incarceration in a lunatic asylum. His brother George, on the other hand, was quite open to the possibility of contacting the dead and he would willingly join in the séances.

It was at one of these séances that Elisa learned the truth about her husband and his predilection towards young girls. Fearful for the safety of her own daughter, she took Alice to live at Rye Top Farm under George's watchful eye until, the report stated, Joseph arrived one day with a shotgun, threatening to shoot the lot of them. Elisa and Alice were forced to return to the marital home and it was two days later that Alice was found dead. The authorities at the West Riding Pauper Lunatic Asylum had recorded that Elisa was suffering from 'mental delusion' and 'chronic melancholia' due to the death of her daughter.

"I wonder why George didn't come forward to give evidence against his brother?" asked Sarah.

"Maybe he was threatened with the same thing," Kylie said, "and don't forget, witchcraft was still a crime in those days, wasn't it?"

"Actually, no." Kevin looked pleased at the opportunity to show off his superior knowledge again. "The Witchcraft Act of 1735 stipulated that there was no such thing as witchcraft though people pretending to be able to summon spirits or cast spells could still be charged with conning people and thrown into prison for it."

All through the discussions, Mrs C had been quietly sipping her herbal tea, but at last she spoke up.

"That was ousted by the Fraudulent Mediums Act of 1951," she chipped in. "We're now controlled by consumer protection regulations. At least they've dropped the fraudulent bit so the judiciary are a little more enlightened these days." She hesitated, looking thoughtful. "As Elisa was adept at holding séances, perhaps we should do the same."

"That's what I said." Gaynor was not going to let Mrs C take credit for suggesting that.

"Mum, no," piped up Martyn.

"Martyn, yes," she replied with the authority only a mother can command. "I think there's a lot more to this than we know."

Kylie was grinning from ear to ear. It was something they had never done before and would undoubtedly be very entertaining.

"Why not?" she said. "Yeh...come on, let's do it."

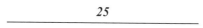

25

"It's always a good idea to join hands," Mrs C was sitting at the head of the table, directing proceedings. This was a first for all of them, especially Kevin and Stuart who both prided themselves on having their feet and their heads firmly entrenched in science.

"There's no need to be anxious, whatever comes through can't harm us...but, of course, you all know that."

"Actually no," interrupted Kylie. "I didn't only pick up Ron in Standedge tunnel, there was something else and it made my life hell."

"I wish I'd known," Mrs C replied, looking at Martyn. "I could have helped with that." And to Kylie, "I promise you, there's no need to be afraid now I'm here."

"Can we please get on," Stuart was sounding irritated.

Sarah responded immediately. "Stuart! Don't be so rude."

"I'm not, it's just—"

Mrs C. banged on the table with the spoon she had been using to stir her tea. "Settle down, please. Nothing will come through unless we all remain quiet and calm."

Everyone fell silent.

"Now then," Mrs C continued, "it's Elisa Bradshaw we want to reach. Yes?"

They all nodded their agreement.

"It's quite likely all of us will pick up something. It's important to keep your mind clear and your thoughts at bay. We will start by imagining we are all inside the Asylum. Kevin has kindly described the inside of the building to us and, in my experience, imagining being in the place is enough. So, that's where we'll start. All close your eyes please and concentrate."

There were candles already lit in the centre of the table and Stuart glanced round at the other six before he too closed his eyes.

There followed an eerie silence, broken suddenly by the sound of Gaynor taking a deep breath and blowing noisily out through her mouth. It brought back memories for Stuart, memories of another one of her annoying habits. She had many. The one that lurched into his mind was her constant chattering when they went to bed. Even after they had done the business she would still rabbit on for at least another hour, stopping him from falling asleep. Fluttering her eyelashes at him all evening meant she was probably hoping for a re-match. He sincerely hoped not.

"Someone's mind is chattering." Mrs C broke the silence and opened her eyes, looking in Stuart's direction. "Stuart?"

Stuart was shocked. Oh my goodness, could she read minds?

"It causes interference," Mrs C went on. "Please try and let your mind go blank. Imagine you are meditating."

Stuart gave her the thumbs up and closed his eyes again.

"Elisa...Elisa Bradshaw...will you come and talk to us? We know what happened to you...it was dreadful...will you grace us with your presence?"

Nothing.

Stuart didn't see how this would work. Every contact he had ever made had been on haunted premises. Mrs C had, however, explained before starting that the spirit dimensions are worlds within worlds, like the layers of an onion, and that spirits are able to pass between the layers and appear anywhere. He had never subscribed to all that mumbo jumbo. As far as he was concerned, dead people could only leave residual energy traces behind. That was all it was. He did not believe that personality survived death.

"It's to do with quantum physics; non-locality and worm holes," Mrs C had patiently, and not very eloquently, explained earlier, whilst making it totally obvious she had no understanding of that area of science at all, nor any area of science if it came to that. But Stuart had been too polite to argue.

"Elisa...we are here, waiting to talk to you. Are you near?"

Still nothing except Gaynor noisily blowing out another deep breath.

"Elisa...yes Elisa...I hear you..."

Was this for real? Stuart couldn't hear anything and his brain was still shifting gear into overdrive. He couldn't get Gaynor out of his head. He opened his eyes but shut them just as quickly when he saw Gaynor looking straight at him with that piercing gaze she'd spent months trying to perfect when they were together.

"Yes dear...we know about your husband...we know what he did...what? Can you repeat that my darling...yes, yes, I have it. Thank you my dear. May the Lord's peace be with you."

137

Mrs C breathed deeply and released Stuart's hand.

"You can all open your eyes now," she instructed. "Stuart, perhaps you would turn on the lights."

There was a lot of shuffling of chairs when the lights came on but no one said a word. All of them were waiting for Mrs C to speak as it was clear she had contacted, or at least believed she had contacted, Elisa Bradshaw.

"Now then," she began, "before I tell you what Elisa told me, did anyone else pick anything up?"

Gaynor raised her hand. "I could see her...you know, in my mind's eye...very clearly, but she didn't look like she did in the old photo Kevin showed us. She was wearing a red shawl over what looked like a school uniform...bit odd really...because the uniform looked modern and she looked too old for it."

"Yes...that is odd...especially as I had the impression she was in a playground near a school and she did come through very quickly which suggests she's still got very strong ties to the earth plane."

"I also saw something hovering around," Gaynor said, fixing her gaze on Stuart again. "It was hazy, smoky. I couldn't tell what it was."

"Yes, I had an impression of that too," Mrs C replied. "We should really have said prayers before we started. Be on the safe side."

Martyn sighed, a deep, disapproving sounding sigh.

"Well come on," Sarah was impatient. "What did Elisa say?"

"She said there's another child that Joseph killed...and the poor thing is buried in George's potato field."

26

Stuart woke early the next day—too early. The meeting with the Board of Governors had been on his mind the whole night and his sleep had been fitful and restless because of it.

He wasn't one to second guess what other people would do but it didn't take a genius to know what would probably happen to him today. He had seen it so many times before.

It was a question of action being taken, any action that would give the impression the school was acting quickly and decisively. Saving face. It didn't matter if the action taken was unjust or inappropriate, as long as the injured parties felt they had been avenged. Finding a scapegoat was something the Principal was well-practised in. He was a politician at heart and would make sure his own reputation remained polished and unblemished.

Stuart had met Haskin's parents on many occasions and they weren't the sort of parents a teacher wanted to have to deal with at Parents'

Evening. They were coarse, abusive and defended their son's bad behaviour whatever he had done. They tried to blame Stuart when Haskin attacked another student with a brick in the playground last year; said he'd been angry because Stuart had pulled him up about missing detention the day before.

As for the Principal, there had been too many pupils expelled in the past few years and he had already made it clear that he didn't want any more. The incident with the brick had been passed over with a gentle slap on the wrists and a 'don't do it again son'. The only thing the Principal cared about were the Stats records and his pension pot.

So yes, Stuart knew the Haskins would be baying for blood and it was his blood that they would get.

Although he had been preparing himself to brave the firing squad alone, he was glad Martyn had offered to go with him. He could help him drown his sorrows in the pub afterwards.

Arriving at the school a little after one o'clock, Stuart and Martyn were greeted in the staff block by a posse of teachers expressing their support. Tom Carter, the Union Rep was also there, assuring Stuart that all the members would stand by him and strike if necessary to get him re-instated.

"Though, of course," he added quickly, "I'm sure it won't come to that."

Stuart shook Tom's hand, thanking him and introducing him to Martyn, explaining Martyn's role in the emergency call out that Stuart had responded to the evening that Haskin was assaulted.

"I was hoping I could accompany you," Tom said. "A Union presence is guaranteed to put the wind up them...and to be honest Stuart, I'm not sure bringing in a murder suspect who is out on bail is the best strategy."

Martyn was about to speak but Stuart got in first, "What would you suggest then, Tom?"

"They have no right to pry into your private life and you are under no obligation, whatsoever, to discuss the personal emergency you were called out to. If you like, say it was a family emergency, they're never going to know any different. From there, we can say that no matter how dedicated you are to your pupil's welfare, your family comes first...and it was outside school hours anyway. You were only on the premises because you had a backlog of marking to do...not enough hours in the day and all that. On top of all that, Haskin gave you no indication, whatsoever, that he was in any distress. On that topic, it's your word against his and who are they going to believe...a delinquent teenager from a bad family who's always in trouble, or you, the epitome of the dedicated teacher? And anyway, bottom line, the assault happened on school premises, which means a failure of the security system and that buck stops at management not you."

"What security system?"

"Exactly."

"Okay," Stuart said, impressed by Tom's spiel, "let's do it."

141

Sarah should have left for work at eight but at nine thirty she was still hanging over the toilet, intermittently throwing up nothing but air. She felt dreadful and crawled back to bed with a hot water bottle. If this is what it's like being pregnant, she wanted none of it.

She would tell Stuart tonight that she had made her decision. He would probably be relieved. They hadn't been seeing each other that long and the honeymoon period was already starting to wane. She also reminded herself that it was him that had wanted to keep their relationship secret from the others—why would he do that if he was serious about her? And to make matters worse, she had seen the way he and Gaynor had been looking at each other last night—throwing each other sly glances.

Kevin had already mentioned to her that the two of them had history. Perhaps he'd been trying to warn her. It was clear Gaynor still fancied Stuart from the way she had been looking all doe-eyed at him the whole night. Everybody must have noticed. She wasn't sure about Stuart though. To give him his due, he didn't appear to still have a thing for her, but you could never tell with Stuart. He kept all his cards close to his chest.

Stuart, though, had a great knack of making her feel sorry for him. And she did...in spades. She just had this pregnancy to worry about, but his job was on the line too and she knew how much that meant to him. He would be devastated if he lost his job. It was far more than a job to him, as he had said so many times—it was a vocation; all he had ever wanted to do.

She pictured him preparing for the meeting, knowing he would be in a state despite his claim to being the calmest person he knows. When she had asked him the other day what form the meeting would take—would it be like a court room or just an informal chat—he had got a bit annoyed and hadn't wanted to discuss it. Reading between the lines, she had guessed that he was probably annoyed at her for even asking the question, perhaps because it reminded him of how far apart they were on the social ladder—he a teacher, she a check-out girl on the tills at the local superstore. Not like Gaynor. She might be a tarot card reader but she had a University education behind her.

But maybe she was putting two and two together and making far more than the right answer. That was something else about her that annoyed Stuart; the fact that she was always second guessing what she thought he should be saying and wasn't. It was something she'd been trying to work on lately because it wasn't just Stuart that had commented on that over the years—quite a few of her boyfriends had said the same thing. But it was hard not to do that when you were getting mixed messages. She just wanted to know where she stood.

Kylie said she should use her intuition more, that on a gut level we all knew how someone felt about us. And Kylie was right, she did know. She just didn't want to accept it, especially with this new problem growing inside her.

Stuart had promised to ring as soon as the meeting was over, but somehow she doubted he would. Whatever the outcome he would probably muster his fellow teachers and head for the nearest pub. It didn't matter. She would ring him around three, by which time hopefully she would have stopped throwing up.

Her phone rang at two thirty but it wasn't Stuart. It was Kylie.

"I was just meditating and I got the impression you weren't doing so good today. Are you alright?"

Sarah admitted she wasn't really. She'd had almost the whole day to convince herself that she and Stuart were over. And to make things worse, when she stopped throwing up and started to feel better, she began to change her mind about a termination. She would manage bringing a child up on her own. Thousands of women did it, so why shouldn't she? She may even be able to finish work, go on social, devote herself to this new little life full time.

"Want me to come round? I'm off today...using up flexi time."

"I'd really appreciate that," Sarah said before she had chance to change her mind. She and Kylie had never been best pals, yet she was closer to Kylie than anybody else. Besides, with Kylie's professed psychic abilities, she might be able to tell her something about Gaynor's intentions, or more importantly, about Stuart's.

"Shall I bring something round for our tea? I've got salmon fillets in the freezer."

"That'd be great...now I've stopped chucking."

"Oh Sarah...poor you. I'll bring some peppermint tea as well."

"Great, see you later." Given the emotional state she was in, the kindness shown by Kylie was almost overwhelming. She was becoming like the sister Sarah had always wanted and never had. Being an only child, she had grown up being told that children like her were spoiled by their doting parents. She hadn't felt spoiled, hadn't felt anything much if truth be told. Her parents didn't even live round here anymore. They had up and moved to Dorset as soon as Sarah had left home to make her own way in the world.

There hadn't been much contact since but that was nothing new, there hadn't been much even when she lived with them. It was a situation that had often made her feel unloved and abandoned. Now it just made her sad. Still, she did wonder if she should ring them. Tell them the news. They might be able to advise her. After all, it is their grandchild.

As she dabbed her eyes, she told herself not to be so silly. Her parents hadn't been any help to her so far, why would that change now? And getting upset wouldn't solve anything. She'd been reading all day from internet searches that hormones run amok when you're pregnant. She would just have to get used to it.

28

The Commercial was empty of lunchtime punters by the time Stuart and Martyn piled in with six of Stuart's work colleagues.

School was finished for the day and they were all determined to drink as much alcohol as was humanly possible in the couple of hours they would normally be on school premises running afterschool classes. On hearing the outcome of the meeting they had all decided that the Principal could run the classes this afternoon, see how he liked it.

"Here's to Mr and Mrs Haskin," said Tom, raising his pint, "and to all who sail past them, as our dear friend and colleague, Stuart Ryder has just done."

There was much frivolity as glasses were chinked together and congratulations offered.

"What a turn up for the books," Martyn said, after downing his pint of cask ale in one go. "Who'd have thought it?"

"Not me, that's for sure," Stuart replied. "But I tell you what, they won't be in a hurry to back up their delinquent son again, I'll bet."

"The lying little toad...shows how thick he is if he expected to get away with lying to the police as well."

"Probably didn't expect the police to get involved. He denied ever saying he'd been interfered with, that was 'head up your arse Principal Paul' getting the facts wrong...as usual. What a muppet."

"Bet he felt a right dick in front of the governors."

"He did squirm a bit," Tom piped up. "Reckon he got carried away with wanting to pull Stu down a peg or two."

"Quite right too." The quip was from one of the younger teachers who had been under Stuart's charge during his PGCE teaching practice.

Stuart clipped him round the head, playfully.

"Oh sir...please sir...Mr. Ryder has just assaulted me..." They all laughed and signalled to the barman that they were ready for another round of drinks.

It was five o'clock before Stuart remembered he had promised to ring Sarah. She would be worried. He should have called her. A quick text would have to do for the time being.

Good outcome. Job safe. OK if I call round later - about 7?

With all the worry and hassle over the Haskin fiasco he'd had no time to think about Sarah's condition, and whether or not he had any view at all on the decision that needed to be made. He really liked Sarah, despite the things she did and said that irritated the hell out of him sometimes. But 'really like' wasn't enough to bring a child into the world

147

together. He didn't love her, at least he didn't think he did. The only sort of love he'd ever known was the infatuation type.

It was true that when he and Sarah had first got together he had been, what Martyn always termed, 'in lust' with her, but it didn't take a psychologist to tell him that that was as far away from love as it was possible to get. And anyway, he had always had it in his mind when he was ready to settle down, that it would be with another teacher, someone in the same line of work, someone his intellectual equal. Trouble was, the only intellectual equal he had ever fancied was Gaynor and he didn't want to go there again.

There were a few single teachers in his school and he had weighed them all up at one time or another. The maths teacher, Jody, was probably the best of the bunch, but she was so incredibly serious. Maths seemed to do something to women, made them look at the world in a different way. He'd asked her out once but she'd turned him down, saying she didn't like going into pubs.

As he stood at the bar waiting to be served with their fourth round of drinks, he decided that the safest thing to do was to leave the decision up to Sarah. It was her body, let her decide. He wouldn't need to make any decisions unless she wanted to keep it and he doubted that would happen. So no worries. He had his job back. Life was sweet.

He had exactly four minutes to savour that sweetness whilst he carried the tray of drinks over to the table where the others were sitting. It was Tom

Carter that brought an end to it, when he said, almost under his breath, "Fuck me...look what's just walked in."

Stuart looked towards the door where three men were standing in semi-shadow. One was caught in a pool of dim light from the lamp over the entrance, a lamp just lit automatically because of the fading light outside. It was McKenzie and he was holding a knife.

29

They were all silent, waiting to see what would happen. Tom had his phone out under the table, ready to ring the police if anything kicked off. McKenzie, knife in hand, sauntered over towards their table. He didn't look happy.

"Guess you're feeling pretty damned pleased with yourself, Ryder," he said at last. "You've no need...I'll get you back for this."

"Oh yea," taunted Stuart, in no mood to be threatened by a toss bag like McKenzie. "What are you going to do? Can I suggest you make sure your story holds up next time, mate? Then again, perhaps your idea of a sexual assault is pulling your own dick."

McKenzie waved the knife at Stuart and took a step closer. "I never touched the kid. I'd never do that. Next time you start throwing accusations round, you'll be for it. And don't fuckin' call me mate."

"What you going to do, McKenzie? Come on, mate...you can tell us...we promise not to expel you...though we might throw you out of the pub."

Tom was at Stuart's side and whispered softly so McKenzie wouldn't hear, "Don't wind him up, Stu. Looks to me like he's off his head."

"What did he just say?" McKenzie demanded to know.

"He said you're a right dick."

"No I didn't," Tom yelled. "We don't want any trouble, McKenzie. Why don't you just leave quietly and we'll say no more about it?"

"Fuck off."

"Sorry, no, that's not the right answer."

"Perhaps this is the right fuckin' answer then," McKenzie yelled as he kicked a vacant chair, sending it scuttling across the floor.

Tom and Stuart both stood up, the others picked up their drinks and shuffled their chairs a bit farther away, all except Martyn who seemed to be trying to decide if he should help defend his friend.

"You ruined my fuckin' life, you did," McKenzie was screaming like an hysterical child now, "and it's fuckin' pay back time."

He lunged at Stuart, sending the table toppling over and stabbing out with the knife, catching Stuart's arm. The knife sliced through the sleeve of his shirt, which was now turning red.

Tom grabbed the arm with the knife and tried to wrestle it free but McKenzie was a strong lad, he had been a prop forward on the school rugby team when he was fourteen and he hadn't lost any of his mass. Martyn, along with the two other male teachers, joined in the fray, one of them punching McKenzie in the stomach. He said later it was like hitting a brick wall. It had no effect on McKenzie, who continued to stab indiscriminately anything that was within arm's reach. All the while, McKenzie's two companions remained standing by the door, no doubt intending to make a quick escape if the police made an appearance.

It was Debbie who put a stop to the fracas—or Miss Glam Arse as she was known in school. Sadly for Stuart, she was already happily married with no plans for infidelity. Calmly walking over to the bar, she picked up a pint bottle of cider that had been placed alongside a poster advertising a special offer—buy Gallagher's Cider and win a holiday in Malaga. Striding up behind McKenzie, she hit him squarely on the top of his head, showering everyone in pear cider.

McKenzie dropped to the floor with the shock. His two companions, realising that things weren't going their way, scarpered, but not before Stuart got a good view of the one with the bushy black beard and mean face. A cold shiver ran through him when he realised the man bore an uncanny resemblance to the apparition he and Sarah had caught on the video camera at Rye Top Farm. Just then, and right on cue, two police officers entered the premises and cuffed McKenzie before he had chance to regain his senses.

It was the Landlord of The Commercial who had rung the police and his detailed statement lay no blame whatsoever at the door of Stuart and his companions, but the police advised it was probably less inconvenient for them all to give statements there and then. After that, they would be free to go.

The likeness of the knife to the one Martyn had been set up with at Rye Top Farm was duly noted. Stuart was advised to go to hospital but the knife wound was superficial and he refused. The police constable took a photograph of it anyway, said it would be used in evidence.

It was when the police asked them all for a description of McKenzie's companion that Stuart realised something was wrong. Everyone described a man, possibly in his forties, with thinning hair and bandy legs. An accurate enough description from what Stuart had seen of him. But no one mentioned the guy with the beard.

"There were two of them," Stuart said. "The other looked older and had a bushy black beard. Mean looking."

The others were looking at him as if he was crazy.

"What?" he asked.

"You're seeing double, mate," Tom joked. "Too much beer."

"What do you mean?"

"There was only one other guy."

The policeman taking the statements looked around the group, "Anyone else see two men arrive with McKenzie."

They all shook their heads.

"Perhaps he wasn't with McKenzie," the police constable said, trying to make sense of Stuart's apparent certainty. "How long was he standing in the doorway?"

"He was there the whole time, standing to the left of the other guy. I can't believe no one saw him." Stuart threw Martyn a glance to check if he'd seen anything, but all he did was shrug his shoulders.

That was it then, it must have been an apparition; the same entity that had appeared at Rye Top Farm, the one that had assaulted Sarah. And something else struck Stuart about that—was it a coincidence that Haskin had claimed he'd been sexually assaulted? Sarah had said it had felt completely real. What if Haskin hadn't been lying? What if the same thing had happened to him?

30

It was nine o'clock by the time Stuart arrived at Sarah's flat. He could tell she was mad at him by the way she flung open the door and left him standing on the step without a word.

It seems she had already rung his house and spoken to Mrs C who had told her he was with

Martyn in the pub and not to expect them home until closing time.

"Before you have a go at me..." Stuart was sure his alibi would quell her anger, hopefully enough so she could tell him she had decided to terminate the pregnancy. He proceeded to tell her all that had happened. He left the man with the beard until last.

"We need to watch the video again, Sarah," he said, pouring himself a glass of milk from the fridge, "and we need to go through again, in detail, everything you felt during that attack."

Sarah said nothing. He waited.

"Have you nothing to say?" he ventured at last.

"Oh, I've got plenty to say," she retorted, not seeming in the mood to be friendly.

"Go on then."

"We were supposed to be discussing this..." she jabbed at her stomach violently and he could see her eyes fill with tears. "You turn up two hours late...okay you've got a good excuse...but you could have texted...and then, when you do turn up, all you do is talk about yourself and what's happened to you. For over an hour! What about me, Stuart? Don't I count?"

Stuart wanted to take a deep breath but he knew, if he did, it would make her even more mad. Instead, he went over to where she was sitting and took her hand in his.

"Of course you count, Sarah. I'm sorry, honestly. It was very self-absorbed of me. But I was attacked by a man with a knife and still feel a bit shaken." She smiled weakly and squeezed his hand.

"I'm sorry too," she said, "for snapping at you. It's just that I'm finding it hard to deal with this on my own. You've been so wrapped up in your job and the Rye Top Farm investigation."

"I know...but actually...I could have lost my job today...and my life as it happens."

Playing the 'poor me' card had always worked on his ex-girlfriends, but this was the first time he'd had cause to try it on Sarah. It seemed to be working.

"I'm being selfish. I'm sorry," she said, looking even more dejected than she had done the night he had tried to finish with her because he thought he'd found somebody else. The fact that his infidelity had never come to light was neither here nor there now.

"That's okay, babe. I'm here now so let's talk."

"What are we going to do about this?"

"Like I said before, Sarah, it's up to you what you do."

That made her mad again.

"Don't put all this onto me, Stuart. This is your baby too."

"When did it become a baby?" Stuart knew he shouldn't have asked that question as soon as her hand flew towards his face. He managed to catch her arm before she hit home. From what he remembered of their earlier conversations, the word baby had never been mentioned.

"Does this mean you want to keep it?"

155

That sent her into floods of tears and gave him the answer he had been dreading. All he could do was hold her close and tell her everything would be alright even though he couldn't see how it could be. He knew he should tell her he would stand by her, maybe they could even get married, but the words just wouldn't come.

"I'll ring home," he said when her tears had reduced to quiet sobbing. "Martyn and Mrs C are staying at mine again tonight. I'll ring them and tell them I'll see them in the morning. I'll stay here with you tonight. Is that what you want?"

She nodded gratefully and dabbed at her eyes.

"I'm frightened, Stuart. I can't have a termination, it would be murdering my own child...but I'm frightened that I might have to bring it up on my own...but worst than that..."

"What?"

"I felt like I'd been raped that night at Rye Top Farm. That's how it felt. What if this baby isn't yours?"

31

Haskin hadn't been in school since the incident, and the Governor's had decided that a visit to the boy's home would be a good idea.

The Principal had been the one to offer his services. At the time, Stuart had kept quiet but after the incident in the pub, and the things Sarah had said last night, he felt an urgent need to talk to Haskin about what had happened to him. With that in mind, he arrived at school extra early to go and see the Principal and suggest that he visit Haskin instead, to apologise for not heeding his plea for help.

The Principal was surprised by his request.

"Why would you want to do that when he had clearly tried to get you fired?"

"The boy has problems," Stuart explained, "serious problems, and this will only have made things worse. We need to build bridges...get him back to school...make him feel safe."

"That's very charitable of you Stuart. As far as I know he's already been referred to a child psychiatrist...but...if that's what you want to do, I won't stand in your way, providing you can assure me that you'll exercise a great deal of care and diplomacy. That's not something you're particularly renowned for, if you don't mind my saying."

Stuart placed his hand over his heart in a gesture of care. "I feel for the lad. McKenzie attacked me with a knife in The Commercial yesterday...did you know?"

The Principal looked shocked. "What the hell?"

"McKenzie used Haskin to get at me. That's why I feel responsible for Haskin's welfare."

"Okay. I can't deny I wasn't looking forward to smoothing things over with his family...they can be confrontational at the best of times."

"Would it be alright if I go this afternoon? Immediately after lunch?"

"Yes of course. I'll arrange cover. And...," the Principal was on his feet, holding out his hand in a friendly gesture of farewell, "...I must say, Stuart, I've been impressed by the way you've conducted yourself over this. You've shown a great deal of integrity. Well done."

32

It was Mr Haskin who opened the door. He didn't say a word, simply beckoned Stuart inside. The Principal had already spoken to Mrs Haskin on the phone to ask permission for Stuart to visit, so at least he was expected.

The lad was slouched on the settee with a coke and a bag of crisps. A large black Labrador was curled up in an armchair that was positioned with the best view of the sixty inch television that was blaring out a mindless daytime TV programme. Mrs Haskin was in the kitchen and shouted through to ask if Stuart wanted a brew. He didn't but said he would love a cup of tea and "thank you very much Mrs Haskin."

"Move your legs," Mr Haskin bellowed at his son, slapping the side of his head. "Let your teacher sit down."

He did as he was told and Stuart perched on the other end of the badly worn and stained settee.

"I just wanted to come round and say I was sorry for not listening to you," he ventured.

"Why?" blurted out his father. "Nowt happened."

"Mr Haskin, would it be okay if I talked with Jayden in private...if that's okay with you Jayden?"

The lad looked mildly shocked, probably because he wasn't used to being shown such respect. This must seem very grown up to him. He shrugged his agreement and his father obediently retreated into the kitchen.

"What happened, Jayden?" Stuart asked. There wasn't time to be beating around the bush.

"Like me dad said, apparently nothing."

"But something did happen, didn't it, or it felt like it had. Is that it?"

Haskin looked Stuart straight in the eye, maybe wondering if he was trying to trip him up like the police must have done.

"What's it got to do with you?" he snapped. "Why would you be interested?"

"The same thing happened to a friend of mine, that's why."

"You joshing me, sir? Like the police, trying to tell me it was all in my head?"

"No, Jayden. I was hoping you'd tell me what happened to you...so we can compare notes like. I want to try and understand what's going on. You told the police McKenzie was involved, how?"

"He was threatening me, following me home from school, saying he was going to send somebody to bugger me."

"Was he alone?"

"No, he always had another fella with him, short arse, balding."

"And what happened that evening...in the toilets, when they assaulted you?"

Just then Mrs Haskin came in carrying three mugs of tea on a tray. She shuffled a little plastic coffee table up to the settee and placed two of the mugs down.

"I've got some nice digestives, would you like one, Mr Ryder?"

"No thank you, Mrs Haskin."

Keeping hold of one of the mugs she began the task of turfing the dog off the armchair. Fortunately it wasn't for moving.

"Mrs Haskin," Stuart ventured. "I would actually like to talk to Jayden alone, if that's okay?"

"Oh no, dear me no. I want to hear what you've got to say."

"Mum, get lost," this was the Jayden that was more familiar to Stuart, aggressive and bullying. "Me and sir want to talk in private."

"What about? I don't like the sound of that. What's going on?"

Stuart stepped in, sensing this was in danger of getting out of hand.

"Mrs Haskin, you have no need to worry. Jayden and I haven't always seen eye to eye about his school work and this is an opportunity for me to get to know him a little better, find out if there's anything the school can do to help. That's all."

"Stop giving him detention for one thing," she snapped. "What good does that do?"

"Mum...for fuck's sake...just go back in the kitchen."

Amazingly, his mother never batted an eyelid at being spoken to in that way and dutifully shuffled off back to the kitchen.

"Were where we?" Stuart said, trying to get his head back in gear.

"You'd just asked me what happened. I'd gone to the boys' toilets on the first floor for a slash. I didn't hear anybody come in but next news I'm on the floor and this man..." Jayden's eyes suddenly began to glisten with tears that were threatening to spill down his face. Stuart reached over thinking to take his hand but then thought better of it.

"Take your time, Jayden."

"No one believes me...I had to be examined...and they said I hadn't been touched."

"Did you see the man?"

"Yeh, I did. The lights weren't on, I hadn't switched 'em on 'cause I knew I shouldn't be there, but there's spotlights outside and one of 'em shines right in. He was like a bear with a big bushy beard and moustache. And he smelled horrible."

"Did he say anything to you?"

The whites of Haskin's eyes were turning red with the effort of stemming the tears. It tugged at Stuart's heartstrings to see such a brazened, tough kid reduced to this. There was no way the lad was making this up.

"No, but I could see McKenzie stood in the doorway. Watchin'."

161

"Listen, Jayden. This was none of your doing and you didn't imagine it. He was getting at me through you."

"Tell the police that. And me mam and dad. They all think I'm crazy. I have to go and see a loony doctor."

"I'm going to tell you something now, Jayden, something that will sound crazy and I want you to promise it won't go any further...promise?"

Stuart wasn't sure what a promise from a kid like Haskin was worth but he had to be upfront with him. It was the least he could do.

"Okay," Jayden said, rubbing away his tears and looking a bit bewildered.

"I'm a paranormal investigator. Do you know what that is?"

A wry smile spread across the boy's face. "What, like that programme on tele? Most haunted?"

"Sort of, yes. We investigate strange occurrences, what most people would call the supernatural, and yes, that includes apparitions; ghosts."

"Cool." Jayden's face brightened, he actually looked impressed. "I've had some weird stuff happen to me. I had an angel in me bedroom once, it had wings and all sorts. It said I was special and had to start behaving meself. And I've seen things too, but nobody ever believed me."

Stuart hesitated. He wasn't sure what to say to that but quickly decided it was probably better to ignore it.

"The man that assaulted you...he's an apparition, what we call a manifestation, but the sort of entity I've never encountered before."

Jayden's mouth had fallen open.

"That's why there was no physical evidence of him assaulting you, but it happened to my girlfriend too and she said it felt completely real. I'm guessing yours did too."

Jayden was nodding his head vigorously. "So I didn't imagine it like they're all telling me I did?"

"No Jayden, you didn't. Trouble is, if you repeat what I've just told you, they'll think you're even more crazy than they already think you are...and I'm guessing I'll lose my job for telling you all this. So you've got to promise me you'll keep schtum."

"I told 'em all in the end that I'd lied about the whole thing just to get at you. Just to get 'em all off me back. I don't wanna go to no loony doctor."

"I'd stick to that story then if I were you. Play the game and you'll come out of it in one piece."

"Is your girlfriend alright, sir?"

"Not really."

"Could I talk to her."

"I don't think so."

"I could join your ghost busting group."

"Definitely not, no way."

"If you don't let me join, I'll tell mam and dad what you've just told me."

"Come on, Jayden. I've spoken to you in confidence...hoping to help you. I'm your teacher for God's sake—"

"You didn't do it to help me, sir. You did it 'cause you wanted to know if it was the same one that attacked your girlfriend."

It was clear there was no fooling Haskin. Stuart suddenly felt like he had dug himself a huge hole that was going to be impossible to get out of.

"And I'll tell you something else, sir. That scroat McKenzie can still get you fired."

"What makes you say that?"

"You know that poison cabinet you have in the chemistry lab?"

Stuart nodded. He remembered the gas mask and somehow knew what was coming.

"I stole the chloroform...stole it for McKenzie. He paid me."

"And the gas mask?"

"Yeh, that too. You'd get into trouble wouldn't you, sir, for not keeping stuff like that safe?"

Stuart's mind had gone into overdrive. He would have to replace the chloroform before the next stock take. How the hell had Haskin managed to get that when he had the only key?

"You're not helping your cause by blackmailing me, Haskin."

"Yeh I am, sir. You let me join or I'll tell."

"I can't drag you into this. Apart from possible physical danger, there's a whole load of psychic shit going on that you're not equipped to deal with."

"I can learn."

"No."

"Mam..."

"Okay! Okay!"

"What is it love?" Mrs Haskin had re-appeared immediately in response to his call.

"Sir would like a digestive after all. Wouldn't you, sir?"

33

It was Saturday afternoon and Stuart had summoned everyone to a special meeting to discuss 'the way forward' as he had phrased it.

"Okay folks, settle down," he said, clapping his teacher hands together, demanding silence.

There wasn't room for them all to sit comfortably around the table and so they were variously sprawled over the lounge furniture and the floor. Stuart was sitting cross legged in front of the TV with Haskin at his side. Martyn and Mrs C were still in residence, all having decided it was more convenient for their investigations and for Martyn's daily check in at the police station. He was still on bail but it was looking more and more likely that he would be discharged, at least according to his bail officer. She had said there had been important developments that should extricate him from suspicion. Stuart suggested that was probably something to do with McKenzie's arrest on Thursday.

Sarah was on the settee wedged between Gaynor and Mrs C. She hadn't been to work for over a week. She'd been to the doctors and he'd given her a sick note for two weeks and some tablets to stop her throwing up. She looked pale as well as tired. Stuart was worried about her.

Kevin had commandeered the armchair and was half sitting, half lying, with his legs over the arm, and Martyn was on the floor at his feet, leaning against the side of the chair.

"Firstly," Stuart began when they had all quietened down, "this is Jayden, one of my pupils from Year 4."

Stuart noticed Mrs C raise her eyebrows questioningly and then quickly narrow her eyes as if she was scrutinising the boy closely. The others showed no reaction.

"Jayden was assaulted on school premises by the same entity that attacked Sarah."

What followed was an audible gasp from them all. It was Sarah who spoke first.

"Oh my God, you poor boy. Are you okay?"

Jayden nodded. "I'm fine. Are you Mr Ryder's girlfriend?"

"You can talk about that later," Stuart butted in, "swap notes, whatever, but for now you should all know that Jayden here was paid by McKenzie to steal chloroform and a gas mask from school."

"He didn't pay me to steal the gas mask. I took that as a precaution."

"Well at least that explains that part of the mystery," Kylie said in astonishment. "No wonder

166

Martyn couldn't remember anything; he'd been chloroformed."

"Twice," Martyn chipped in.

"Me too, mate," Stuart added. The night Sarah was attacked. There's no other explanation."

"Were you there, Jayden? The night I was attacked?" Sarah's eyes were piercing into Jayden's face. He was looking sheepish and not answering. "Well?"

"Yeh, I were there."

"Were you wearing the gas mask?"

Haskin nodded. "I didn't want to be chloroformed."

"So McKenzie didn't know you were there?"

"Yeh he knew. He took me along. Paid me like. I've been practising on cars. He wanted me to trash yours, sir, so it wo'n't start. I disconnected the starter motor."

Stuart's mouth fell open. "Why would you do that?"

"First he said it were just a car-jackin. We did that but then we went to that house and he said he wanted you to stay there cos there was something there that were important. He didn't want you leaving. But when I looked through the window and saw what was going on, I reconnected yer starter motor and scarpered. That's why McKenzie came after me in school. He'd been threatening me for days."

"I'm speechless," Stuart said.

"We should probably report all this to the police," Kevin said. "Like immediately."

Haskin jumped to his feet. "Yer can't do that, yer'll get me arrested. They'll do to me what they did to McKenzie. Yer can't tell 'em," and turning to Stuart. "Please, sir, I trusted you."

"McKenzie has already been arrested. There's no point dragging Jayden into this. Or me for that matter. I'll be in serious trouble if it's found that I allowed chloroform to be stolen from my classroom. How did you do that, by the way?"

"You'd opened the cabinet so I dropped a beaker on the floor and sneaked it out while you weren't looking."

Kevin was holding up his hands. "I really don't like this...it's unprofessional and not the way we do things at Waterford."

"This isn't the Waterford group, Kev. We do things our way here. Now, we need to get on with discussing the way forward after the revelation that came through Mrs C at the séance. For Jayden's benefit, Mrs C appeared to have contacted the wife of a child murderer, one Joseph Bradshaw."

"There was no 'appeared' about it," Mrs C interrupted with a hint of reprimand strong enough to compete with Stuart's teacher voice.

"Sorry. The message was that there was another body in George's potato field. George was Joseph's brother. We're back in the nineteenth century here by the way."

Kevin raised his hand. "I've done some research into that, pulled up an old 1850s map of the area around there. Can't be sure which was the potato field but I think I've got a good idea. Potatoes don't need particularly good soil. I drove round there on Thursday. The remains of Hobhole Farm are still there, as are the field boundaries. The field itself isn't accessible by road but we can park on Gellfield Lane, it's not far to walk."

"So let me get this straight," Stuart was confused. "Rye Top Farm and Hobhole Farm were owned by the same family?"

"Seems so. The property we call Rye Top Farm was where George lived. Hobhole Farm was Joseph's farm. As far as I could ascertain, Hobhole Farm was left abandoned and fell into disrepair after Joseph died, leaving the ruins we see now."

"Okay, we need to get up there. Have a look round, do some EVPs. Tomorrow suit everyone?"

"I know a guy who has some portable geophys equipment," Kevin said. "He'll probably let me borrow it. He owes me a favour."

"And I've got a metal detector," chirped in Jayden, "if that would that be any good."

He looked pleased with the response he got from the others. Stuart reckoned that was the first time he had ever seen Haskin smile.

"Just don't tell your parents where you're going," cautioned Stuart. "And definitely don't tell them who with."

"Do we know who owns the land round there, Stuart?" asked Kevin.

"Appears to be open ground. It's on the edge of the moors. Never even seen any sheep grazing there."

"Could do with checking before we go round there with geophys and detectors. We'd need permission."

Stuart shrugged, "Nah, I don't think so. Who's going to see us anyway?"

"On your head then."

"Fine. My head's big enough to take it." That made them all laugh

"Okay, let's move on to McKenzie and his bearded companion." Stuart was determined to keep order. "It seems very clear now that this entity is connected to McKenzie. It first appeared to me and Sarah at Rye Top Farm and, unbeknown to us, there was a dead body upstairs; a man who we presume McKenzie killed...though the police have still to catch up with us on that. It's next appearance was to Jayden on school premises and, on the same evening, to Martyn at Rye Top Farm. On all these occasions the entity had an apparent physical presence and assaulted both Sarah and Jayden...though there was no evidence of any physical contact in either case."

"Does that mean that this thing, whatever it is, messes with your mind, making you believe there's been contact?" It was Gaynor who spoke, quiet until now.

"Could be...but I'm sure both Sarah and Jayden will confirm it felt very real to them. And let's be clear about this...both assaults were rape, so whether it really happened or not, the after effects are the same...right guys?"

Stuart was looking from Sarah to Haskin and back to Sarah again. He was about to mention Sarah's pregnancy but when he saw that her head was dropped onto her chest and she wasn't making eye contact, he decided against it. It was her place to tell the others, not his. Was she ready to tell them? He had no idea. Though he guessed she was finding it hard to keep quiet. She probably wanted to scream out that the pregnancy was very real and that she still couldn't understand how it had happened as she swore she had not forgotten to take the pill, nor had she been throwing up until the day she discovered she was pregnant.

Kylie was on the floor at Sarah's feet and Stuart saw her reach up to hold Sarah's hand in a comforting gesture. Kylie knew about her condition. After all, it had been she who had told Sarah before she even knew herself.

The lengthening silence would soon have everyone wondering what was going on. He should continue.

"The fourth appearance was in the pub on Thursday. No one saw him except me, not even Martyn. He was standing in the doorway with McKenzie's balding accomplice. By the time the police arrived, he had gone and I was too busy defending myself to notice when and how he had disappeared. Taking everything into account then, I would suggest that this entity has attached itself to McKenzie. What does everyone else think?"

"I think that might be a sweeping assumption." It was Kylie who was speaking. "Who else was present at all the appearances, or at least nearby?"

Stuart was stunned into silence. He knew what Kylie was suggesting because she had hinted at it before. Surely she couldn't believe that?

"You mean Stuart?" Kevin was the only one brave enough to speak out. Kylie didn't answer. She didn't need to.

Mrs C was the next to speak. "I can do a psychic check of your aura Stuart...if you like? Just to check."

"Check what?"

"I'll check whether you have an intrusion...a discarnate entity that could have attached itself to you."

Stuart experienced a strong aversion to that suggestion, almost a repulsion, and that worried him. Why would he not want Mrs C doing that? Having what she called an intrusion was better by far than what Kylie had insinuated on more than one occasion. Could it be that, subconsciously, he was thinking Kylie might be right; that this thing was a projection from his own psyche and not a real entity. But could he trust Mrs C? Surely he could. She had been living in his house since Thursday so he had known her long enough to assess whether she was a charlatan. She certainly believed herself to be genuine.

"Okay, let's do it." He felt he had no choice.

34

Mrs C decided the best place to conduct the examination was in Stuart's bedroom and so they left the others downstairs, with Martyn making drinks for everyone and Kylie passing round the cake and biscuits she had brought.

Mrs C directed Stuart to take down the large print of David Bowie and position himself in front of the now blank wall, facing the window. She stood on the other side of the room and closed her eyes.

"Just getting into the zone," she explained. "Won't take long, so just relax and try and let your mind go blank."

That was easier said than done. All Stuart could think about was seeing the bearded man in the doorway of the pub, and the image would not go away.

At last, Mrs C opened her eyes, resting her gaze on what seemed to be a point behind Stuart, somewhere in the far distance. He couldn't help his logical mind thinking how ridiculous this was. He was a science teacher for God's sake and one of his pupils was sitting downstairs. If any of his colleagues ever found out about this, or God forbid, Jayden's parents, he'd be sacked on the spot. He was sailing too close to the wind. He needed to stop and take stock. Maybe even withdraw from the group for a bit.

"There's a lot of anxiety in your aura, Stuart, with lots of red flashes. Can you try and calm yourself, just for a moment."

"Sorry." He took a few deep breaths, trying to focus all his attention on the tidal flow of air as it moved in and out of his lungs.

"Okay, that's fine, you can stop now." She signalled for him to sit down on the bed, and walked across the room to sit beside him.

"There's rather a large hole in your aura," she announced with a gravity in her voice that worried Stuart even more.

"What does that mean?"

"It means you are wide open for an attachment. You're like a house that's got a room to rent...an open invitation for an unwanted tenant."

"You mean it's me that this entity has attached itself to?"

"I'm not saying that. I can't see any attachment...but that's not to say this entity isn't capable of coming and going as it pleases. Maybe, just at the moment, it's not at home."

Stuart was in a stunned silence. What did this mean for Sarah's pregnancy? If he told her this, she'd really freak out.

Mrs C patted his hand gently, "Don't worry, Stuart. I can fix this."

"How?"

"Energy medicine. I can close the hole in a jiffy, but then you must make sure it doesn't open up again."

"How will I do that?"

"I'll show you. It's all about balancing the chakras and keeping the aura intact."

"So you're saying it's an actual spirit, a real entity? Only Kylie has kept saying it's a projection from someone living."

"It's hard to discern between those things," she said, "they both have an ephemeral existence on the astral plane."

"So how will we find out?"

"We may not need to."

"But if we do?"

"Well now...if it's already attracted to you, I suppose we could invite it in but I wouldn't recommend it. Invited guests, unlike squatters, are very hard to get rid of."

She laughed out loud when she said that, giving Stuart a mischievous glance. They both knew that she was thinking of her and Martyn's unexpected and extended stay in Stuart's house.

"The thing is," Stuart ventured, "we really need to know who or what this entity is. I can't believe it's a projection...surely it would make more sense if it was a ghost or some sort of residual spirit energy. Wouldn't it make sense if it was Joseph Bradshaw?"

"We would have to confront it to find that out, Stuart. And that's far too dangerous. Let's just deal

175

with what we know for the time being and keep you safe. That's the main thing."

35

They all re-grouped again at Stuart's house the following morning, hoping for an early start—early enough to avoid any hikers or dog walkers that may be tempted up to the fields at the back of Rye Top Farm because of the unseasonably mild weather.

Jayden brought his metal detector, showing it off proudly to the others, explaining how it all worked. Stuart had never seen him so animated, nor so eloquent. It made him feel guilty. He had always had Haskin down as a trouble maker, a no-hoper, a waste of space yet here he was now, settling into a group of strangers, all much older than himself, on an equal footing. He could be twenty four instead of fourteen. When all this was over, Stuart promised himself he would mentor the lad, make sure he did something with his life, or at least get him through his exams. That is, if he still had a job at the end of all this.

Kevin had kept his promise and brought along a geophys device, borrowed from an archaeologist friend. His explanation that it was a ground penetrating radar system, with multi-channel settings left all of them perplexed, except Stuart who was fascinated to at last get his hands on one of these machines. He always liked to give his students real life examples of the theory the curriculum dictated they learn, and this would be a great addition to his lesson on X-rays. He would take lots of photographs on his phone and make them into a PowerPoint presentation. Of course, he would have to lie about the purpose of their search—this would simply be the prelude to an archaeological dig. Kevin went on to explain that the machine would pick up any anomalies such as post holes, building foundations and, of course, graves. They were looking for the remains of a body after all.

They arrived on site and ready to go before 8am. Kevin had brought along a copy of the plan of the area. He had found it in a book published by the local historical society, and on sale at the village museum. Dated 1880 it clearly showed both Rye Top Farm and Hobhole Farm. A scrutiny of the field system on the plan, and comparison to the fields that lay before them, Kevin quickly ascertained what he suspected might have been George's potato field.

"Who said there was a body buried here?" Jayden asked, his metal detector slung over his shoulder as they trekked up the hillside, through ankle-breaking couch grass and deep bogs hidden by swathes of rushes.

"Mrs C. She's a spiritualist. She made contact with Joseph Bradshaw's wife."

"What's a spiritualist?"

"Someone who can contact the dead."

"Ghosts you mean?"

"No dear, not necessarily." Mrs C had overheard the conversation and was eager to put the young man straight. She fell in at his side, linking his arm to avoid mishap. Stuart expected him to pull away but he didn't.

"We don't really talk in terms of ghosts, Jayden. We like to call them spirits...it's that part of us that lives on in a disembodied fashion...that means without a body. Some spirits are unhappy and stay close to the earth plane and can manifest into what we call ghosts...but most exist quite happily on the astral plane. There they make their own reality until they decide it is time to move on."

"Move on where?" Jayden asked.

"To higher levels of existence, or sometimes..." she stopped walking and pulled Jayden a little closer to her. "...sometimes they come back to act as guides and mentors to those living on the earth plane."

"What like angels you mean?"

Mrs C laughed and squeezed his arm. "Well yes, I suppose so. Though quite often they have no conscious memory of the role they have accepted."

"So, who's God then?" Jayden asked as they carried on walking. "And is He up there, on a higher level?"

"Whatever God is and wherever He, or She, is...no one knows. That is beyond our understanding. Everything we know about life after death has come to us through the spirit world."

"From people on the astral plane?"

"That's right. We can make contact with them while they're on that level of existence. But it takes a lot of energy on their part and so they have to have something very important to impart to us. Usually it's to comfort a loved one. In this case, Elisa wanted us to know that her husband murdered three children and that a fourth is buried here."

"Creepy. What about demons?"

"Well, that's a different kettle of fish altogether. And not one for discussion at the moment."

Mrs C unlinked his arm as they scrambled over the crumbling field boundary, a dry stone wall that had long since been left to the mercy of the weather.

"Right, this is the field," Kevin announced once they were all safely on the other side. "Jayden and I will sweep the field in a systematic fashion. I'll start bottom right, you start bottom left Jayden. Mrs C, you can find yourself a quiet corner and see if you pick anything up. Those of you with EVP Apps on your phones, make sure your data and WiFi are switched off...don't want to get any false readings. Who does that leave?"

Gaynor and Kylie both raised their hands.

"I've brought my dowsing rods," Gaynor said, "I've had good results from them in the past."

"Okay, why don't you follow on behind Jayden?"

"I'll stick with Sarah, if that's okay?" Kylie said. Stuart was pleased to hear that. Sarah still looked troubled and he didn't want her left alone. He would be accompanying Kevin, helping to interpret the geophys data that they hoped would come through on the display screen. Neither of them were familiar with this piece of equipment, so they would need to refer to the handbook frequently.

"Okay, let's go."

If Stuart felt peeved that Kevin had taken command of this expedition, he didn't show it. He actually felt relieved to have some of the burden taken off him. He had enough to weigh him down and wasn't really in the mood for organising others, especially when he was beginning to feel responsible for what had happened to Sarah and Haskin.

He'd gone to bed early last night with a book on transfiguration. It was about how some people were able to change how they look; take on the appearance of someone or something else. He needed to know if it could have been him that raped Sarah that night. Perhaps he'd had a black out, or memory loss—it happened to people under stress all the time. And if it had been him that attacked Sarah, had he also attacked Haskin? The fact that there had not been any physical evidence of rape in either case did nothing to allay his fears.

As he glanced back across the field at Sarah, huddled on the wall with her coat pulled tight around her, he wondered, not for the first time in the past twenty four hours, whether he should kick all this paranormal stuff in touch. It was getting too complicated, too messy, too dangerous.

At the end of three hours they had covered the entire field without any success, not in the task of finding a body anyway. Jayden, to his credit, had found one George III coin that could well have belonged to George Bradshaw himself, a threepenny piece dated 1968 and what Kevin described as a 1940s bit of tat—a belt buckle that had probably fallen off a ploughman's horse. It was still treasure to Jayden and he brushed off the dirt before putting it with his other finds in his jacket pocket.

"Okay, we need to have a rethink," Stuart said when they were all gathered under the tree drinking the hot coffee supplied by Kylie in three separate flasks.

Kevin spread the plan of the farmland on top of the wall and he and Stuart pored over it trying to figure out where else the potato field could be.

"What about this one?" Stuart's finger was resting on the plan. "Must be that one over there." He was pointing to an area farther up the moor.

"Could be...shall we go and do a reconnaissance whilst the others are resting?"

They set off in the direction of the moor leaving the others to enjoy a well-earned rest.

"What is it with you and Sarah?" Kevin asked when they were well out of earshot.

"What do you mean?"

"It's obvious there's something going on, mate...and she looks well pissed off."

"We're seeing each other...it's no secret."

"Best tell Gaynor...I think she's got her eye on you again."

"No chance."

"So why does Sarah look like she's just discovered she's lost her winning lottery ticket?"

"Can't say, Kev."

"Can't or won't?"

"Not up to me, mate."

"There is something then? Is it to do with what happened at Rye Top Farm that night."

Stuart didn't answer and was grateful that Kevin changed the subject when he next spoke.

"See that area over there? There's a patch with no heather. Let's check it out."

The sound of running water told them there was a hidden steam in their way, bordered on either side by vast swathes of rushes. That meant bog. They both knew it was possible to cross peat bogs by standing on tufts of rushes but then you could just as easily sink in up to your knees in an instant, or twist an ankle so badly as to need mountain rescue. So they went with care and it took a while. When they eventually reached the patch, all they found was the dried and rotted carcass of a sheep, blackened by the peat on which it lay.

"We'll have trouble getting the geophys equipment up here," Kevin said, turning the remains over with his foot, "and even if we do, I doubt we'll be able to wheel the trolley through all this."

"Can you grow potatoes in peat?" Stuart didn't have a clue about gardening and he didn't think Kevin knew much more.

"Mmmm...it slides doesn't it...peat...so probably not ideal."

"Good for burying bodies though..." They were both aware what that comment referred to and it wasn't something anybody round these parts mentioned very much anymore. It brought back too many bad memories, especially for the older villagers.

"Mrs C was definite about it being in George's potato field so I don't think this is it, do you?"

"I wonder who that is up there?" Stuart was pointing up the hillside towards the Pots and Pans monument on the brow of the hill. "He seems to be watching us."

A figure was standing at the side of the monument in a confrontational stance, legs apart and hands on hips.

"Probably just a hiker."

"He's not dressed like a hiker."

Kevin followed where Stuart was pointing.

"Wow Stuart, you've got good eyesight. I can barely make him out."

Stuart screwed his eyes up to get a better view. "He's wearing a long jacket and flat cap...and he's got a beard."

Without another word, Stuart set off running up the steep incline. He was still having trouble accepting that he'd seen the ghost of Joseph Bradshaw in the pub, but if this was the guy, he wanted to see him up close.

"Don't take your eyes off him," he shouted back at Kevin, "I want to know his every move."

"Hang on, Stuart," Kevin yelled back. "It's a bloody sheep."

Stuart stopped in his tracks, chest heaving, trying to catch his breath. He looked up towards the monument. There was no one there, just a couple of sheep grazing at the side of the low stone wall that surrounded the blackened memorial tower.

His bewilderment was cut shorted by Jayden's excited voice coming from a field way down the hillside, just at the back of the ruined farm. The others were already gathered round him.

"Come on," shouted Kevin. "Looks like he's found something."

They were down the hill in a lot less time than it had taken to go up and on reaching the others Stuart pushed through the circle of onlookers. Jayden was holding something up that was glinting in the morning sun, waving it about like a trophy at a football match.

"What is it?"

"I got a reading for gold," he was yelling, "and I just started to dig."

Stuart could hardly believe what he was seeing. It was a gold pendant, square and chunky, about an inch in diameter.

"Nice one, Jayden," he shouted. "Now try pulling the other one."

Meanwhile, Kevin had taken hold of the chain and was examining it closely.

"This isn't a joke." His tone was solemn, incredulous. "This is old...it's a religious piece."

He passed it to Stuart to examine. On one face was what looked like the Virgin Mary, clutching a cross as big as herself, and on the other side were five bleeding hearts. There was writing on each of the four sides.

"John...Woodcock...Jesuit...1646." He turned to Jayden. "This is yours right? You're just having a joke."

"No way. Like I said...my detector went crazy. I know the gold noise when I hear it."

"We'll need to report this," Kevin said. "It could be worth a fortune. We need to find out who owns the land."

"I thought Jesuits had to take a vow of poverty. How come this one had a gold pendant?" It was Mrs C who spoke. "Seems a bit odd."

"And what's it doing here?" Martyn spoke up for the first time. "Was it buried on its own or was it round somebody's neck?"

They all fell silent.

"Where's Gaynor?" Kevin asked. "She was here a minute ago. I saw her reading a book about medieval theology last week. She'll know what this is."

"She's gone," Sarah said. "Left in a hurry. Something about a video conference she'd forgotten all about."

"Best get the shovels and start digging." Stuart said at last, still preoccupied with the figure on the hill. Kevin hadn't seen him, just like Martyn hadn't seen him in the doorway of the pub last Thursday. What the hell was going on?

They all took turns at sharing the four shovels they had brought—all except Sarah who kept herself quietly in the background.

Sarah wasn't stupid. She could tell Gaynor had been lying about why she left so suddenly. She'd seen her face when Jayden had held up the pendant he had found. Gaynor had looked guilty. She was hiding something. And the things she had said earlier, had left Sarah more confused than ever.

"I know you and Stuart are an item," Gaynor had said. "And I know what Stuart's thinking, and it's not true. This isn't about me and Stu getting back together; this is about proving to the world that other beings exist in other dimensions."

"What's that got to do with Stuart?" Sarah had asked.

"Stuart is the key, the linchpin. Without him none of this would have come to light. But he doesn't know it. He's a descendent of Joseph Bradshaw, did you know that? If you come round to mine tomorrow night, I'll prove it to you. And the man you've been seeing, the one who assaulted you, who you've been calling Joseph Bradshaw, is a demon called Abaddon. I believe it first manifested at Hobhole Farm. You might, in the coming weeks, accuse me of using Stuart to my own ends. I'll not deny it. I need him to get to the truth of what's been going on here but I promise you, there is nothing going on between us."

It was at that point that Jayden had found the pendant and Gaynor had left, leaving Sarah feeling violated and angry. She didn't want anything to do with Gaynor. Why would she believe the wild assumptions of the queen of tarot cards? She didn't believe in the cards and she certainly didn't believe in Gaynor.

Wandering over to where the others were busily working, she sat down on a broken patch of wall. Perhaps if she stared at Stuart long enough, her intuition would kick in and tell her how he really felt.

Mrs C was taking pride in supervising the area they were digging, exclaiming every now and then, "Be careful, dig gently, you don't want to crush any bones."

They all agreed that the soil here must have, at one time, been conditioned to make it arable as the peat was crumbly and loose and a much lighter colour than up on the moor. It made it easier to dig but made it less likely they would find anything. After an hour they had dug a large trench and found nothing.

"Okay, it's safe to say the pendant was buried on its own. Jayden, keep it somewhere safe...don't lose it."

"As if."

"And let's get back to searching for the body we came here to find. Martyn, will you and Kylie fill in the trench? The rest of us will sweep this whole field

187

and then maybe that one around the side of the ruins."

"I hope the police don't come snooping round here," Kylie commented as she and Martyn started to pile the soil back into the hole. "I noticed Rye Top still has the crime scene tape round it. If they see this, they'll think somebody's been digging up a body."

"Fair comment," Stuart had overheard her. "We'll just have to hope they don't work on Sundays."

"Hang on," said Sarah, holding out her phone in the direction of the tumbled down gable end of the farm house. "I've got EVPs coming through."

They all stopped what they were doing to listen. Stuart was leaning over her shoulder so that he could see any text that came through. For a long time there was nothing but static and the red histogram that seemed to be going crazy. Then a rasping voice sounded that went on for at least five seconds, causing a series of words to flash up on the screen.

Mine . . . thief . . . bury . . . gain

Then nothing.

"That's weird. Is it telling us the pendant was stolen and then buried? Or is it accusing us of stealing it?"

"Okay, note it down, Sarah, and stay here, see if you get anything else...we need concrete stuff or we're gonna end up just going off on wild goose chases. I really want to stay focussed on finding this body. The rest of you, let's get on with the search."

With that Stuart set off to where Kevin had already started searching with the geophys equipment. If there was a grave here, Stuart knew that was their best chance of finding it. He and Kevin made a good team. He hadn't realised before how alike they were, at least in their methods of investigating the paranormal. And the Waterford Society was a far more professional outfit than their little band of wannabe ghost busters. Maybe he wouldn't give it all up completely. Maybe he would become an affiliate of the Waterford group—that way he could keep a little distance and yet make a more professional defence if ever his clandestine activities were discovered by the educational authorities. It would also release him from the responsibility of Jayden Haskin—that was definitely something he had to extricate himself from.

"There's something here," Kevin's voice, calm and pronounced, interrupted his thoughts. They examined the screen together.

"See this," Kevin's finger was tracing the outline of a depression on the display. "That shows the soil has been disturbed and in-filled."

"You mean it could be a grave?"

"Could be...though it's quite small and shallow. And I'm guessing this was once an arable field."

"We are looking for a child."

"Okay...hey Martyn...over here with your spade."

Martyn had dug two feet down when Stuart pulled him back, pointing into the hole, "What's that?"

"Hang on," Martyn threw down the spade and reached in to pull whatever it was free. Brushing off the soil, he held it up for Kevin and Stuart to see.

"Well it's definitely bone," Stuart said, "but it's not human. Looks like the thigh bone of a horse to me. Can you dig a bit more out to be sure?"

The next thing that came out was part of a jaw bone and fragmented pieces of spinal column.

"Definitely a horse," Stuart said. "Probably cheaper to kill it here than take it to the knackers' yard. Might as well fill it back in, Martyn."

"Hang on, what's that?" Kevin had just spotted something sticking out from the side of the hole about eighteen inches down.

"Looks like roots. Probably left over from the last crop grown here."

"I don't think so."

Kevin and Martyn leaned in closer to get a better view but Stuart was already lying flat on the ground with his head inside the hole and his eyes only inches away from whatever it was.

"They're not roots," he yelled, "they're fingers . . . it's a bloody hand."

Kylie had already joined them to see what all the fuss was about.

She gasped when she recognised what they were looking at. "That doesn't look like an old burial to me."

"Okay..." Kevin said, taking control before anybody else had chance to speak. "We need to ring the police, guys."

Hearing the commotion, all the others had hurried over and were now gathered round as Sarah took out her phone.

"Hang on," Kevin interrupted, "we need to get our story straight. Are we going to tell them we were purposely looking for a body or are we just going to say we're out for a day's amateur archaeology."

"Whatever we say, I reckon we'll be in shit street," said Martyn, "especially me. I'm on bail for murder as it is."

"I think you should make yourself scarce, Martyn," was Kevin's advice. "You too Mrs C. I'll handle the police...they know me well enough through my work to know I wouldn't be up to anything illegal."

"What? You're just gonna tell 'em you're here in a work capacity? Writing an editorial for the weekly rag about local nutters who go round looking for bodies as a hobby."

Kevin smiled, a huge broad smile, "That's a great idea, Stu. I think I'll run with that."

"I think it's important to be honest," Sarah pushed her way to Stuart's side, taking hold of his hand. "The police already know we're paranormal investigators, we've nothing to hide. Just tell them the truth, that we got information about a body being buried here through paranormal means. If we start lying or telling untruths, we're gonna slip up at some point and then we will be in trouble."

"Sarah's right," Kevin agreed. "Best to keep it all out in the open."

Stuart was feeling increasingly uncomfortable. "If Jayden is here when the police arrive I'm well and truly shafted."

"Okay, Jayden, you leave with Martyn and Mrs. C. Okay?"

Jayden didn't look at all happy with that suggestion.

"And you'll need to leave the pendant with us. It's treasure trove and we're going to have to declare it."

"That's not fair," he yelled. "I found it, it's mine."

"Come on Jayden, we've got to play by the rules here. Depending on who owns the land, somebody must, the pendant will be put up for auction and you'll get fifty percent of the proceeds. Nobody's going to swindle you out of that...but these things have to go through the proper channels. Okay?"

Jayden pulled the pendant from his pocket and dropped it into Kevin's outstretched hand.

"Good lad."

"Hopefully," said Stuart, tussling Jayden's hair, "if your mum ever finds out that I've involved you in all this, a wad load of cash might mean she'll be a bit more forgiving and not insist I lose my job over it."

"I won't grass on you, sir." Jayden looked a lot older than his years when he said that and there was something about his manner that told Stuart he could trust him, whatever might happen in the future.

"Are you sure you want to do this?" Mrs C was looking worried. It was seven o'clock and she had already been complaining it had been a long day. Not as long as his that was for sure.

At least she and Martyn had been able to sneak off and be back at his house before noon. He'd been tied up with the others at Hobhole Farm ruins until turned five o'clock, answering police questions, giving statements. The police had even taken the gold pendant, saying it might not be an archaeological find but could be important evidence, seeing as how a religious man was murdered at Rye Top Farm only a short distance away.

The officer in charge had not been pleased that they'd all handled it, thereby ruining any chance of forensic examination. So yes, it had been a long day. Still, Mrs C had got the evening meal ready, chicken curry, his favourite, and it was the best he'd ever tasted. The others had long since gone to their own homes and he now wanted her to try and contact Joseph Bradshaw through him.

"I really don't think it's a good idea," she was still protesting. "Why don't we wait until the others can be present."

"Why? What difference will that make?" Stuart asked.

"Safety in numbers."

"Come on, Mrs C., I heard you tell Jayden that ghosts can't harm us."

"I lied."

"How so?"

"I knew someone, in the spiritualist church, who thought he couldn't be harmed. Someone asked him to check out their house, because there were odd things happening and they thought it might be haunted. So they asked him to go round and perform an exorcism."

"You mean David Gray? He wasn't killed by a ghost, Mrs C. That was likely McKenzie."

"And was McKenzie a killer when you knew him?"

"No, but people change. He was a kid then."

"It's not that long ago."

Stuart shrugged. He didn't really understand what she was getting at.

"I need to find out who or what this entity is and the only way I can do that is to face it and, hopefully, communicate with it."

"And what if we summon it and it comes and I can't get rid of it?"

"That's not going to happen."

"I'm sorry, Stuart, but for a paranormal investigator you're a little naïve."

"It's called being grounded, Mrs C."

"No, it's called being stupid."

Stuart was shocked by her abruptness. She had always been so polite and kind and old school. And what was that he could see in her eyes—was she angry, afraid? Whatever she was, she had made him feel like a naughty child and he really didn't like that.

"So you won't do it?"

"Not tonight, no."

That sounded pretty final, especially as she signalled the end of the conversation by switching on his television and pretended to be engrossed in Emmerdale. But Stuart was not going to let this drop. He needed to do this, if not for himself then for Sarah. He'd seen how worried she was today, how unlike herself. They both needed to know what had happened that night at Rye Top Farm.

"What about when Martyn's finished his bath?"

"No."

He picked up the remote and pressed the power button. The TV screen turned black.

"That's a bit rude, Stuart. I was watching that."

"It's my TV," he replied, sounding like a spoiled child even to himself, "and my house."

Mrs C looked a little put out. She placed her mug of tea down on the coffee table and stood up, obviously preparing to leave the room.

"If that's how you feel, we should leave. I'll go and tell Martyn to hurry."

Stuart felt terrible. Whatever was he thinking? It wasn't like him to be so rude. But what if it wasn't him, what if it was Joseph Bradshaw acting through him again.

"I'm sorry," he apologised. "That was so rude of me...please forgive me. I just want to talk."

She sat back down. "Go on then. Talk."

"When's your next meeting at the spiritualist church?"

"Tomorrow evening."

"We could do it there. I could run you both home after school. We could have tea at yours."

Mrs C said nothing for a while, she was clearly running through the pros and cons of this suggestion.

Eventually she spoke, "We could do that I suppose. Though it wouldn't be a case of summoning the entity...we can't be doing that, not there...we would just have to see if he came through...and if he does, at least we're in a protected environment. I would have to warn the others though...put them in the picture about what's going on."

"No problem with that."

"Some of them will want to get involved...given that David was one of our group until recently. How would you feel about that?"

Stuart wasn't sure how he felt about that as he was already having second thoughts about being so openly involved in all this paranormal stuff. He had heard about spiritualist churches and had the impression of a load of elderly people in competition with each other over who had the most psychic power. Though David Gray had only been in his twenties as far as he knew.

"They could provide an important conduit," Mrs C continued, "and a safe one."

She was right. Until Mrs C had joined their little band they hadn't got very far with their investigations; all they really had were the EVPs and Kylie's dream. This could open things up.

"I should probably pass it by the others first."

"Invite them along if you like. We're always looking for new members. A donation is expected though...you'll need to warn them...a couple of pounds each."

"That's okay. I'll ring round now."

He pressed the power button on the remote again and the TV crackled back to life,

"Sorry," he said again.

Mrs C waved him away with her hand, eyes locked once again on the screen.

38

"Whatever you said to that Haskin boy obviously worked wonders," the Principal said as he popped his head around the classroom door the following day before the nine o'clock bell had sounded. "I've just passed him in the corridor...he's like a different boy. Well done."

"Yes, it went well," Stuart answered, not welcoming the interruption. He was desperately trying to catch up on his marking. He'd promised Year 5 they would have their essays back today and he wasn't even half way through them.

"I'm thinking of making you the School Liaison Officer for our more difficult students. How would you feel about that?"

Stuart looked up. Praise from the Principal was as scarce as rain in the Sahara. He didn't want the position but he knew that to turn it down would mean he would never be offered another one.

"It would carry a small stipend," the Principal added.

"I'd be honoured." Stuart replied, hoping his lack of enthusiasm wasn't too obvious.

"Splendid. I'll set the wheels in motion. Carry on."

It was very hard for Stuart not to stick two fingers up at the Principal's back when he was walking away but he was glad he hadn't when Haskin appeared at the door almost immediately. It was okay to act like that outside school but here he had to be every inch a responsible adult and he certainly didn't want Haskin appearing to be pally with him.

"What?" he said, carrying on with his marking.

"Just wanted to say thanks for yesterday, sir, and to ask what happened to me gold."

Stuart laid his pen down reluctantly.

"Come in, shut the door."

Haskin did as Stuart asked, shutting the door quietly. Stuart couldn't help thinking he did indeed seem like a different boy.

"The police have it. They think it may be connected to the murder at Rye Top Farm. Hopefully, you'll get it back...eventually...don't know when though. I'll keep you informed, don't worry."

"Thanks, sir. Oh and I've got an appointment with the loony doctor this afternoon. Is it okay to mention what really happened?"

"That's up to you. It's not my place to advise you on that."

"It's just that you said before that I should stick to my story about making it all up."

"You must do whatever you think is right, Haskin...though bear in mind that most psychiatrists don't believe in the paranormal. Now if that's all..." Stuart motioned to the pile of papers resting under his hands.

"Yes, sir, Thank you, sir."

As soon as the bell went at three thirty, Stuart dismissed his class and headed straight for the door. It would take a good hour and a half to get to Dewsbury and he had to collect Martyn and Mrs C from his house first. Sarah wasn't coming; said she wasn't in any mood for séances so the only other person was Kylie and she had promised to be at the house so they could all travel together.

Sure enough, they were all there ready and waiting. Mrs C had even made a pile of sandwiches to take with them.

"We have to be there by seven," she explained as they loaded up the car, "and the M62 is a nightmare at rush hour. I don't think we'll have time to get home and get something to eat first."

As it turned out, the traffic wasn't too bad and they arrived at the Ebenezer Hall in plenty of time. They were greeted at the door by a lady who looked a lot like a corrupted version of Lady Gaga. Mrs C introduced Martyn first, and there was great pride in her voice when she told the woman that her son was a freelance consultant for a large retail outlet. Stuart and Kylie exchanged puzzled looks but then, realising the cryptic deception, had to turn away to stifle a laugh.

"And these are two friends from a paranormal group in Saddleworth. They're currently investigating a manifestation but have reached an impasse." Then turning to Stuart. "You're hoping to be given information about this entity tonight, aren't you?"

Stuart nodded. "Hopefully." He couldn't think of anything else to say and was beginning to wonder why he had suggested to this.

The woman patted his arm. "We'll do our best. Come."

They were led into the main hall where austere wooden chairs were arranged in rows in front of a raised platform. Some of the seats at the front were already occupied by grey and silver-haired women who were busily engaged in conversation with their neighbours.

"We'll sit here," Stuart said, indicating the back row seats. Mrs C looked mildly disappointed but ushered them along the row before taking the seat beside Martyn.

It wasn't long before all the seats were taken which meant that their view of the Medium that had taken the podium was slightly obscured.

"That's Mr Jones," Mrs C whispered to the others. "He's very good...a regular on the Spiritualist circuit. I'm not sure who else will be reading, usually someone from our own church...there's usually at least two."

"Do you ever take it, Mum?" Martyn sounded slightly afraid of what her answer might be.

"Oh yes, dear. We take turns."

He turned away, making eye contact with Stuart and raised his eyebrows. Stuart ignored him. He wasn't comfortable either but this was a religious service of sorts and he felt the need to be respectful.

From what he could see, the man on the podium was pretty average looking, probably in his fifties. His shirt was open at the neck to reveal a carpet of greying hair and a heavy gold medallion. Stuart thought how he looked very much like a 1970s working man's club singer, the sort of tribute act that still frequently provided the entertainment in his local pub.

Proceedings got underway with a hymn, *Come Gentle Spirits To Us Now*, quickly followed by a philosophical reading by an elderly lady who didn't look that far away from the Pearly Gates herself. Then came another hymn, *Gentle Jesus, Abide With Me*, followed by prayers and then a collection; all donations welcome. Almost an hour later, 'our most esteemed medium, Gary Hardacre' took the stand.

His sermon began with a brief summary of his background; "For the benefit of the new members here tonight." He introduced his wife, who was sitting on the front row and she duly turned around and proffered a friendly wave. He said she was a healer whose speciality was easing back ache and helping to heal those with aging, painful knees.

He then went on to give an account of his first experience with spirit; or his 'calling' as he termed it. He was nine years old and sleeping in his bed when suddenly a thick mist appeared from under his closed bedroom door.

"I wasn't frightened," he said. "I was amazed, fascinated, and I knew, right there and then, that I had been chosen."

Kylie stifled a laugh as she whispered in Stuart's ear. "You'd think he'd have questioned whether the house was on fire first."

A gaunt looking lady in the row in front of them, turned her head and issued a reprimanding, "Ssshhh!"

Stuart was beginning to feel his eyes close when he was startled back to wakefulness by Mrs C reaching across Martyn's lap to smack him hard on his leg. She was pointing to the front.

"I have a message for you," the man Gary was looking straight at him. "Do you wish to receive it?"

"err...yes...please." Stuart stumbled out his consent. This was it. This was what he'd been hoping for.

"There's a man standing behind you. He's referring to you as sir, does that mean anything to you?"

"He's a teacher," Mrs C shouted out. Stuart glared at her.

"Ah yes...but he's mocking." Gary suddenly looked uncomfortable. "I'm sorry but he's a rather unsavoury character. I don't wish to continue with him."

Mrs C was on her feet immediately. "Please Mr Hardacre. This is very important. This spirit has manifested to this gentleman on many occasions and is causing many bad things to happen. We need to know who it is."

Gary closed his eyes and placed his hands on the podium as if to steady himself.

It was so quiet in the hall that Stuart could hear the distant buzz of traffic on the M62.

"His name is Stuart." Gary said at last.

"No dear, that's this gentleman's name," shouted out Mrs C. "We want the name of the spirit."

Gary was concentrating hard, eyes tightly shut. He had begun to gesticulate with his arms, as if trying to warn someone off.

"I'm getting Joseph, and something about a tunnel. There's been digging and I'm being given a Scottish name...McKnight...McKent"

"McKenzie?" Stuart had blurted out the name before he had chance to stop himself.

"Yes, McKenzie. You need to protect yourself from this spirit." Gary's voice was now urgent. "We all do."

With that he opened his eyes. "Mabel, Enid, Alice...please come up here. We need to banish this spirit immediately."

There was a hushed panic amongst the audience. One or two of the ladies rose from their seat, wanting to leave, only to be told to remain seated by those around them.

"Please join hands and close your eyes," Gary instructed. "We will begin by calling in our spirit guides."

There came strange noises from the audience; whoops and whistles overlaid on a background of noise that sounded to Stuart like a hundred voices trying to talk in a dream. He opened his eyes. Kylie and Martyn were both sitting quietly, eyes tight shut, but Mrs C was making the same strange noises as the others, clutching at Martyn's hand.

Stuart looked towards the front of the hall. There seemed to be a fine pale grey mist rolling around, and it was turning darker with every second. He blinked thinking it was probably his tired eyes. No, it was still there. Suddenly, someone pushed his head forward and down onto his chest with such violence that he saw stars. Recovering himself immediately, he swung his head round to look behind him. There was no one there. Instinctively, without any thought, he grabbed Kylie's hand on his left and Martyn's on his right.

"Stuart, what's wrong?" It was Kylie. Her eyes were open and she was looking scared.

Stuart tried to answer but found he couldn't. He could feel his mouth moving but nothing but nonsense was coming out.

"Mrs C." Kylie yelled. "What's wrong with Stuart?"

In a moment, Gary and another man were at his side pulling Stuart's chair out from the row. The women, Mabel, Enid and Alice weren't far behind and the five of them joined hands in a circle around Stuart, who was still sitting on the chair.

He felt the world spinning, slipping. He was dizzy, confused. He could hear voices but they weren't from the people around him. Then he heard Mrs C scream, "It's on him, do something."

The next thing that happened would puzzle Stuart for the rest of his life, never really knowing if it happened or if he had just imagined it. He felt himself being pulled away. He could see the people around him. Kylie was crying. Martyn had his arms wrapped around his mum who had her hands over her face, apparently too afraid to look. Stuart felt light, almost buoyant, yet something was still pulling. And then others came and pulled at the other side. He was in a tug of war and he was the rope. He was stretching, retracting and stretching again. They were pushing and pulling in a weird distortion of reality. There was singing, like a heavenly choir, but there was also a roaring and bellowing that sounded like a wounded animal. He wondered if that was him. His mouth was still moving but it didn't feel right. His lips felt swollen, rubbery.

He felt something moving inside him, something that didn't belong to him. It was coursing through his veins, sliding and slithering like a snake. He felt it coiled around his neck, hissing inside his head. And then the world turned black and he was standing in a void. There was no ground, no sky, nothing but a deep black void of nothingness. And there, standing beside him, was the bearded man with lifeless eyes that looked like black pools of coal slurry. He opened his mouth to speak, infecting Stuart with a fetid stench of death. This was Joseph Bradshaw and he had killed many times, more times than Stuart could ever know. And he would do it again, and again, and again...because he could, even though he was long dead; he had friends and allies.

"The girl belongs to me now," Bradshaw breathed out the words, like a hot desert wind. "She has already accepted my gift, it's inside her."

"No, no," Stuart screamed but he heard nothing, only the hissing of the snake coiled around him. Something was moving in the blackness, approaching from behind the entity. It was close now, close enough to reach out and touch.

"This is just for you," Bradshaw hissed. "Enjoy."

It was a young girl, no more than six years old. She was crying, wanting to know where her mother was. Stuart knew her name was Cassie without her telling him. Cassie Thornley, last seen on the 10th

November two years ago, waiting for her nan to collect her from outside the school gates. Behind her was another child, a girl aged nine, Juliet Winters, and behind her yet another child, this time a boy called Nathan Peters. Joseph Bradshaw was laughing, telling Stuart that there were many more and did he want to meet them all?

And then a voice, soft but urgent, "Stuart...come Stuart...take the hand..."

Stuart looked about him. There was no hand except Joseph Bradshaw's, reaching out to him, telling him to take hold. He was confused. The voice was gentle and kind, the voice of a good person.

"Can you see the hand?" the voice again, more urgent than before. "It's where the light is Stuart. It's reaching out to you from the light."

There was no light. Joseph Bradshaw moved closer. Stuart could feel the heat of fire inside him bringing with it a smell like a steaming slurry pile. But wait...what was that...there was a faint glimmer like a lonely star in an infinite universe. He tried to move towards it but Joseph Bradshaw was blocking his way. And then, out of the void, came a host of creatures like him, evil and fetid, slime dripping from gaping mouths, fingers groping in the void, seeking out their prey. They were all around him. There was no escape.

Stuart felt his energy being sucked away. His legs buckled and he sank down and down into more nothingness. But then he landed, as if on a cushion of air, and was lifted up into a white light that was everywhere, a white void that was loving and peaceful.

And then he was back in the hall, lying on the floor with all the people round him, hands joined, singing, praying. Mrs C was kneeling at his side, her hands laid on his chest.

"You're safe now," she said on seeing his eyes open. "That was a close call, Stuart. We've never encountered anything like this before."

The medium Gary knelt down beside her, helping Stuart to a seated position.

"This is a particularly malevolent spirit," he said. "We managed to prevent an intrusion, but only just. I will need to seek advice from someone far more experienced in these things than I am."

An elderly lady, with a kind face and a blue rinse, pushed through the circle and handed Stuart a mug of tea. He took a sip and grimaced. It tasted like she'd tipped the whole sugar bowl into it.

"For the shock, dear," she said.

"Did you see him?" Kylie asked. Stuart nodded. "I saw him too, clear as day..." she turned to the others. "Did anyone else see him?"

No one had, at least not in human form. One or two, including Gary reported having seen a black formless entity that was spitting fire. One lady said she had seen only his face; the black beard and eyeless sockets.

"Did anyone see the children?" Stuart asked, his voice trembling. This reaction was unfamiliar to him and he felt like he was going to begin crying at any moment.

"I sensed there were others there with him, innocents, but I couldn't make contact," came an answer from a lady who looked younger than the others. She had tears in her eyes and had her arms folded over her chest for comfort and perhaps protection.

"There were three," Stuart said, "but I sensed there were more behind them. They gave me their names. I think they must be children that he has killed, or maybe through someone else...someone who's living."

"I've heard of that happening," Gary sounded even more tense now the danger was over. "And I think everyone here this evening needs to be on their guard. I have a terrible feeling that this entity will attack again, trying to find the weakest link."

"He tried to make me go with him," Stuart said almost to himself, "I wonder if that's what he did to McKenzie. And there's something else..."

A few of the ladies had been quietly chattering amongst themselves but everyone stopped talking to hear what else he would say.

"My girlfriend, Sarah, is pregnant and Joseph Bradshaw said it's his child and that Sarah belongs to him."

There was a gasp from everyone but the loudest was from Kylie who rushed to his side and took his hand.

"We should go," she said. "Now. Sarah needs us."

39

It had been a busy first day back at work and all Sarah wanted to do was make a cup of tea and put her feet up for five minutes before sticking a Tesco ready meal in the microwave. Normally, she'd have been looking forward to a glass of wine but since the news that had tumbled her world down around her, she hadn't touched a drop.

She knew something was wrong as soon as she walked in the door. The hall light was on for one thing. When she'd left for work that morning it had been daylight and she'd have had no need to switch lights on. On walking through to the lounge, which was at the back of the apartment, she saw the curtains were closed. That definitely wasn't right. She distinctly remembered opening them this morning. The lounge faced south east and the sun had been shining at eight thirty. She remembered thinking how pretty the maple tree looked in the park opposite, dripping its golden boughs over a freshly mown stretch of green lawn.

She checked her watch. Stuart would be halfway to Dewsbury by now but maybe he'd called in earlier. She had given him a spare key some time ago, in case she ever locked herself out, which she did quite often, but he had never let himself in without her permission. She should ring him but then thought better of it. Perhaps she was mistaken about the light and the curtains. She certainly wasn't feeling herself lately.

Filling the kettle, she flicked through the TV channels. One of her favourite movies was on Channel thirty two at seven. That's what she would do; chill out and have an early night.

The film was halfway through when she heard a noise coming from the bedroom. At first she wasn't sure because it sounded like someone snoring and she wondered if her neighbour had his parents staying. As the bedrooms shared an adjoining wall, which was not insulated against noise, it meant she did sometimes hear what went on in his bedroom, though she'd never heard snoring before. But that must be it, she told herself, and turned up the volume on the TV. She was, however, in the habit of muting the sound whenever the adverts came on and, when she did this, there was no question about where the noise was coming from.

Jumping up from the chair, she rushed towards the bedroom, flinging the door open wide and hitting the light switch.

40

It was fortunate there were no traffic police patrolling the M62 that night as Stuart and Kylie made it back in half the time it had taken to get there.

There was no answer at Sarah's door despite lights being on. Stuart peered through the letter box. The tell-tale flicker of light from the television was leaching out into hallway. He shouted Sarah's name, many times but there was no answer.

"I have a key," he told Kylie, rifling through all the keys on his key ring before finding the right one. It slid home easily and the door swung open. They hesitated before stepping over the threshold, neither speaking but both knowing that each was terrified of what they might find. Inside was a silent as a grave.

It was like walking into the Marie Celeste. Everything looked normal. The remains of a TV dinner was on the coffee table, next to a half finished mug of tea. The TV was set on the movie channel but the sound was muted. Stuart called Sarah's name again. He opened the bathroom door and switched on the light. Empty. The bedroom door was closed and he knocked gently and called Sarah's name again before opening it. A triangle of light from the hall spilled into the room and across the bed. That room too was empty.

"I'll ring her," Stuart said, taking out his phone.

"No need." It was Gaynor coming through the front door, closely followed by Sarah.

"What's going on?" Stuart wanted to know.

"I just called round on the off chance, to see how Sarah was. I'd done a reading...I knew she was in trouble. Good job I did."

"Why what happened?" Stuart reached out and took Sarah's hand, drawing her to him.

"He was here," Sarah gulped.

"Who?"

"That man, with the beard...he was here, in my bedroom. He pounced on me...and I mean pounced...he leapt up like he wasn't human. I was screaming, but then he was gone but I could still feel him, clawing at my back. Just like you described in the tunnel, Kylie. I ran outside. I was terrified...and then I saw Gaynor."

By now she was sobbing uncontrollably and all Kylie could do was hold her close and tell her everything would be alright.

"We've been sat in my car, wondering what to do," Gaynor explained. "I wanted her to come home with me but she wouldn't. She said you'd be coming round later."

Stuart found it hard to believe that Gaynor had wanted to check up on Sarah; she hardly knew her and anyway, wasn't she a rival in love? Perhaps she'd found out Sarah was pregnant. Perhaps Sarah had told her.

This fiasco was getting more complicated with every move they made. He couldn't deny what had just happened to him at the spiritualist church. He had made contact with Joseph Bradshaw, and Joseph Bradshaw had a black, bushy beard, just like the entity that had mock raped Sarah at Rye Top Farm; just like the man who had been here tonight. And the things he had said about Sarah suggested there must be a connection between that and what had happened here. But what Sarah was describing was

213

almost the same as Martyn had described when the entity had attacked him. And now she was saying that it was like what had happened to Kylie as well. Stuart didn't want to label what she was saying as hysteria but somehow it all smacked of an over-active imagination.

"Did you see anything, Gaynor?" he asked.

"Sorry, no. I'd just parked up when I saw Sarah run out of the house, screaming."

"Did you check inside?"

"I did, after I'd settled Sarah into my car. I went back to shut the front door. She'd left it wide open."

"You went inside?"

"Only for a moment, just to check there was no one there."

"You were gone ages," Sarah said, her voice still trembling.

Gaynor laughed. "No I wasn't. You were in shock, Sarah. It's hard to judge anything when you've had such a fright."

"So you checked the whole flat?"

Gaynor nodded. "Everything looked fine. No signs of a struggle or anything. Sarah did say she was very tired."

"What are you saying?" Sarah snapped. "That I imagined it all? That I fell asleep and dreamed it? Is that what you're saying, Gaynor?"

Sarah was becoming angry and Stuart couldn't blame her. Even if Gaynor's insinuation was justified, and Stuart had to agree that it was, she had no right to say so in front of Sarah.

The calming voice of Kylie, always the diplomat, broke the tension. "Let's go inside. I'll make some tea. Thank you Gaynor for taking care of her but you can leave Sarah with us now."

With Gaynor gone, the three of them sat down to drink hot tea and talk about the events of the evening.

"We should ring the police," Stuart said. "They'll need to know about the other children, whether they believe me or not is their problem, not mine. At least I'll have told them. And I think we should tell them about this too, Sarah. It's all connected. This man needs to be caught."

"It wasn't a man, not a regular man."

"I still think it could be a projection," said Kylie. "A mental conjuring if you like. And if it is, someone's doing it, and they're doing it on purpose. This isn't unconscious."

"They won't believe me."

"That's up to them," Kylie said, "but I agree with Stuart. This needs sorting."

41

Stuart and Kylie were sitting in the interview room, which was brightly lit by fluorescent tubes, making it feel cold and unwelcoming.

Was it really only yesterday that they had discovered the body behind the ruins of Hobhole Farm? Statements had been taken in the field, a term the police had used, not him, and Stuart had come clean about everything that had happened since that first paranormal investigation that he and Sarah did at Rye Top Farm. He had been left with the impression that the police were humouring him, assigning him to the category of 'just another nutter.'

He was here now, determined to make them take the information he had received from Joseph Bradshaw seriously. He had just signed a formal statement giving the names of the dead children he had contacted at the spiritualist church. It was this statement that was on the table in front of Inspector Mallick. Maybe now they would sit up and take this seriously.

"Okay, here's what we have so far." The inspector looked a little uncomfortable as he glanced through the papers before him. "McKenzie is still in custody. He's been charged with the murder of David Gray, the young priest who was murdered at Rye Top Farm. You'll be glad to know that the evidence is over-whelming, so your friend is off the hook."

Stuart breathed a sigh of relief. At least that was one problem solved.

"We've also been able to confirm that the gold pendant you found belonged to the murdered man. It will undergo forensic examination once everyone else's fingerprints have been taken for elimination purposes."

"What about the children...the names I've given you?"

The inspector ran his pen over the statement, hovering over the names of the children.

"I can confirm that the body you discovered in the field behind the ruins of Hobhole Farm was indeed that of the missing six year old girl, Cassie Thornley."

Stuart was stunned. He remembered Cassie. She was the pretty, blonde haired child who had been crying for her mother.

"We have yet to find the bodies of Juliet Winters and Nathan Peters."

The inspector was piercing Stuart with an accusatory expression when he said that.

"My head is telling me you could have pulled these names from anywhere...missing children are big news. Nathan Peters disappeared over twenty years ago, Juliet thirty years ago. Cassie was more recent. Now I don't believe in all this stuff you've been doing, but my gut is telling me to put scepticism aside for the time being."

"He said there were many more." Stuart said at last.

"Who said?"

"Joseph Bradshaw."

"The ghost you mean?"

"He wasn't a ghost...we call them spirits, or maybe projections." It was Kylie speaking up.

"I'll get in touch with the man who held the séance," the inspector continued without comment.

"It wasn't a séance," Kylie interrupted again. Stuart wondered why she was being confrontational. "It was a spiritualist meeting."

Inspector Mallick looked a little impatient with her. "Semantics. However, probably against my better judgement, I have decided to sanction further such investigations...only because the parents of these missing children need closure. And I tell you, this is a brave decision and not one taken lightly. If this goes wrong we'll be the laughing stock of Greater Manchester."

Stuart wondered how he could be concerned about that when so much was at stake. It made him weep to think of the horror of all those young lives brought tragically, and perhaps violently, to an end. Probably the inspector was hardened to it.

"As this is a murder investigation...a multiple murder investigation," he said, correcting himself, "there will be no talking to the papers, no disclosure. Do you understand?"

Stuart nodded. "Though one of our members who's been involved in all this is a freelance reporter. I don't know whether he's made our paranormal investigations public yet."

"Name?"

"Kevin Venkman."

"Ah yes."

Stuart assumed from that response that Kevin was known to the police. He had said many times that he had contacts in the local constabulary, that's how he managed to scoop all the best stories.

Inspector Mallick signalled to the young constable standing by the door. "Get hold of Kevin would you, ask him to come in...like immediately."

"It's two o'clock in the morning, Gov."

"I know what time it is. Just do it."

"Yes Gov."

The inspector went back to looking through the papers on the table.

"I'll arrange a meeting with...what was his name? Gary Hardacre? And as it was you, Mr Ryder, who received the...what shall we call it? Communication? Perhaps you should be there too. Can you agree to that?"

It really wasn't something Stuart wanted to go through again, especially when he was still trying to cope with all Sarah was going through. He wanted to be with her not sitting here helping to find the bodies of children killed over a generation ago.

"I need to be with my girlfriend. She's in need of a lot of support at the moment."

"It will only be a couple of hours...tomorrow evening?"

Kylie reached over and squeezed Stuart's hand. "All of this is connected to Joseph Bradshaw in some way and this could be a way of finding out...show us how to fit all the pieces together."

"I'd rather not," he said, pulling his hand away, "but I guess I should. The man who may have raped my girlfriend and forced an entry into her flat tonight was pretending to be Joseph Bradshaw, a man who's been dead for nearly two hundred years.

A monster who killed children. I need to know what the connection is and why me and my friends are being targeted."

Inspector Mallick was shaking his head. "The description your girlfriend gave of the intruder is nothing like Joseph Bradshaw, deceased. We've managed to find an old photograph of him. Want to see it?"

Stuart felt the hairs on the back of his neck stand up, accompanied by a cold shiver down his spine. He nodded. The inspector rifled once more through the papers on his desk and handed Stuart a sepia coloured photograph mounted in a cardboard frame.

It looked nothing like the man he had assumed was Bradshaw since that first night at Rye Top Farm. He passed the photograph to Kylie.

"This isn't him," she said. "Joseph Bradshaw has a black beard and a full head of hair."

"I assure you, that is Joseph Bradshaw. Married to Elisa. Had a daughter, Alice."

"What the fuck's going on?" Was all Stuart could think of to say.

"That's what we're going to find out," answered the inspector. "Believe me, we'll do everything we can to catch the man who broke into your girlfriend's flat but just for the next twenty four hours, let's concentrate on finding the bodies of these children. Okay?"

Inspector Mallick looked at his watch. "You both need to go home now and get some sleep. Stuart, a police car will collect you at 5.30pm tomorrow evening. I believe the spiritualist church is in Dewsbury? If the arrangements need to be changed after speaking to Mr Hardacre, I'll let you know."

"Can I come?" Kylie chirped in.

The inspector rose from his chair and smiled for the first time that night. "Why not, the more the merrier."

It gave Stuart the impression he was still taking it all a bit too lightly.

42

The following evening was the weekly tea dance at the Ebenezer Hall.

When the police arrived with Stuart and Kylie they were quickly ushered into a back room where a small, select group of ladies had been assembled by Gary Hardacre—hand picked for their mediumistic skills. Mrs C was amongst them and she greeted them warmly with a kiss on the cheek, eager to know how Sarah was doing.

"She's gone to stay with her parents for a while," Stuart explained. "I don't think she'll be going back to her flat anytime soon."

"Dreadful business, and very worrying given that the information came through such a malevolent spirit. I've suggested to Gary that I try and reach Elisa again. After all, it was she who told us to search the fields around Hobhole Farm...and I really don't think any of us want to face that malevolent entity again...least of all you, Stuart."

Stuart was just about to say that was exactly what he wanted to do, to find out who or what this entity was because, according to the police, it wasn't Joseph Bradshaw. However, Gary was now clapping his hands and asking for silence. After introducing the two plain clothes detectives, he showed the men to seats positioned by the door and asked everyone else to take their places around the table.

"Stuart, I want you to sit here between myself and Mrs Curtis. Kylie you may sit next to Irene." A middle-aged woman with auburn hair who was sitting directly opposite Stuart, raised her hand and waved at Kylie.

Gary proceeded to give an introduction to the aim of the evening, briefly explaining why the police detectives were present. As he talked, the lady with the blue rinse, who Stuart and Kylie had been introduced to on Monday evening, lit six candles and placed them at the centre of the table.

"Lights please," Gary said when all the preparations were complete. "And for the benefit of our guests here tonight, I ask that we all remain silent and seated throughout the proceedings...no matter what happens. Join hands please."

A prayer of gratitude was said followed by a request for protection against any malevolent spirits that may come through.

"It's now time for you all to call in your spirit guides," Gary said in hushed tones. There was a long period of silence, interrupted only by the sound of deep breathing. Stuart glanced over at the two detectives, wondering what they were making of all this. The candlelight didn't offer much illumination but they appeared to be maintaining a serious composure.

Then Mrs C began her invocation. "Elisa. Elisa Bradshaw. Can you come and talk with us again please. We need your help, dear."

Silence.

"Elisa. We found the child's body, exactly where you said it was. Cassie's parents are so grateful that they've found their beautiful daughter."

Silence.

"Elisa...are you here?"

"I've got something," Gary had suddenly moved his position and was sitting upright in his chair, hands splayed wide on the table. He turned his face to Stuart and began to speak, though in a voice that was not his own. It was deep and threatening. "I told you I'd have her. Didn't I tell you? (Laughter)...do you not believe me? (Laughter) Do you not yet know...I am your worst nightmare (Laughter) . . . the old lines are always the best don't you think—"

"Elisa I can hear you..." Mrs C's voice was loud enough to drown out what was issuing from Gary, "yes, yes...I understand."

And then it was as if the hounds of hell had been let loose in the room. Gary was shouting incomprehensible words that sounded like blasphemy yet were rhythmic, like a mantra. He was

223

thrashing about with his arms, looking like a wild man. Chairs were toppled as some of the ladies ran for the door.

Stuart could hear Kylie shouting his name but she was a long way away, too far for him to answer, too far away to come back.

There was a rising crescendo from those who were still in the room. They were singing the Lord's Prayer. The candles were flickering and dying, one by one.

A darkness was approaching, reaching around Stuart, engulfing him. And then the man with the black beard was at his side again, arms open, ready for a welcoming embrace. He was laughing so hard there were tears rolling down his face onto his beard, glistening black like stars in a moonless sky. There were red sparks like fire moving in a circular motion around his head. Stuart could see Sarah in the distance behind him. She was sobbing. Or was that Kylie. He couldn't tell.

"Welcome Stuart," the entity was saying. "There's no going back now."

"Who are you?" Stuart asked the question in his head, knowing his mouth could not form the words.

"You know who I am. We're made from the same stuff you and I...you've always known it."

43

When Stuart came to he was lying in a hospital bed. The rest of the ward was hidden by a curtain that was pulled all the way round. It was night time but a dim light was shining through the curtains, illuminating the yellow daffodils that were there to provide a cheerful back drop to the misery of illness.

There was a cannula in his left hand leading up to a bottle that he assumed contained a glucose solution. He knew that's what they give to people in shock. And he was in shock. He knew that much.

His mind went back to the Ebenezer Hall and he remembered what had been said to him by the bearded man who they had all referred to as Joseph Bradshaw. And the thought felt familiar, as though he had thought it many times, for many years, maybe many lifetimes. But trying to focus his thoughts was like trying to catch a pig covered in grease, which when cornered, ducked and dived and then slipped away. The police must have got it wrong; got the wrong photograph. He knew the bearded man was Joseph Bradshaw. Everything that had happened had confirmed it. Joseph Bradshaw, a murderer of children, of his own daughter. That wasn't him. He wasn't Joseph Bradshaw. He would never do anything like that.

But then what was he doing here? And why was there a policeman standing guard at the door to the ward. His eyes couldn't see him but his mind knew he was there. Clear as day. What had happened? And why couldn't he remember being brought here?

There was a panic button hanging down the side of the bed. He grabbed hold of it and pressed.

225

The following evening the group were gathered at Kylie's flat, all except Sarah and Stuart.

Sarah had been in touch to explain she wouldn't be around for a while as it was her intention to stay with her parents in Dorset for the foreseeable future. Stuart was still in hospital in Leeds having had, what was described to Kylie, a complete mental collapse. The admission of guilt he had made during the horrendous spiritualist meeting had prompted the two police officers present to read him his rights as he was carted off to hospital. Of course, the whole idea of Stuart having murdered Cassie Thornley was ridiculous but such an admission of guilt could not have been ignored. His parents were putting his admission down to the stress of the trouble he'd had at school, defending himself against false accusations from Jayden Haskin.

It was clear Stuart hadn't told his parents what had really happened and Kylie thought it best for everyone if she played along with that.

The only other absentee was Jayden. No one but Stuart had contact details for him and none of them knew how to get hold of him short of standing at the school gates, which all agreed wasn't a good idea.

Kylie had been out and bought the usual nibbles but no wine this evening. It didn't seem appropriate somehow.

Martyn and Mrs C were sitting side by side on the settee, dipping into a bowl of peanuts. Gaynor and Kevin were on straight back chairs in front of the TV. They had been the first to arrive and had made a beeline for the chairs that Kevin had placed in front of the TV. Kylie saw that it was a statement of power, sitting higher than everyone else and at the front, making it clear they would be leading the meeting. It seemed a bit of a liberty when only she and Mrs C knew what had happened at the spiritualist church on Wednesday night.

Kylie had also invited Josh along. They'd seen less of each other lately and she reckoned it would be good to have an objective view of what had happened over the past few weeks from someone who didn't believe in the supernatural. After all, with all the murders and Sarah's intruder, there was always a chance that there was nothing paranormal about any of it, though she found that hard to believe. He was comfortably lounging in the armchair, already looking bored. The only one of the group that Josh had time for, was Stuart and, as he wasn't here, Josh was sitting in silence, sipping his beer and only half listening to the conversations.

"Shall we start?" Kevin announced. "First of all I just want to say how sorry I was to hear about Stuart and Sarah. What a week it's been. I was pulled in on Monday night, early hours, not sure any of you know that. Inspector Mallick just wanted my assurance that I wouldn't publish anything about them getting involved in paranormal investigations. Obviously I gave my word on that. My job depends on cooperation with the police."

227

"We're here to find out what happened at the séances," said Martyn. "Not to listen to you spouting off."

"Apologies I'm sure. I understand why we all might be a little tense..."

"Oh you forgive me then...that's big of you."

"Martyn, sshhh." Mrs C gently tapped his arm. "We're not here to fall out."

Josh yawned.

Kevin motioned towards Mrs C. "Mrs C do you want to go first?"

She shuffled in her seat, making herself more comfortable before beginning.

"I think you all know what happened on Monday night." They all nodded. "I won't go through that then. Wednesday night, however, was a different kettle of fish. 'Course I can only speak from my point of view...Kylie will have other things to say."

"Get on with it, mum."

"I asked Gary to be here tonight. He's the medium who led the proceedings on both occasions, but he said he had a prior engagement. I don't think he did but there we are. But I did talk to him and he gave me a detailed account of what happened to him on Wednesday night. He is adamant that he was taken over by the entity you've all been calling Joseph Bradshaw...said he felt the growth on his face...you know, of the beard. He has no recollection of what he said but we record all our sessions and have it on video. Would you like to see it?"

Kylie had already set the equipment up and took great delight in asking Kevin and Gaynor to move their chairs away from the TV.

"Without an infrared camera the visual is not very clear," explained Kylie, "but you can hear Gary...though obviously it doesn't sound like him."

She clicked the play button and went over to the door to switch off the main light.

Gary, Stuart and Mrs C. were in the centre of the frame, clearly visible whilst the candles were being lit. When the light went out, their faces could still be seen in the flickering candlelight. The video played on to the moment when Gary began to speak in the strange voice. It sent a chill through the room. Even Josh sat up and took notice, leaning forwards, peering into the screen. Just as Mrs C began to talk over Gary on the video, Kylie paused it.

"What do you see Josh?" She asked. "Describe it to us."

"Okay, I see Stuart...at least I think it's Stuart though it's hard to tell now because he seems to be in shadow when he wasn't before."

"What about Gary?"

"Who's that? The guy on Stuart's right? Must confess, didn't notice he had a beard but it's certainly not possible to miss it in this shot."

"Gary is clean shaven, Josh."

"Nah, look..."

"It's called transfiguration," butted in Mrs C. "He's taken on the persona of the entity."

Kylie clicked the rewind button and stopped it back at the beginning of the video to prove to Josh that Gary had no facial hair.

"Okay...now go back to where you had it before." Josh appeared to be hooked.

There was no doubt about it, Gary appeared to have suddenly acquired a long, bushy black beard and wild hair that fell over dark eyes.

"And that is exactly the same man that was on the footage that Stuart and Sarah took at Rye Top Farm," said Kylie. "In that shot he appeared to have been assaulting Sarah and it was a man with this same description that was in her flat on Monday night."

Josh sat back in his chair but said nothing as Kylie pressed the play button again.

"This is me talking to Elisa," Mrs C said. "She appeared with such rapidity and was clearly terrified to be in the presence of...let's continue to call him Joseph Bradshaw until we know any different...her husband...the murderer of their child and at least two other young girls. Now I had asked Elisa where the two children were buried whose names were given to Stuart on Monday night, and she showed me...she said the place didn't have a name but I saw the area clearly. I've passed this information onto the police...as you know Kevin, two police officers were present at this meeting."

Kevin nodded, "Have they followed it up...found the bodies?"

"Not yet, but it's quite a large area...they've been out there digging since yesterday. It's only a matter of time."

"Now look what's happening to Stuart," Mrs C was pointing at the TV screen. Stuart appeared to be fading in and out, becoming almost transparent one minute and then solidifying again. It was almost like watching a computer generated image of a ghost. There was a lot of noise which Kylie said was some of the ladies panicking and leaving the room, but there was also a lot of static and what sounded like EVPs. All of a sudden, Stuart seemed to be hauled out of his chair by unseen hands. But it didn't look like Stuart; it was Joseph Bradshaw and he was laughing. As the video rolled on, his chilling words were clear for them all to hear. "I killed Cassie Thornley." He appeared to be drooling, licking his lips, saliva dripping from the black beard. "I killed them all, enjoyed every last one."

And then the video abruptly ended.

"There was no one near the recording device," Mrs C explained. "It had been placed on a high shelf out of harm's way and could only be reached by standing on a chair. Apparently it switched itself off."

"This is explosive stuff," Kevin said, clearly in shock. "I've never seen anything like this before."

"We've not finished," Mrs C said. "Listen to what Kylie has to say."

Kylie was sitting on the arm of Josh's chair and she reached out for his hand before beginning.

231

"I was sitting at the opposite end of the table to Stuart so I had a pretty good view of him. Just before Gary started speaking in that terrible voice I saw something leave Stuart, from his mouth, a sort of vapour, and it covered Gary...that's when Gary seemed to turn into Joseph Bradshaw."

There was a stunned silence.

Kylie waited a moment before continuing. "And then I saw it go back into Stuart. I've suspected for some time that this...let's call it an entity...was a projection from Stuart."

"The term is a homunculus," Kevin jumped in, eager for the opportunity to show his knowledge. "The manifestation of a thought form. I've come across these before though never like this. They don't usually last. They're pretty transient. This one must have been worked on for a long time for it to be so solid and for us to be able to see it. I know Stuart. We all do. He wouldn't do anything like that."

Josh started to laugh, quietly at first but then he got progressively louder.

"You are joking?" he said at last. "Tell me you're joking."

Kylie tapped the back of his head. He was lucky she didn't hit him a lot harder.

"This is serious, Josh. You saw the video."

"You're honestly telling me that Stuart is some sort of black mambo, a witch doctor...poor sod's in hospital and you're here accusing him. Come on guys, at least wait 'til he's here to defend himself."

Mrs C interrupted. "No one's accusing anyone of anything. We're just trying to understand what's going on. The astral plane is full of the thought forms of everyone who has died. Some will persist for hundreds of years, some will disappear in a few weeks or months but none will disappear entirely—there's always a faint residual echo that can be reanimated if you know what to do, but it takes more energy than one person can produce. This isn't something you can do on your own."

Josh answered again with a wide smirk. "So we're accusing Stu of being in a coven now?"

Gaynor was all but jumping up and down on the edge of her seat with excitement. "I was reading something the other week about lamas of Tibet having the ability to produce exact replicas of themselves—called tulpas. It means they can be in two places at once...bi-locate."

Even Josh took that on board. "I read about that in Castaneda. Don Juan Matus could do that."

Mrs C looked more serious than they had ever seen her. "A thought form needs to be recharged with energy if it is to persist. But it's really dangerous to keep recharging them and no one in their right mind would do that."

"Why not? What will happen?"

It was Kevin who answered. "They'll start to exhibit a rudimentary intelligence of their own and that means they'll be beyond the control of the person who created them. I had this with a haunting I was called out to last year. The girl said her house

233

was filled with a disturbing presence after she and some mates had been experimenting with a Ouija board."

"So is Joseph Bradshaw a ghost or a thought form?"

"Or a demon?"

"Whatever it is, it's malevolent and we need to be extra careful from now on. These entities can be more dangerous than real people."

"I think we should consider all possibilities." It was Kevin who was speaking and he was looking at the others with a grave expression. "We're in uncharted territory here...our main problem is that we have real events, including murder don't forget, intermingled with paranormal stuff. Before we start making wild accusations or jumping to imaginary conclusions, we need to separate the two."

"I have more information as well," Gaynor said, "too much to go through now, but why don't we all meet at mine tomorrow evening...I'll divulge all then. Oh and by the way, I've been recording this session." She pointed to a small camcorder that had been placed on a shelf at the back of the room. "Hope everyone's okay with that."

"You really should have asked everyone's permission first, Gaynor."

"Sorry. It's all the excitement. We're on the verge of a major breakthrough in paranormal research. I can feel it. So, is everyone okay with me recording it?"

They all confirmed that they were.

"Do we know what the police made of the séance on Wednesday night?" Josh was directing his question to Mrs C. He was interested to know if they had made any comment on the night.

Mrs. C was shaking her head. "They left in the ambulance with Stuart. They read him his rights, for what good that did; he was virtually out cold."

"And no word since?"

"Nothing."

"Perhaps you could follow up with Gary Hardacre, Mrs C?" suggested Kevin. "I'll go and visit Stuart tomorrow...if I'm allowed. See how he's doing...see when he's going to be discharged. If he's going to be discharged. Shall we meet again tomorrow evening? At Gaynors?"

"Might be difficult for us," said Martyn, meaning him and his mum. "Haven't got my car back yet."

"You don't want it back, son...it's had a dead body in the boot."

"You can stay here tonight if you like," Kylie offered. "You can have my bed Mrs C. I'll have the settee. Martyn, you're on the floor."

Just then there was an almighty crash from the bedroom.

"What the...?" Kylie jumped up to investigate. When she returned to the lounge, her face was ashen. "It's back. The thing from the tunnel...it's found me."

Josh leapt up and went into the bedroom to investigate.

"Kev, spirit box. Quick." Gaynor shouted, apparently not even trying to hide her excitement at this new development.

The bedroom was in chaos. Wardrobe doors open and clothes flung everywhere. A broken mirror lay on the bed.

Kevin rushed to the doorway holding the spirit box in the direction of the bed. "Scanning on AM. Is there a spirit present in this room?"

Martyn pushed past him, EMF detector in hand. The display was flashing red, going crazy.

"Did you hear that?" Kevin yelled.

Bad shore had flashed up on Martyn's detector.

"Are you Joseph Bradshaw?"

I am Legion

"Let me speak to it." Mrs C had pushed her way past Kevin and was holding out the Christian cross she always wore around her neck. "Why are you here?"

Havoc

Murder

There was no need for Martyn to look at the text flashing up on his device. The words were coming through clearly even though the static was almost deafening.

"I command that you go back from wherever you came from," Mrs C continued, oblivious to the fact that she was blocking the view finder of Kevin's equipment. Without warning, she was pushed against the dresser by an unseen force causing her to lose her balance.

"Can we please clear the room," Kevin instructed. "We need to set up our instruments properly. Gaynor, get the movement detector and the camcorder."

"It isn't safe," Mrs C shouted, being helped to her feet by her son, while tugging at Kevin's sleeve. "We must leave. There's nothing we can do."

"Martyn," Kevin yelled, "please remove your mother from my arm."

"Look, look..." Mrs C was pointing to the floor under the window where a dark shadow was creeping towards them. "Sweet Jesus save us, Mary Holy mother of God protect us—"

"For Heaven's sake, Martyn." Kevin sounded out of patience.

"I see it, Mrs C," yelled Josh, stepping towards the manifestation.

Martyn pushed his mother into the lounge. He had never seen her in such a state.

"We have to go," the abject terror in her voice was clear. "Leave them to it. Kylie, Josh, you come too. We must leave."

"No way," Josh was smiling as he turned to answer her. "This is dope. I wanna see what happens."

"I wouldn't get too close to it if I were you, Josh," Gaynor warned in a voice that was as fluid and as calm as a lake on a sunny day. "It's looking for a new host to inhabit. Here...catch." She threw a teddy bear that had been tucked up in Kylie's bed into the shadow. Instantly, all the equipment fell silent and the shadow was gone.

"How did you do that?" Kevin asked.

Gaynor tapped the side of her nose. "A little trick I picked up in Mexico."

Bending down she lifted the teddy from the floor. "I'll take this—we can experiment with it later."

45

When Mrs C and Kevin turned up at the hospital, Stuart wasn't sure he could manage any more visitors. He'd already been questioned by the police all morning. They'd been at his bedside first thing demanding answers to questions he didn't understand. He was tired, so very tired.

They kept asking him about McKenzie—what was his relationship to the lad? Had McKenzie ever been to his house? Was it Stuart who had supplied McKenzie with the chloroform that was used to abduct Martyn? Where was Stuart at the time Cassie Thornley's disappearance? Where was he on the evening of David Gray's murder?

He had asked them what they'd seen at the meeting at the spiritualist church but they wouldn't say, maintaining that they were only interested in his version of events. Did they think he had something to do with it?

"How are you doing?" Martyn's Mum pulled one of the chairs closer to the bed. "What a to do. Never seen the like before. Gary couldn't believe what happened."

"He wasn't the only one."

"What do you think happened, Stuart?"

"I've already told the police everything I know. I don't want to go through it again."

"Please tell us. We need to hear it too."

Stuart sighed, a long deep sigh and closed his eyes. "I'm too tired."

Mrs C reached out and squeezed his hand. "Please Stuart, it's important."

"All I know is that I was attacked by Joseph Bradshaw...and he spoke to me."

There was a long pause that was too long to be comfortable.

"Tell us what he said. Please Stuart."

"He said there was no going back...and then he said...he and I are made from the same stuff."

"Malevolent entities like this tell lies, Stuart. Forgive me for saying but you and Kev here have no experience of things like this. I have and so has my church. We can help."

"I know what Kylie thinks—"

"And probably so does the entity—maybe it picked up that thought from her."

Kevin was throwing warning glances at Mrs C. Stuart saw and wondered why.

"What do the others think?"

It was Kevin who answered. "It's all just conjecture at this stage but we appear to be dealing with a thought form, that and maybe transfiguration.

239

We all saw how you and also Gary Hardacre took on the appearance of the man we've been calling Bradshaw."

"The man was Joseph Bradshaw despite what the police have said. I know it was."

"I'm not sure it matters who he was," Kev was pacing the floor at the foot of the bed. "To be honest, a part of me wants to bow out of this. We're in over our heads. I think we should just let the police get on with it."

"You can't do that!" Mrs C sounded shocked. "You're a paranormal investigator and a journalist to boot. Besides people have been hurt, so we need answers. Are you frightened?"

"He's not frightened," Stuart answered for him. "He doesn't believe it. His rational head has already accepted that I'm a murderer. Isn't that right, Kev?"

"Not exactly."

"Exactly what then?"

Kevin was staring at the floor, shifting from foot to foot.

"If you've something to say, Kev, for God's sake just say it."

"Okay," he said, thrusting his hands deep into his pockets. "I've thought long and hard about this and whichever way I look at it, you and your little band of investigators are implicated in at least two murders and the police are out there digging for two more bodies as we speak. I know what they think and I can't afford to jeopardise my relationship with them."

240

Stuart sighed again and said, almost under his breath. "Fine. Just go."

Mrs C followed Kevin out of the room. Stuart could hear them whispering; she was trying to dissuade him from leaving. But he knew Kev. He was stubborn and wanting to distance himself from anything even slightly suspect was no surprise. What help had he been so far anyway? They didn't need him and whatever he might come up with to explain all this away would never wash.

Joseph Bradshaw was real and Stuart knew he was still there. He could still feel him, somewhere, close-by, watching, waiting.

But he was so tired. He needed to sleep, not think any more. Just rest. He closed his eyes and drifted away.

46

Gaynor had everything laid out on the table in readiness for them all arriving.

The things she'd uncovered had been hard to keep to herself but she wasn't yet ready to tell them everything. She had told no one what she had been up to, not even Kevin.

What they did know was that she had spent the last two weeks tracing the lineage of the Bradshaw family from the nineteenth century to the present day. Her research had begun in the records office at the local library and had progressed to a genealogy website well used by anyone serious about tracing their family history.

With the information she now had, everything was beginning to make sense and she had formulated a plan about how it all hung together. It was this plan she was going to present to the others tonight but she wouldn't tell them that this was only half the story. That would come later. She didn't want to chance anyone stealing her glory. This was big, and she had proof, nearly all the proof she needed, but not quite. There was still work to do.

It was a shame Stuart couldn't be here. Then again, he may not be best pleased with what she had to say. There were still loose ends, some of them involving Stuart, but she was hoping the others could shed light on those, especially Kylie who, despite her ineptitude at doing research, would be a strong ally when it came to offering support for Gaynor's ideas. Sarah too should have an input but Gaynor knew there was no chance of that. None of them had any idea how long it would take her to recover from her ordeal but Kylie had told them all yesterday that Sarah was pregnant with Stuart's baby. They didn't even know if she intended to keep it. Swapping notes with Kylie last night about it, they had both agreed that if it was them, they would likely arrange a termination, otherwise the poor child would be a constant reminder to her.

Gaynor's house was in Ashton, not too far from where Kevin lived, and the two of them had met here many times to discuss future projects and iron out problems within the paranormal group. There had never been any paranormal activity in this house and so when she heard the back door open she just assumed it was Kevin coming in through what he called 'the tradesman's entrance'.

"Hi Kev," she shouted through. No answer. "Kev?"

Still nothing.

As she turned to head for the kitchen a cold wind swept past her, blowing into the air all the neatly laid out papers in a melee. Through the paper storm she could see a tall figure standing in the doorway.

His wild black hair and bushy beard cast his whole form into shadow. He reached out an arm and took a step towards her.

47

The police had found a small wax model of a bearded man under the stone flags in the yard at the front of Rye Top Farm. No more than a curiosity, it had been bagged for forensics along with a small black pouch of human hair.

The bodies of Juliet Winters and Nathan Peters, the remains of the two missing children referred to by Stuart, were found a short distance away in a grazing field adjacent to the remains of Hobhole Farm along with the remains of at least six other children. The official autopsy report was still awaited but Inspector Mallick had already been advised by the pathologist that it was likely all the children had been sexually assaulted.

Further excavations were underway in the fields that lay above Standedge Tunnel; fields that once belonged to Hobhole Farm. A statement had already been made to the press that human remains had been found there but until investigations were complete, there would be no further comment except to say that the remains were historical, having been in the ground for at least a hundred years. It was rumoured that up to ten skeletons had so far been recovered.

The DNA profile on the contents of the pouch didn't bring up any match in the police database. When the wax figure had been analysed and its composition ascertained, the police called in an expert in the occult from Edinburgh University.

It was obvious, even to sceptic coppers, that this was some sort of black magic voodoo doll. Only too willing to oblige, the Professor had got on the next flight to Manchester. It was comforting for the inspector to know that even academics worked on a Saturday when needs must.

The figure itself had been moulded from beeswax, mixed with powdered offal and dried pig's blood. The stomach had been hollowed out and a disgusting concoction of blood, spittle, semen, urine and faeces had been placed inside before being resealed and buried. There was a DNA match for that macabre mixture and he was sitting in the cells awaiting trial for the murder of David Gray.

However, he was keeping silence on the matter of the wax figure, refusing to explain.

The effigy had been carefully placed on a white cloth in the middle of the table. Professor Clarin was examining the detail, magnifying glass in hand. Inspector Mallick sat in silence, patiently waiting for the Professor's pronouncement, which seemed to be taking an awful long time.

At last the Professor sat down, placing his magnifying glass silently onto the table.

"I've only ever seen one of these before," he began, "in Haiti, in ninety six. I've seen similar effigies hung from trees in cemeteries, intended to open lines of communication with the dead, usually the recently departed. Sometimes they are nailed to the tree upside down, the intention being to make their creator stop caring for someone who has done them wrong. But you say this one is packed inside with human tissue? That makes me think it may be a *pwen*, a far more serious invocation."

"What? You mean like conjuring up spirits?"

"I understand your reticence and your scepticism Inspector, but there is far more 'twixt heaven and earth than—"

"Yes, yes, get on with it."

If the Professor was insulted by the inspector's impatience, he didn't show it. "They're used in classical voodoo though there are numerous anecdotal recordings of their being used far more widely and in different contexts. They are filled with components that the *Iwa*, or spirit they want to invoke, will find appealing. The one I saw was being used as a tool for healing and guidance. This, I suspect," he waved his hand over the effigy, "is a different matter entirely."

"Does it work? This business of conjuring up spirits?"

"Curiosity can drive people into places where angels fear to tread, Inspector. Raising spirits and bringing them into manifestation is a very risky business. As someone more knowledgeable than myself once said, 'A fool and his soul are soon parted.'"

"Can we get on with it?" Inspector Mallick said making a point of looking at his watch.

"In modern parlance, these so-called spirits, are usually nothing more than thought forms—often referred to as a homunculi."

"When you say 'nothing more', you mean they're not real?"

"Believe me, they are very real but not in the sense that they are dead people who have retained their personality. It is believed, and we have ample evidence for this, that when we die we can leave some residual energy of ourselves behind. If this persists and is accessible, it can be reanimated in a new form for good or ill."

"And could the...reanimation...commit murder?"

The Professor laughed. "Dear me no...at least not in a physical sense. I guess it would depend on whether or not frightening someone to death constitutes murder. I would say though that if this effigy was intended to invoke a malevolent manifestation, it is likely that it will have wreaked havoc, especially in its creator who would have an intimate connection to it and could likely have been driven insane. These creations respond to the unconscious mind of their creator and how many of us understand what goes on in there."

"So the person who's done this might not even know what's happening?"

"That's correct. Though these forms must be fed energy if they are to persist and that is something that would have been done consciously. Though if they are worked on for long periods I believe they can become, to all intents and purposes, autonomous. They become stronger the more they are recharged and that makes them very dangerous. Once they're set free, if they start to run out of energy, they will take it from the nearest source—usually the person who manifested them but not always."

The inspector looked thoughtful. It was clear he was having trouble computing this bizarre information.

"Okay, run it by me again," he said. "How does this work exactly?"

48

"Why are you here?" Gaynor took a step back, unsure how to deal with this. It had seemed so easy

247

being in control. She knew what she was doing, but this wasn't on the agenda. "I said I'd send for you when the time was right."

The bearded man didn't speak. He took another step towards her.

And then another. If he came any closer she would be backed up against the settee, trapped, no escape.

"What do you want?"

He stopped. The black eyes were moving, surveying the room. He raised his arm, pointing to the armchair. The limp figure of Kylie's discarded teddy was slumped over the arm.

Gaynor sidled over to it, never once taking her eyes off the intruder. She picked it up. Her camcorder and EVP recorder were lying beside it. Diverting her eyes for a second, she switched them both on with a well-practised sleight of hand and placed the camcorder on the back of the chair as she tossed the soft toy over to him. A rotting, gnarled hand reached out and caught the teddy. It didn't have the effect it had had in Kylie's flat. A vivid image of some sort of voodoo doll flashed into Gaynor's mind.

The monster turned the soft toy over and over, this way and that, scrutinising every detail. Lifting it to his face, he sniffed it and then, opening his mouth so wide that the jaw seemed to dislocate, he placed the head inside his mouth. His teeth were decayed, with many missing, and his breath was fetid and rotting. He ripped the head off with his teeth, spitting it out onto the floor and threw the body at Gaynor.

"There are others." His voice was coming through on the EVP, cracked and laced with static electricity. "Destroy them."

"I don't know what you mean," Gaynor answered, her calm resolve all but gone. This wasn't going how she'd planned. The cards had hinted at such an effigy and she'd come across the idea when she'd been researching thought forms. There must have been one for this manifestation to be so powerful. "I don't know where to look."

The man pointed at her before placing his rotting hand against his hollow cheek and pushing his head down onto his shoulder. The sound was of bone splintering and breaking followed by an unholy scornful laughter. Withdrawing his hand, he pointed a threatening finger at her once more.

"There's another way," she was holding onto the back of the settee, digging her nails into the fabric. "I'll sort it, I promise."

His mouth opened and an unearthly growl issued forth, carrying with it the remnants of words she most feared. "You're mine," he said. It was unmistakable.

She let go of the settee and slid down onto the floor. When she looked up, he was gone with no trace of him ever having been there. She prayed the camcorder had caught it all.

Gaynor made her way to the kitchen. She would make herself a good, strong cup of coffee, maybe add a dash of the whisky that had lain untouched in the cupboard for months.

She needed to come clean to the others. She couldn't deal with this on her own any longer. But would they believe her? Somehow she doubted Kev would. Perhaps he wouldn't come as he'd already made it clear on the phone that he thought they should extricate themselves from Stuart's group. There was too much to lose, he said, and they couldn't afford to get on the wrong side of the police. But he didn't know what she knew and now, more than ever before, she needed his help.

This would make the paranormal annals. It would be a case that would be talked about for years to come, perhaps forever. It could lead to all sorts of new research avenues. Imagine, proof of life beyond life; energy forms with autonomous existence that probably exist in the multi-dimensional universe that physicists were so fond of talking about. Who wouldn't want to know about that?

Her visitor, who they were all referring to as Joseph Bradshaw, wasn't him at all. Joseph Bradshaw had long since taken on another mantle. How she wished it was him, that would be so much easier to deal with. The sensible thing to do would be to get an exorcist and send him back to the light but they'd tried that before. Isn't that what David

Gray had tried to do? And Martyn too. It didn't work with entities like this, obviously, or he wouldn't have materialised in her living room. She'd gone too far. Put herself in danger, and maybe the others too.

The doorbell rang, making her jump. Keep calm, deep breaths she told herself.

It was Kylie and Josh. Gaynor hesitated before letting them in. She didn't agree with Josh being here. He wasn't a member of any group and the way he had behaved in Kylie's flat had been stupid in the extreme.

"Can we come in?" Kylie asked. She sounded suspicious.

Gaynor took a deep breath and opened the door wide. "Sure. But why is Josh here?"

"Is that a problem?"

Josh took hold of Kylie's hand. "I'm here for support. You know what she's been through."

Kylie seemed to make a point of releasing her hand from his grip. "I have the whistling in my ears again. Something's wrong. I wasn't going to come tonight. It's a warning."

"It's fine. Really." Gaynor lied. "Come in, make yourselves at home."

She pointed through to the living room and was just about to close the door when a small red car pulled up outside. It was Martyn and his mother.

"You got your car back then?" Gaynor shouted.

"Hell no," Martyn said giving his mother a peck on the cheek. "It's a gift from my beautiful mama."

251

"We should wait for Kevin," Gaynor said when they were all inside and seated.

Mrs C was shaking her head. "I was with him this afternoon, visiting Stuart. Kevin won't be coming."

"That's a shame," Gaynor replied, hiding her disappointment. She would ring him later. Explain everything. Get him back on board.

"Okay. Where to start..." Gaynor said, settling herself down in front of the others. She hadn't had time to rehearse what she was going to tell them and she wasn't sure how it was going to be received. Would they be angry that she had kept so much from them?

"Well we could start with Ron," Mrs C was pointing towards Kylie. "He wants to be heard."

Gaynor began to protest. She didn't want any distractions. What she had to say was too important.

Mrs C abruptly stood up and was pulling Martyn to his feet. "He's saying we need to leave."

"No, please no," Gaynor was beside herself.

"Kylie, Josh...now." Mrs C's voice had an unmistakable urgency. She was bustling them all towards the door.

"You need to hear this." Gaynor's protestations were falling on deaf ears.

Mrs C turned back as she was leaving the room. "You need to stop whatever it is you've been doing. You've no idea what you're messing with."

Leaving through the front door, Mrs C was instructing the others to get in the cars as she hurried down the path.

"It's got Stuart and now it wants Martyn!" Gaynor screamed out the words. "I'm trying to protect him."

Mrs C stopped and turned back to face Gaynor who was standing in the doorway.

"What do you mean?"

"That's what I had to tell you all. It wasn't just a random attack when Martyn's car was stolen. He was targeted."

"Who by?"

"It was the entity you've all been calling Joseph Bradshaw. He was acting through McKenzie."

Mrs C had taken a couple of steps back up the path towards Gaynor. "You need to leave this house. Get your coat, lock up and get in the car with Kylie and Josh."

Hurrying away to speak to Josh, she banged on his window.

"Pen and paper? Quickly."

Josh fumbled through the fascia, handing her what she'd requested.

"Here," she said, scribbling down an address. "It's my church in Dewsbury. We all need to go there now. Wait for Gaynor, she's coming with you."

50

It was past midnight by the time they arrived at the spiritualist church. A thunder storm had erupted as

253

soon as they had reached the M62 and the wind was now lashing rain against the windows, rattling them in a ferocious dissonance.

Eight of the more experienced members of the spiritualist church were already there, waiting for them in a fog of burning incense. Wooden chairs were stacked up along the walls and on a table lay a pile of Bibles waiting to be distributed to everyone present. A huge circle had been drawn in chalk on the weathered floorboards. In the centre there had been placed an altar with various sacred objects carefully laid out; a Christian cross, a rosary, a chalice filled with water and a large quartz crystal as big as a man's hand.

"Thank you all for coming at such short notice," Mrs C said in greeting to those who were waiting. "We have never had to deal with anything like this before and I ask you all for your patience and forbearance. I have no idea what will transpire but we need to be ready for all eventualities. Father Joseph..." a bespectacled man in a dark suit and dog collar stepped forwards, "...I'm trusting you to keep us safe."

And turning to the rest of the group, she added, "Father Joseph is from Saint Thomas's. He is licensed by the catholic church to perform exorcisms."

"What the heck is all this about?" It was Josh and he was sounding none too pleased. "Are we in danger? Is something bad going to happen?"

"When we're all gathered inside the circle and prayers have been said, Gaynor will explain. Won't you Gaynor?"

Gaynor bowed her head. She felt unjustly shamed. She should tell them that exorcism wouldn't work. She should tell them it could make things worse, but she just couldn't find the words.

"I suggest we all grab a cushion from the store room," announced an elderly lady with pink hair and bright red lipstick. "We may be here some time. Peter, can you fill the water carrier and you'll find a tin of biscuits under the sink."

"I'll get blankets," offered a lady with blonde hair scraped back in a tight bun, "and I'll check the doors, make sure they're all locked."

Mrs C nodded in appreciation.

"What's going on, Mum?" Martyn asked, walking over to stand at his mother's side.

Mrs C looked at him, managing a smile that wasn't very convincing. "I'm not sure. Let's wait and hear what Gaynor has to say."

She took his hand and squeezed it

When everyone was back in the room, the lady with pink hair instructed everyone to remove their shoes and step inside the circle.

"In the name of our Lord Jesus Christ," she began when everyone was settled comfortably on the cushions, "may the Archangels gather around us. Michael be at my right hand, Gabriel at my left, Uriel before me, Raphael behind me and above my head, the presence of the Holy Spirit. Father Joseph, would you lead us in prayer please."

The prayers lasted a good fifteen minutes, during which time Kylie had had to constantly poke Josh in the ribs to stop him falling asleep. Gaynor sat apart from them all, eyes cast downwards, silent. When the prayers were finished, Mrs C invited her to tell them what she had planned to tell them earlier.

"You all thought Stuart was McKenzie's prime target because of what happened to Haskin, and to Sarah. He wasn't. It was purely by chance that Stuart and Sarah went to Rye Top Farm that night and got involved. McKenzie recognised Stuart and had an old score to settle, so he used the entity to punish him. You all know McKenzie has been charged with David Gray's murder?" It was a rhetorical question which no one volunteered to answer.

"David Gray had gone to Rye Top Farm to perform an exorcism."

"No dear," Mrs C interrupted. "He went to give a blessing, that's all."

"Maybe that was what he intended doing, but it didn't pan out like that I'm afraid."

"How do you know all this?"

"The entity you keep calling Joseph Bradshaw told me."

"If it's not Joseph Bradshaw, who is it?" It was Kylie who was asking, leaning forward, remembering the night of the séance when the medium Gary Hardacre took on the appearance of the entity and attacked Stuart.

"Maybe you should ask your familiar. What's he called? Ron?" Gaynor replied coldly. "He must know. He's from the same place."

Kylie cast a questioning glance at Mrs C who hesitated a long time before responding to Gaynor's remark.

"It is a demon of the highest order—" She held up her hand for silence when Josh began to protest. "It matters not whether you believe. It is not a ghost, nor a spirit. It is pure energy and it is evil. It will destroy all it comes into contact with." Mrs C was looking directly at Gaynor when she said that, unforgiving, accusing. "Please tell us Gaynor, how long you have been in dialogue with this malevolence and why?"

Gaynor straightened her back and took a deep breath. "This is the proof the world needs of other realms of existence. You and your friends here, you only touch the surface. No one believes you. It's all done on faith. I will have proof...proof that I can show to the scientific community. My research will change everything. I started with the Bradshaw family genealogy. Joseph and Elisa had a son, Edward, as well as the daughter, Alice, who was murdered. Edward had two daughters and one of them, Hannah, married Peter Waite. They had a son, Frank. Frank and his mother bought Rye Top Farm in 1973."

"So you're saying that the man who invited us to carry out an investigation at Rye Top Farm is a descendent of Joseph Bradshaw?"

"Yes, and this thing you're calling a demon was attached to him. But I think for a time it attached itself to Stuart as well. I don't understand why Stuart didn't suspect something was wrong, especially with what happened to Sarah. It's been feeding off him and getting stronger."

"Why would it do that? Why pick Stuart?" Kylie asked.

"Because Stuart is also related to Joseph Bradshaw though through Joseph's second wife, Catherine. Joseph remarried in 1879 when he was sixty years old. He had three more children, a boy and two girls. The boy, Peter had a daughter, Suzanna, born in 1901. She married Edward Ryder. Their son, James, is Stuart's father. That means Frank Waite and Stuart are second cousins once removed. Joseph Bradshaw is Stuart's great, great grandfather."

There was an audible shocked intake of breath. Only Josh spoke.

"Does he know?"

"I doubt it."

"This is bullshit! What are you accusing him of?"

Gaynor shot him a piercing glare. "You know nothing, Josh."

"What's this got to do with my son?" Mrs C's face was ashen.

"Perhaps Kylie can enlighten you? Kylie?"

Kylie's expression was as stunned as Martyn's.

Gaynor continued. "Only priests are allowed to do exorcisms, you know that. And what Kylie brought out of that tunnel was way beyond your capability to get rid of. You should have known that. You all should. Kevin's right, you're all amateurs. You didn't get rid of it Martyn. You left it at Kylie's old flat, weakened to be sure, but still there."

There was a stunned silence as the others tried to piece together what Gaynor was telling them. Nothing seemed to make much sense.

"So you're saying it's the same entity? This bearded man is the same entity that attached itself to me in Standedge tunnel?"

"If you'd checked up properly," Gaynor went on, "you would have known that McKenzie's sister had moved in to your old flat and was having a real bad time of it. From what I can gather, it attached itself to McKenzie when he visited her as soon as he came out of borstal. He wanted to move in with her but she wouldn't let him. McKenzie's bad news and whatever he did, strengthened the malevolence beyond anything we can imagine. It gained so much energy from him that it was able to manifest. I can only guess that the form it took, the man with the beard, was straight from McKenzie's imagination. So what may have started as a thought form, or homunculus, became imbibed with the energy of this demon. I'm assuming McKenzie got scared and called in the priest to exorcise it. That obviously didn't work and I'm guessing that the next job it gave McKenzie was to get rid of Martyn for trying to destroy it."

"You didn't answer my question, Gaynor. How long have you been in contact with this malevolent entity?"

"Since that evening in Kylie's flat."

Something in Kylie's voice told Mrs C she was lying but she remained silent, not wanting to unsettle the group by wild accusations.

"I'd done my homework," Gaynor continued. "I knew what to expect. I was intrigued to find out more. There's no empirical data about stuff like this. What we know is either anecdotal or spurious. It's important stuff and if you want to make new discoveries, you've got to be prepared to push boundaries."

Mrs C was shaking her head in disbelief. "You have no idea what you've been messing with, you stupid girl."

Gaynor was about to protest but then thought better of it when she saw the way they were all looking at her.

"I've kept a detailed journal and I've got hours of video footage," she offered by way of defence. "I'll be thanked one day."

"Wouldn't hold yer breath." The sarcasm in Josh's voice was apparent to everyone.

"And I don't know why you've brought us here," Gaynor went on. "These type of entities are not bound by space and time like we are. They can materialise anywhere and if you think this," she said, sweeping her arm around, "will protect us, you're deluded."

Mrs C was almost screaming at Gaynor now. "Your stupidity astounds me. Do you honestly believe that you have the experience and the energy to deal with this? Well, do you?" She got to her feet, not waiting for Gaynor to answer. "These people do and they understand how dangerous it is. This entity must be destroyed and if you have an ounce of common sense you'll keep quiet and pray no one gets hurt tonight."

51

Detective Inspector Burman sat back in his chair, looking intently at Inspector Mallick who was sitting opposite. "Are you honestly telling me you believe all this shit?"

"The lads saw it with their own eyes, gov. And if it wasn't for Mrs Curtis we would never have found those bodies. So yes, I'm inclined to give them the benefit of the doubt. And I don't know how, or why, but somehow, McKenzie is up to his neck in this stuff."

"Have you made any more progress with him?"

"Nah. Duty solicitor answers every question for him with the usual, 'my client has no comment'."

"Try again, but this time have Professor Clarin from Edinburgh present. Maybe he'll get something out of him. If that doesn't work, knock it on the head. I think we've got enough to take to the CPS."

The wax figure was lying on a sheet of white paper in the middle of the table, looking even more grotesque under the harsh fluorescent lights. It's gut, filled with McKenzie's lurid mixture, was now open to the air and some of it had spilled out onto the paper, imbibing the air with the smell of decay. McKenzie was staring at it. His complexion was pallid, eyes glazed.

"My client has decided to cooperate," the duty solicitor announced. "He is ready to answer all your questions."

Inspector Mallick shuffled his chair forward, elbows leaning on the table. He nodded. "I'm glad to hear it. Let's get this unholy mess cleared up, McKenzie. Tell me," he swept his hand over the effigy, "what was this all about?"

"We were fucked. We had nothing. Just out of remand, we'd no money. There was no help. We had to do something."

"So you moved into Rye Top Farm. You were squatters?"

McKenzie nodded.

"Please answer for the tape."

"It was empty. Going to waste. So yes, we were fucking squatters."

"And then what?"

"Weird shit kept happening. Footsteps when there was no one there. Bangs and scrapes like somebody was dragging something round inside. We had a scrap one night, found a loose floorboard upstairs. When we lifted it up, we found that."

"What did you do with it?"

"Nothing at first. Didn't know what it was."

"But you do now?"

"It told us, not like normal talkin' but we knew. Told us it could do things for us, get us things. But we had to take its stuffin' out and put other stuff in."

"What stuff?"

McKenzie dropped his gaze to the floor. "Stuff. You know what, you've checked. I can tell."

The inspector chuckled. "We certainly have. I never knew shit and semen commanded such power."

McKenzie banged his fist on the table. "This ain't no laughing matter. After we'd done that it said we had to blow in it and seal it up and then bury it in the front yard. And it worked. It took a few weeks but it worked in the end. Suddenly, things started happening. We'd find money in the street, and food. We even got a couple of women round. But then it changed. The thing that had been making all the noise, started materialising."

"The thing?"

"It were a demon. It said so."

"You're telling me this is a demon?" the inspector picked up the effigy, holding it up in front of McKenzie, who visibly shrank away.

"You need to destroy that. And the other one." His voice was trembling.

"There's another one? Where?"

"It's what the demon told us. It's in Standedge tunnel."

The inspector smiled. "Really? So it's one of a pair. How very quaint."

"I know you don't fuckin' believe me but it's the truth"

Inspector Mallick nodded. "I believe you, McKenzie. I've seen him. I believe we've also got him on video."

McKenzie's mouth had fallen open. "So you know. You know I didn't kill that priest."

"Unfortunately we know no such thing. You're still charged with his murder. And just for the record, David Gray wasn't a priest. Tell us what happened."

"We got scared. I'm still scared."

The inspector motioned towards Professor Clarin who was sitting next to him. "This man knows what to do about all this stuff. You've no need to be scared while you're in our custody."

"It wanted us to go and get the other one from the tunnels." McKenzie was pointing at the effigy.

"Do you know why?"

"To make it stronger."

"Did you?"

McKenzie was shaking his head. "No. We were going to, we did try once but we chickened out. I can face anybody man, get the better of anybody, but not this. No one can."

"Tell us about David Gray. What happened there?"

"We didn't know what to do when the thing started materialising...we were scared shitless. We'd rung a spiritualist church and asked about it. They said they'd send someone. They sent him..." McKenzie was visibly shaking and the inspector noticed his eyes filling with tears. McKenzie was right. This was serious stuff.

"Tell us what happened. Take your time."

"He told us not to interfere. Not to do anything, no matter what we saw. He started with some sort of prayer...I don't know...I'm not religious. We were upstairs in the front bedroom. There were bangs and shouting. Me and Tommy...we were huddled together in a corner. Never bin that scared. And then the priest sort of changed. His face went all weird...like he was bluebeard and then he wasn't...kept changing."

"Bluebeard?"

"That's what we started calling it...it didn't give us a name. We asked it like...loads of times."

"Go on."

"He went downstairs and then came up again...went in the bathroom. And then we heard screaming. I rushed in...couldn't just sit there, doin' nothin'. The priest...." McKenzie stifled a sob, keeping it locked in. The inspector had seen more hardened criminals than him break down but never had he seen one so frightened. "...he had a kitchen knife and he was stabbing himself."

Inspector Mallick chuckled. "Well, I've heard it all now."

McKenzie's fist came down hard on the table. "If you'd bin there, yer wo'n't be laughin'."

"You can see how this looks, can't you McKenzie? It's hardly going to stand up in court."

"We knew we'd be blamed. Obvious ain't it? But it's the truth. I swear it."

"We found David Gray's body in Martyn Curtis's car. You put it there?"

Silence.

"Please answer for the tape."

"Yeh. We figured if we fitted somebody else up for it we'd be off the hook."

"Why Martyn Curtis?"

"We were supposed to kill him...but we couldn't...no way. We might be thugs but we're not killers. After we'd nicked his car, we dumped him and went back to the house, with his phone. Said we'd done it but it knew we hadn't."

"Why did it want Martyn Curtis dead?"

"It had a grudge against him. It's his hair and stuff in that pouch." McKenzie was pointing to the small, black velvet pouch lying on the table next to the figure. "He came to me sister's flat, reckoned he wanted to rent it but we knew he'd been there before and done things."

"Things?"

"Against Bluebeard. Me sister reckoned he tried to get rid of it from the flat. Me and Tommy, we think it followed us to Rye Top Farm. And honestly, when Curtis turned up at the house a couple of days after we'd car-jacked him, me and Tommy, we saved his life that night. Bluebeard went for him. He'd have done what he did to the priest, but we got him out of there."

The inspector was looking through the papers in the file. He pulled out a report showing the photograph of Jayden. He held it up in front of McKenzie. "And what about Jayden Haskin? How does he fit into all this?"

"I don't know what happened to him."

"You were threatening him."

"I knew Stuart Ryder was gonna be at Rye Top Farm. He'd got me put away. I had a score to settle. Young Haskin, he's like me. I got him to half-inch some chloroform from school. I were threatening him cos he was getting clever with me. Wanting more money, wanting this, wanting that. I just wanted to frighten him good and proper. I didn't know the thing had followed me. It'd only ever bin Rye Top. It did the same as what it did to that girl who was with Ryder at the house. That's when I knew we had to stop meddlin'. Hurtin' grown-ups that's one thing, but not kids, never kids. But it was already too late. It didn't need us anymore, it had Ryder and to be honest we were glad to be free of it."

"What do you mean, it had Ryder?"

"I'm not sure. I don't know how it works. All I know is that we were sent to The Commercial and I saw Bluebeard go for him, sort of merge into him like he tried to do with David Gray. Only difference was, the priest stopped him and Ryder didn't. I've not been bothered with it since."

The inspector turned to the professor with a questioning look.

"With enough energy, and a constant supply of it, these type of manifestations can and do persist, and I suppose it is possible that they are able to move from person to person, a bit like an infection. There are reports of such manifestations becoming autonomous and adopting a unique identity. Are they real or imaginary? I can't answer that. I've never come across anything like this before but, to be honest, I do think we should take this seriously."

52

Inspector Mallick placed four photographs on the table in front of McKenzie.

"For the tape, I'm showing McKenzie photographs of Cassie Thornley, Juliet Winters and Nathan Peters. Do you recognise any of these children?"

Mckenzie shook his head.

"Please answer for the tape."

"No. But isn't that the one who went missing. She was in the paper."

"For the record, Mr. McKenzie is pointing to the photograph of Cassie Thornley."

He pushed the photos closer to McKenzie. "They all went missing. Their bodies have been recovered from the fields at the back of Rye Top Farm where you and your mate were squatting."

McKenzie rubbed his hands over his face. "You don't think? You can't? I would never hurt a kid."

"You threatened Jayden Haskin...with a knife I believe."

"Just trying to scare him. I've told you that."

The inspector took a polythene bag out of a drawer in the table. Removing the contents, he held a pendant up in front of McKenzie. "Seen this before?"

McKenzie nodded. "It belonged to that priest."

"The one you murdered?"

"No. I told you what happened."

"Do you know where this was found?"

"In the field at the back of the old ruin, behind Rye Top Farm."

"That's right. Same place as the bodies of those three children. Do you know how it got there?"

"Me and Tommy, we buried it, near that thing we'd made. We thought it'd get rid of Bluebeard. We were scared man. We'd have done anything."

"It's solid gold. 17th century. Did you know? Worth a lot of money by all accounts. I'm surprised you didn't try and sell it."

"We were going to but someone told us to use it in a ritual like, to protect us from Bluebeard."

"Who told you?"

McKenzie shrugged and cast his eyes downward. "Never knew her name. She never said."

"She? Description?"

The inspector lay the pendant down on the table. "We've had it inspected by the V and A. Belonged originally to a Franciscan priest who was probably executed for his faith. Been in David Gray's family for generations."

"She said it was powerful. She said it'd keep him away if we buried it. I think it gave it more power meself."

"Can you describe the woman?"

"We promised never to tell and I'm no grass."

"You're going to go down for a long time, McKenzie. I really don't think keeping information from us is going to help your case."

"Don't know her name. She turned up in a cloak with a hood...had some sort of veil covering her face. And it was dark."

The inspector laughed. "You're having me on, right?"

"Do I look like I'm laughing?"

"Where did you meet her?"

"Outside the vicarage on Gellfield Lane. Then we walked up to them old ruins."

"How many times did you meet her?"

"Just that once."

"What happened?"

"She did a bit of a ritual, with candles and stuff, and then we buried that."

"Did she arrive in a car?"

"No. On foot."

"You'd recognise her voice again though?"

McKenzie shrugged again. "Dunno."

"Did she have an accent?"

"I'd say she was local."

"You said she had candles and things, so she must have had a bag?"

"Yeh, from Tesco."

"How did you contact her initially?"

"We went to that shop in the village that sells all that weird stuff, wanting to know what we could do to get rid of it. The woman said she'd help. Don't even know if it was the same woman who turned up."

"Which shop was this?"

"The tarot shop on the High Street."

53

The rain was still lashing against the windows of Ebenezer Hall, rattling the windows and chilling the air.

Mrs C was sitting on a cushion beside Martyn. She reached out for his hand.

"Tell us what happened that night in Kylie's flat," she said.

"I attempted what I thought was a proper exorcism. And it seemed to work. No one got hurt. Nothing untoward happened."

"It was all my fault," chirped in Kylie. "It attached itself to me in Standedge tunnel. Ron warned me it was a demon but I didn't tell the others that. It just sounded too stupid and at the beginning I wasn't listening to him. I'd been so frightened. I just thought it was my imagination out of control. The others convinced me it was a poltergeist or something. What Martyn did definitely helped...it wasn't half as bad afterwards."

"You must have drained it of some of its energy," said the lady with the pink hair. "It wouldn't like that at all."

"And then that night that Stuart and Sarah went round to Rye Top Farm," Kylie continued. "I knew something was wrong. I knew something had happened to Martyn because the figurine he brought back from Mexico was smashed on the floor."

"You blamed me for that," Josh chirped in but was ignored.

"Next time I saw Stuart, I could see there was something wrong but I couldn't put my finger on it. I didn't connect it with what had happened to me. I'd spoken to Sarah about what had happened to her and it was different. It wasn't the same. Ron's whistling seemed to be telling me that the man who attacked her was a projection coming from Stuart. It made sense. The thing only ever manifested when he was there."

"Not quite true," Martyn said. "Stuart wasn't there when it attacked me at Rye Top Farm. I was there on my own—well, I thought I was, but McKenzie must have been there. Apparitions can't bundle bodies into cars, abduct people and frame them for murder."

"So, it's McKenzie? It's him it's attached to?"

"Was. Clearly not anymore. He's been in custody since the fracas in the pub."

"It's latched onto me." Gaynor's announcement silenced everyone. "I invited it. I wanted to study it. You should thank me Kylie because it was looking for you. It's what's commonly referred to as an intrusion. These things are attracted by the vibrations given off by those aspects of our lives that need changing. They are our vulnerabilities and that's why such entities seek us out. That's what they're attracted to because it makes for easy pickings. When a spirit entity enters the energy field of a person, it can come in with such force that it dislodges part of the soul, making the person melancholy, sometimes changing their entire personality."

"Of course, they can be persuaded to leave their host," the lady with the pink hair had shuffled forward on her cushion, eager to join in the conversation. "Or in your case, Kylie, Martyn must have done a good job of evicting it. But they leave a hole behind. Like an empty room in a house. That's where your familiar Ron came in. He moved in and patched that hole."

"So what are you saying? That I've still got an intrusion, albeit a benign one?" Kylie looked panicked. This wouldn't be what she wanted to hear.

"Yes, dear. But we can do something about that...," the lady paused, her eyes resting on the space behind Kylie. "Dear Ron, you have no need to be afraid. We thank you with all our hearts for protecting Kylie from this monstrous aberration and we ask that you continue to do so until it is safe for you to leave. But be assured, passage into the light is a joyful occasion. You will be free...and at peace."

"Is that what you saw in Stuart's aura, a hole?" Kylie asked Mrs C.

"Yes. I believe this entity has been coming and going at will, perhaps between Stuart and McKenzie, feeding on both. Though now Gaynor has opened herself up to it, it has a bigger choice of hostelries."

"We need to get rid of it. Send it back where it came from." The lady with the pink hair was looking worried. "Father Joseph, can you do it?"

"I can try," he replied, "though I'm not sure—"

"You can't," Gaynor interrupted. "It won't work. This is beyond anything any of you have encountered before. It needs to be sent back to the source of its power. There was a doll. Some sort of talisman figurine that McKenzie had. He told me he'd buried it in the grounds of the farm."

"How do you know that?" Martyn voiced everyone's shock. "Are you saying you've had dealings with McKenzie while all this has been going on?"

"He called me in to help get rid of the problem."

"When? Why didn't you tell us?"

"It really doesn't matter now."

"It matters to us!" Martyn was shouting. None of them had ever seen him so angry. Mrs C grabbed hold of his arm, afraid he might strike out.

"My intention was to find the doll and take it to my mentor in Mexico," Gaynor's composure was infuriating to them all. "He will know what to do. I've been keeping a video diary because I know this is going to be big. There's proof here of everything we've ever believed in. I know—"

"It needs to be found and destroyed," Father Joseph interrupted. "It's a travesty and an abomination."

Gaynor was shaking her head. "Absolutely not. That would be the worst thing we could do. That's what it wants me to do because that will set it free. We can't let that happen. Whoever has the effigy has some degree of control over it whether they know it or not."

The conversation was interrupted by a loud banging on the door at the front of the building. They all froze. There it was again.

"Shouldn't we answer it?" Josh asked.

"Oh no, dear," said the lady with the tight bun in her hair who was clutching the sides of the cushion she was sitting on. "We must not leave the circle, not under any circumstances."

"This is like something on Netflix," Josh complained, sounding more irritable by the second while the banging continued.

"I bet you're thinking of the Devil Rides Out," chirped in the lady with the pink hair. "The Dennis Wheatley film. The four horses of the apocalypse appeared. It was all based on fact you know, nothing was made up."

275

"Can we please be quiet and listen," Mrs C demanded. "Someone's shouting."

"Unbolt the door. Mrs Curtis. Can you hear me? It's important."

"Ignore it," said the lady with the bun. "It's the demon. That's what they do to get you to break the circle."

Mrs C was already on her feet, stepping out of the circle. "That's only in the movies, dear. I think we can safely say, that is Gary."

Everyone held their breath while the door was unbolted, even Josh who, despite his bravado, wasn't sure what was real and what wasn't.

As the door creaked open, Gary Hardacre tumbled in followed by a billowing cloud of dry leaves.

"You must stop this immediately," he yelled as he strode across the hall. "It's far too dangerous. Get rid of these markings on the floor...and get rid of her." He was pointing at Gaynor. "My guides have spelled it out good and proper. We're in uncharted territory here and no matter what we do, or what we believe, this is way beyond our capability."

Mrs C was looking agitated, even confused. "But I thought—"

"Well you thought wrong, Mrs Curtis and I'm surprised at you, putting everyone in danger like this."

Stepping into the circle, he yanked Gaynor to her feet. "I've no idea what your game is but you're not welcome here. Leave. Now!"

"But..."

"Now!"

Josh was on his feet, beckoning Kylie to follow him. Gaynor couldn't walk home. They would have to drive her.

54

Stuart's eyes flickered open as a bright shaft of sunlight flared out from behind a cloud and danced across his face.

A silhouetted figure was standing in front of the window, perfectly still, perfectly silent. The daffodil covered screen fluttered in the cooling breeze coming from the slightly open window. The nightmare momentarily flashed back into Stuart's memory. Joseph Bradshaw, the smell of him permeating every recess of his dreaming mind. He was about to call out, shout for help. He was in hospital and so there would be someone nearby, but then the figure spoke.

"Good morning, Mr Ryder. Hope I didn't startle you."

It was Inspector Mallick.

"Of course you bloody startled me, standing there like that, staring at me. What do you think?"

The inspector pulled up a chair, making himself comfortable before explaining the reason for his visit.

"You'll be glad to know that despite your confession concerning Cassie Thornley, you will not be charged with her murder."

"You've spoken to the officers who were at the séance?"

"I have."

"And they saw him? Joseph Bradshaw?"

"They saw what Mrs Curtis has described to me as a transfiguration. Yes."

"And?"

"And what?"

"What do you make of it?"

The inspector laughed, a sarcastic, almost embarrassed sort of chuckle. "I really have no idea. My job is to find out who murdered those children and bring him or her to justice, not to accuse the dead. I'm here to ask you about Frank Waite, the owner of Rye Top Farm."

"What about him? I don't really know him."

"Was it him that contacted you or did you get in touch with him?"

"He telephoned. Said his mother's house had been empty for some time and he'd been trying to sell it. He suspected it was haunted. He wanted us to carry out an investigation. He thought it might be his deceased mother."

"And you jumped at the chance to investigate because that's what you do? Did he give you any indication about what sort of things were going off there?"

"Not really. He just said that the previous tenants had reported odd things...and he also said that some of the viewings had been disrupted because potential buyers had heard rumours of it being haunted."

"When you went to the house, did you not think it odd that there was no 'For Sale' sign up?"

Stuart's eyes widened. The thought had never occurred to him. "We didn't notice, never thought about it...it was dark. What are you saying?"

"The house was never put on the market. There was no agent and no potential buyers."

"Why would he lie about that? What was the point?

The inspector shrugged. "Perhaps it wasn't him who rang you. Perhaps it was someone pretending to be him, someone who, for whatever reason, wanted that house investigated. How did he get the key to you?"

"He left it under a stone by the front door, along with some cash...fifty pounds. We don't charge a fee, just expenses, most of the time not even that. We never discussed payment so I was surprised he gave us anything. He told me to keep hold of the key, and said he'd contact me again in a few weeks to pick it up and get our report."

"Did he?"

"No. He didn't seem interested in how long it would take either or how many visits we would make. Usually with a callout like that, we'd just do one sweep over one night and I told him that."

"So you never saw him? You've no idea what he looks like?"

Stuart shook his head.

The inspector slipped his hand inside his jacket and pulled out a photograph which he handed to Stuart.

Stuart's mouth dropped open. He was holding a photograph of a man with a weathered, rugged complexion and a bushy, black beard.

"Oh my God. This is the man we've kept seeing. Joseph Bradshaw."

"That's Frank Waite."

"I don't understand."

"You're not on your own there," said the inspector, taking back the photograph. "But we need to speak to him urgently. I was hoping you could give me an address or contact point."

"Sorry, no. Though the call will be logged on my phone."

"We've already checked that. The call came from an unregistered number, no longer active."

"You think he murdered those children?"

"Let's just say we're hoping he can help us with our enquiries."

"We checked up on Joseph Bradshaw, you know, as part of our paranormal investigations. He lived at Hobhole Farm, the ruins behind Rye Top Farm. It wasn't proven at the time but it seemed likely that he killed his own daughter and other children too. It's probably their remains that you're finding up near Running Hill. He had his wife incarcerated in a lunatic asylum to keep her quiet."

"Why were you checking him out?"

"Some of the stuff that happened to me and Sarah in that house led us to him. I can send you the transcripts if you like, and the results of our research. Things happened that night that we haven't told you about."

"Like?"

"Like the sort of materialisation you saw at the séance, a man that looked like that photo you've just shown me. We caught it on video. It pounced on Sarah...she said she felt like she'd been raped, psychically."

The inspector looked puzzled. "But she wasn't? It wasn't a real man?"

"She said not but the rest of us weren't so sure. I was there, right next to her, but I felt like I'd been drugged or something. The whole thing was weird and we were never able to suss out what really happened. And there's something else...it was after that, that Sarah found out she was pregnant."

The inspector raised his eyebrows. "Yours?"

"I guess...but it's weird. She's on the pill, never misses."

The inspector got to his feet. "Okay, let me have everything you've got...as soon as you can."

"Have you shown that photo to Jayden Haskin?" Stuart asked.

The inspector shook his head. "No, why would I do that?"

"You should. The lad wasn't lying when he said he'd been assaulted. It was the same as my girlfriend."

The inspector looked thoughtful and nodded. "Okay. I'll do that. The storm trooper guarding the door has been removed by the way, you're free to be discharged if the doctor's happy."

With the Inspector gone, Stuart experienced an overwhelming sense of relief. Things were starting to fit into place, not everything, not by any means, but if Frank Waite had modelled himself on Joseph Bradshaw, surely that would explain a lot of the confusion they'd experienced so far. And if Frank Waite had murdered the three children found in the fields behind Rye Top Farm, did that mean that something else was at play here? Something benign, or someone that wanted Frank Waite exposed. Was that the reason for all this? But that didn't change the fact that there had been real materialisations of a man that looked exactly like Frank Waite. Was it he who had produced a homunculus? Was he the one who was adept in such practices? And what did all that have to do with Joseph Bradshaw?

55

"You okay, sir?"

It was Haskin, standing on Stuart's doorstep at nine o'clock on Saturday morning. Stuart had been hoping for a lie-in—hospital accommodation wasn't very conducive to a good night's sleep.

"I'm fine, really. What do you want?"

"I've been doin' some research about that tunnel you all went in, the one where Kylie got zapped. I've got a map. Wanna see it?"

"Can you not come back later, at a more reasonable time?"

"It's important, sir. Honest."

Stuart was in no mood for this and he shuffled from foot to foot, sighing deeply. "Nothing's that important at this time on a Saturday morning, Haskin." But then he remembered the last time he turned Haskin away and thought better of it. "You'd better come in."

Jayden laid out an ordnance survey map over the coffee table. A faint double, dashed line had been highlighted in yellow on the map.

"That's the canal tunnel," Jayden said, following the line with his finger. In neat handwriting along the bottom margin, he had written the details of the tunnel's construction and he proceeded to read it out loud.

The tunnel goes from Diggle to Marsden and runs for over three miles. There was no room for people or horses so the horses would be led across the moors to the other end of the tunnel and the men would lie on their backs on the deck and leg the boat through on the walls of the tunnel.

"That's where the term 'Leg it' comes from, sir." Jayden said, tapping his finger on the map. "I legged it after nabbing this map from the Post Office. A woman saw me, she was yelling blue murder but she didn't catch me."

Stuart didn't answer, but instead rubbed his hands over his face in exasperation. He was tempted to mention the entity that seemed to be following Kylie round but thought better of it. Hadn't Kylie said he was a legger?

Sweeping the map onto the floor, Jayden produced a large folded sheet of paper from his jacket and spread it out carefully on the table. It was an enlarged sketch map of the area showing all the contour lines and grid markings. Clearly painstakingly copied from the original map.

The words 'Rye Top Farm' were written in capital letters with an arrow pointing to the sketch of a building. The house was lying about a mile from the Diggle end of the tunnel. Just a short distance away were the sketched ruins of Hobhole Farm.

"See these?" Jayden asked, pointing to a patchwork of lines he had drawn in pencil around the tunnel. These were the fields that belonged to Hobhole Farm and you can see the tunnel runs right underneath them." Pointing to another section of the map, he added. "And these are the other tunnels and the connecting passages."

"You sure about this?" Stuart asked, hardly able to believe that someone like Haskin had the intelligence to produce anything this detailed. It would have taken some degree of surveying and map reading skills, and a knowledge of grid references.

"Oh yes, sir. I went down to the library and copied a map of the tunnel that was used when it was being built, and then I went up there with that ordnance survey map."

"The map you stole from the Post Office?"

Jayden shrugged and carried on. "It's easy to follow the line of the main railway tunnel, 'cause of all the air shafts and spoil heaps above ground. And I could tell its position by looking at the fields and contours and comparing it to the old map. There's also this," he was pointing to a cylindrical object he had sketched on the map. "It's the Cote Pit ventilation shaft. The canal tunnel lies below the railway tunnel here. To get the location of the other tunnels, there's three railway tunnels under that hill you know, I had to go down there and map it out for meself."

Stuart sat back in his chair in shock. This lad was full of surprises.

"You went into those tunnels...on your own?"

"Yes, sir. I ain't afraid o'no ghosts." Jayden seemed proud of his Ghostbuster joke. Stuart assumed it was directed at Kevin and laughed.

"Can't deny I'm impressed. Though not about the stolen map, obviously. And providing you're right of course and these grid references are accurate."

"I swear it. And these little sections, look, here and here, these are connecting passages, there's loads of 'em running between all four tunnels. Did you know that, sir? It's a real labyrinth under them hills. Are you going to call a meeting, sir?"

"Things are in a bit of disarray I'm afraid. You know more bodies have been found up there?"

Jayden nodded. "I saw it on Facebook and it was all cordoned off when I went up there. And I know you've been in hospital and I bet it's something to do with this."

Stuart nodded. "Quite a lot has happened since that day we were there, digging. That pendant you found, by the way, belonged to the priest who was murdered at Rye Top Farm."

"So does that mean I won't get anything for it?"

"I'm afraid so. It'll go to his family."

"But this is important, isn't it, sir?" Jayden was pointing to the sketch still laid out on the table, his excitement undiminished.

"I suspect it's very important. It's always seemed that the entity that attacked Kylie in the tunnel was something to do with what happened at Rye Top Farm, but I just couldn't find a connection. Rye Top's connection to Hobhole Farm and the fact that the field systems stretched as far as the tunnel, could be the link. The police believe all they're dealing with is a murderer, and I think they suspect Frank Waite, the owner of the house, but there's more to it than that. Much more."

Jayden got to his feet. "Shall I put the kettle on while you get dressed? And then you can ring the others, get them round here."

Stuart couldn't help laughing. Here was Jayden Haskin, the uncontrollable delinquent of Saddleworth School, suddenly transformed into someone who wouldn't be out of place in the Principal's office. He had changed in a matter of a few weeks. There was something about him now that was altogether decent and good.

"Sure," Stuart said. "I'll get right to it."

56

Stuart, Jayden, Martyn, Mrs C and Kylie were all assembled in Stuart's lounge before two o'clock that same afternoon.

Stuart's laptop was open on the coffee table. Sarah was on screen, sitting in the lounge of her parent's home in Dorset. Everyone wanted to know how she was and to pass on their love and concern. She assured everyone she was fine and hoped to be back soon. No one dared mention the pregnancy, especially not Stuart. That would come later, when there was just the two of them. So far, every effort he had made to speak with her had come to nothing. Either she wasn't on-line or her parents said she was sleeping and didn't want to be disturbed. She'd obviously given them instructions that she didn't want to speak to him.

They were all really pleased to see Jayden again, asking how he had been and what he'd been up to since they last met.

Pleasantries over, the meeting began though not until Stuart had explained why Kevin and Gaynor were absent.

Jo Harthan

"Kevin has bowed out in an effort to maintain his credibility. I believe he thinks everything that's happened is explainable in non-paranormal terms. Gaynor, on the other hand, took it upon herself to do a solo investigation, believing that a close encounter would propel her into the paranormal research hall of fame. As far as I know, and from what you've all told me, the entity we've been referring to as Joseph Bradshaw is now in close communion with her. God help her is all I can say. I certainly didn't want her here today."

"She was always bad news." Sarah's voice came through loud and clear from the laptop. "And think about what happened to me that night. She was there, I reckon she sent it. I wouldn't trust her as far as I could throw her."

"She wouldn't do that," Stuart said. "Why would she?" Even as he spoke he wondered if he should be sticking up for her. Did any of them really know what Gaynor had been up to? And she did have her sights set on getting back with him, Kev had told him as much. If it was her, she had succeeded in getting rid of Sarah that was for sure.

"And don't forget what Gary said the other night." Mrs C was perched on the edge of the settee, eager to contribute to the discussion. "You weren't there Stuart. He arrived at church just as we were about to start an invocation and exorcism. And thank God he did. He warned us to stop, said it would only make things worse because Gaynor was there inside the circle with us. We should have left her house

288

without her that night...I just wanted to make sure everyone was safe. I didn't know she was the danger...but I should have known, shouldn't I?"

"Don't beat yourself up about that, mum. Nor anybody else for that matter. We're all just trying to figure this out and, to be honest, it's been like walking through a maze, blindfolded."

"One thing I can tell you all," Stuart continued, "is that Inspector Mallick showed me a photograph of Frank Waite the other day, the guy that owns Rye Top Farm, and it was the man, apparition, demon, whatever you want to call it, the thing we've been seeing. That thing we've been calling Joseph Bradshaw."

"Is he implicated in the murders?" Martyn looked concerned. "When we talked about somebody projecting an apparition, do you think it was him?"

Stuart was shaking his head. "I honestly don't know what to think."

"You weren't there Stuart when Gaynor told us about the genealogy research she'd done." It was Kylie who voiced what the others were thinking. Someone had to tell him.

Stuart said nothing but waited expectantly for her to continue.

"Both you and Frank Waite are related to Joseph Bradshaw. I believe Gaynor said you were second cousins once removed or something."

There was a stunned silence. They were all waiting for Stuart's response.

"So is that important? What are you saying, Kylie?" Stuart remembered only too well the intimations Kylie had made many times about the projection being from him.

"I don't know, Stu, honestly." Kylie's eyes were cast downwards. "I just kept feeling there was a bad egg in our omelette somewhere. It was probably Gaynor."

"I promise you it wasn't me, Kylie."

"No, dear, it wasn't you." Mrs C's hand patting his was clearly an attempt to reassure him. "You were playing host to it for sure, intermittently, not all the time. But you wouldn't know that. It wasn't your fault."

"I certainly didn't know I had any connection to Frank Waite but it must be pretty tenuous. We're not even the same generation. Does anybody have copies of Gaynor's research?"

They all shook their heads. "It was all verbal. She never showed us any of her notes."

"But she did mention Frank Waite's mother, Hannah Bradshaw. She was Joseph Bradshaw's granddaughter," said Kylie. "Do you remember, Martyn? Didn't Gaynor say she'd died under suspicious circumstances?"

"Threw herself under a train or something..."

"I think she said she fell down an air shaft."

"Couldn't do that by accident, it'd have to be—"

Jayden was flushed with excitement as he interrupted the conversation. "Do you know there's railway tunnels above that canal tunnel you lot went in?"

Stuart smiled but he sounded more subdued than before.

"Now would be a good time to tell them all about your discovery, Jayden. It might have a bearing on this. Show us the sketch you made."

If Jayden was nervous about presenting in front of them all, he didn't show it and they all listened intently to what he had to say. When he had finished, Mrs C was gushing in her praise, making Jayden flush with pride.

"My, my...what has happened to you, young man?" she said. "You are positively glowing with good energy...and so eloquent. You have clearly stepped into the role you were meant to take."

It was obvious that Jayden wasn't used to such commendation by the way he shuffled awkwardly back to his seat as the others offered words of admiration. Stuart was glad for him. The lad deserved some recognition.

Congratulations over, Stuart took the floor again.

"We need to start at the beginning. Back in the tunnel that night Kylie was attacked. There's a connection between what happened there, Martyn's efforts to get rid of the attachment and what happened to Sarah and me at Rye Top Farm. What Jayden discovered could be the link. We just have to fit all the pieces together."

Two weeks of wild speculation followed—the result of séances, EVPs and, in the case of Jayden Haskin, the results of research into railway archives that had thrown up many anecdotal reports of strange, paranormal activity while the tunnels were being built between 1794 and 1811.

Some of the incidents reported were so startling as to be disbelieved by the local constabulary at the time. One of the examples Jayden had found was of an Irish navvy employed with a hundred others to dig out the first tunnel. He claimed to have seen the devil emerging from the wall of a newly excavated section. His report described a grey man with leathery skin, a goat-shaped face and malformed limbs, with eyes as black as coal. It caused the sides of the tunnel to collapse, resulting in the death of three men. Despite his testimony, the incident was reported as an unfortunate accident. A local doctor was quoted as saying, "Working underground for long periods can cause a malady in the head such that strange things are seen and thought to be real."

They speculated that perhaps this was the same entity that they had been dealing with. Maybe it had been released when the tunnels were being dug? But that sounded too incredible even for the less sceptical Kylie. All it did was make it even more difficult to fit the pieces together.

It was late one evening when Stuart received a telephone call from Kevin Venkman.

"You remember the investigation my outfit did at the lunatic asylum in York? Gaynor went back there last week and dug deeper. She's uncovered a diary, written by Elisa, Joseph Bradshaw's wife. I think you might want to see it."

Stuart agreed to a meeting on the proviso that Gaynor did not attend. They already knew that she had been questioned by the police about the murder of David Gray. The fact that she had kept quiet about her involvement with McKenzie from the start meant she was not to be trusted and was clearly a dangerous acquaintance to have if she was still in contact with the malevolent entity. Kevin agreed that there was no need to involve her and he promised to bring them all up to speed on the developments in that quarter.

The meeting was arranged for Saturday afternoon at Stuart's house and they all waited in solemn silence for Kevin to arrive. He brought with him a paper transcript of the diary, explaining that Gaynor wanted to protect her copyright over the original as she intended publishing the photocopied entries in the book she was planning to write.

Once everyone was settled, he read out the contents to the eagerly awaited audience.

"Entry dated 1st December 1849...just over a week before she took her own life. Which actually, Gaynor is now disputing. You'll understand why when I read you the diary. Okay, here goes.

'My husband Joseph is possessed of the devil. He acted towards our daughter Alice, in a way no father should, causing her much consternation. He has sinned against God and the church, made worse when he silenced her because she grew petulant. I believe he has done the same to others also, being grossly unhinged and taken over by the devil that befriended him whilst still a boy and green of eye. He told me they were met when he went into the tunnels under Pule Moss; tunnels not long dug out when he went to explore them. Once, in great lament and remorse, he told me of a waxen doll his mother had instructed him to make when he was but fifteen years old. He was to take it down into the tunnels and bury it deep so that the devil may be bound there forever. And they accuse me of witchcraft! It is her they should incarcerate here, not me. I have written to the jailer, though writing is hard because my poor hands are calloused and dry from the washer room, begging him to find the doll and so prove all that I say. But he says it is the imaginings of my sick and grieving mind. I cannot bear this hell much longer though I am fortunate my husband does not visit me, for if he did, my very soul would be in danger as this thing, this devil, can change its place of abode at will. I will not let it in but it's only a matter of time before it comes to destroy me for it grows stronger by the day.'

A stunned silence followed as they all tried to assimilate Elisa's words.

At last Kylie spoke. "So this entity, that attached to me in the tunnel, it was this, the same one she talked about? Was it in the tunnel all along, waiting for a new host?"

Kevin was shaking his head. "I don't think it's that simple. Did you know Frank Waite turned up at a police station in Southampton yesterday? Handed himself in and admitted to the murder of those children they found."

No, they didn't know.

"I think McKenzie's hoping he'll cop for David Gray's murder too; he's still protesting his innocence even though he's been charged."

"So you think Frank Waite was behind what happened to us?"

"I'm not sure anyone possessed by a demon can be deemed to be responsible for anything to be honest. Elisa says in this diary that the demon can chose who it possesses, perhaps it wanted a change of residence, perhaps Frank wanted rid of it. Perhaps we'll never know but Gaynor did do some thorough research on the Waite family. Hannah Bradshaw, Frank's mother, was Joseph Bradshaw's granddaughter and Gaynor suspects that the entity transferred to her on the death of Joseph in 1898. She would have been thirteen at the time of his death and it wasn't long after that that she was accused of causing the death of a neighbour's dog. Nothing proven but there are accounts of her being seen scouring the hedgerows for Wolfsbane, Larkspur, foxglove and water hemlock to name just

295

a few. She married Peter Waite in 1903, the same year that Frank was born. It's probably safe to assume they had to get married. Peter died shortly afterwards in mysterious circumstances. Poisoning was suspected but never proven. There were many such accusations made against her throughout her life."

"So if Frank was born in 1903...that would make him over a hundred years old."

"Exactly. And I have his mother's death certificate here...she only died in 1995 aged an astonishing hundred and ten."

Kylie's mouth dropped open. "Do you remember, Stuart, we found her grave up at Heights. Hannah Bradshaw...the inscription must have been in her maiden name. We discounted any connection because it was a relatively recent burial. And I've read about that. About how intimacy with the devil can confer longevity."

"Which leaves me to conclude that Frank took on the mantle when his mother died and probably continued with their murderous pursuits."

"But how does all this relate to what happened to us?"

"I reckon it was in the tunnel when you four went in that night...either it or Frank Waite. Did Waite want to get rid of it? Is that why it attached itself to Kylie? When he invited you to do an investigation at Rye Top Farm, was it to lure Martyn there? Perhaps the entity wanted revenge. It had already killed David Gray when he had tried to exorcise it, perhaps it wanted Martyn dead too. You might have had a lucky escape, Martyn, being set up for killing someone instead of being murdered yourself."

"So where do you suggest we go from here, Kev?"

Stuart was again amiable to advice from a trusted contact. If the last few days had shown him anything, it was that they needed the expertise and resources of the Waterford group.

Kevin turned to Kylie, addressing her directly. "Are you still having problems?" he asked.

She shook her head.

"Is anyone having problems?"

"No. Martyn's mum has been checking us all nearly every day, just to make sure we're all clean. So far so good."

"Then I suggest that you forget about this for the time being and thank your lucky stars that it didn't turn out worse for you all."

"How can we do that?" Stuart was sounding annoyed with Kevin's patronising tone.

"Easy. Just leave it to the police."

"What about Gaynor?"

"She's gone to Mexico to consult with her mentor. She's confident this can be sorted and the malevolence can be laid to rest...though she did warn me that she may need our help to finish the job. That's all I can tell you at the moment."

"Is it attached to her? Has she taken it with her?"

"As far as I know, she's been working with a professor from Edinburgh and they have it all under control. She'll be in contact with you all in due course, for permission to quote names and events, though she has promised the police that she won't publish anything, anytime soon. In the meantime we all just need to lie low and not speculate. It's easy to start gossip and rumours, please don't forget we have three dead children here, and many more unidentified remains. We don't want the families upset by talk of demons. Are we all agreed?"

They all gave their word. Sarah was due to arrive back from Dorset any day. Stuart knew he would have enough to deal with then, without talk of demonic possession.

58

The Green Fig was empty when Stuart arrived. He had booked a table by the window. At least if he didn't enjoy their breakfast conversation, he could look out over the Pennine hills as he reflected on his future.

The thought of what Sarah was going to say had given him indigestion for days. He'd tried to ask her on the phone but she wouldn't be drawn. He had no idea whether she had come to a decision about the pregnancy or not. He hoped she had, at least then they could get on with things. The indecision and not knowing was killing him.

She arrived just as Michael Jackson was blaring tunefully out of the radio about the kid not being his.

"How are you?" he asked, hoping he sounded sympathetic and loving despite feeling like he wanted to run away. "I've ordered your favourite. Hope that's okay."

She nodded as she sat down opposite him. She wasn't smiling.

"So, what's new?" How pathetic did that sound? He just couldn't think of anything else to say.

"I got rid of it. I've had an abortion." The words cut into him like a knife. Sharp, unexpected. The decision had been made. The problem had been excised. He should be happy.

He didn't feel very happy.

"Sarah...I'd have stood by you, you know that."

"Stood by me?" She sounded angry. "Did you really think I would want to share my life with someone who was standing by me because he had impregnated me with the seed of a demon?"

"What!"

"I've spoken to Gaynor...yes your ex who did all the research about Joseph Bradshaw's family."

"Come on, Sarah. I know she said I was somehow related to him, but you don't honestly believe that I'm anything like him? Do you?"

"We keep secrets from ourselves, Stuart. You may think you don't, but you do. I saw the way you kept looking at Gaynor. You still have feelings for her. She tells me that you thought she was trying to get back with you. She wasn't. The only interest she has in you is that she thinks you're the linchpin for all this. She explained it all to me, how we all start out living by the map handed to us by our culture, but more importantly, our DNA. If we don't recognise our motives, we continue to propagate our flaws."

"I can't believe you're saying this." Stuart was in shock. "That's Gaynor talking. What exactly are you accusing me of?"

"When we were at Rye Top Farm, the manifestation or whatever it was, said to me 'I knew I'd get inside you.' You took me by force that night, Stuart, and you are related to Joseph Bradshaw."

Stuart was stunned. The events of the séance in Dewsbury came rushing back into his mind with the overwhelming force of a tsunami. All his self denials were imploding, being washed away in the rubble of confusion. He had become Frank Waite that night, and everyone present had seen it, the transfiguration. And it had told him, it had said it was him. Had the same thing happened that night at Rye Top Farm. Was Sarah right?

He could feel an impenetrable barrier growing between them. Her eyes were cold and accusing when she next spoke.

"Kylie knew from the start but I didn't listen to her. She kept quiet for fear of upsetting you."

"So what are you saying, that I'm some sort of monster who goes round raping women? Perhaps you think I killed those children too?"

"That's for you to decide, Stuart. The only thing I'm accusing you of is getting me pregnant without my permission. I've no idea how you did it, me being on the pill and all, maybe you don't know either, but you did do it, make no mistake about that."

Shuffling her chair back, she got up to leave.

He reached out to take her hand. "Sarah, please don't go. I need to figure this out. There's no one else I can talk to."

Her expression softened and she sat back down but withdrew her hand from his. "You should probably talk to Gaynor. She's seems to have it all figured out. Maybe she can help."

Stuart didn't answer. Gaynor was the last person he wanted to talk to. He remembered that night they'd had a blazing row; he couldn't even remember what about. They'd been seeing each other quite some time and she had said something that had pushed buttons that hadn't been pushed for years. He remembered the rage he'd felt and how hard it had been not to hit her. And there was another time, long ago when he was still a child, maybe nine or ten. There had been something in his bedroom, egging him on, encouraging him to do things he shouldn't have been doing to a girl from school. He couldn't even remember her name. There was no one else in the house. She'd been screaming, asking him to stop. But he hadn't. Couldn't. He'd been terrified she would tell someone but she never did.

It was shortly after that, that he'd started going down to the stream that ran through the woods, looking for frogs. Pulling their legs off somehow satiated the obsession he had for girls.

But he'd changed all that, he'd grown up, kept it all under control. Hidden it away just like Sarah was saying. He felt his eyes filling up with tears and was trying desperately hard to make them go away.

He lifted his gaze to hers. "I'm ashamed of things I did when I was a kid. But I didn't know any better. And when I grew up I just thought that's what kids did. I'm not like that now. I would never hurt anyone or anything."

"I know that, Stuart. I'm sorry I was so abrupt. I didn't mean to accuse you. But you needed to know."

"I'm frightened," he replied.

"Me too. We unleashed something in the tunnel that night that none of us were up to dealing with. Gaynor believes it was after you all along but maybe it wasn't strong enough then, maybe Kylie was the easy option. And then Martyn trying to exorcise it meant that he became a target."

"And we were set up? Lured to Rye Top Farm."

"Maybe it had decided to use you as an accomplice? When you and I turned up there, we were handing it dinner on a plate. As it grew stronger it was probably able to use the biological connection to take possession of you, albeit only temporarily. Kylie told me the same thing happened at the séance you all went to when I wasn't here."

"Martyn's mum said she found a hole in my aura."

302

"Yes I know, Martyn told me."

"You know me. I didn't believe in all that spiritual stuff."

"You do now though?"

He nodded. "I can't cope with this. It's all too much."

Sarah reached over and took his hand. "Then leave it up to Gaynor. She knows what she's doing. She'll sort it."

59

The frost was lying hard on the ground outside the tunnel entrance at Marsden.

It was Sunday evening—a time when most people would be relaxing with their feet up after Sunday dinner. No one in their right mind would be out here on a night like this.

Gaynor had already secured permission for their expedition so the gates, which were usually kept locked by the canal authority, were standing open in readiness. Two small boats were tied up by the bank. In Gaynor's bag was the effigy that McKenzie had used, on loan from Professor Clarin. If he was expecting her to return it, he would be disappointed.

"Okay, listen up," she said when they were all assembled. "The most important thing to know is that fear will feed this thing, so no matter what happens we stay strong. Anyone who has the slightest doubt about that needs to leave now because any chink in our armour could be devastating for all of us. Understood?"

"Why this end?" Kylie asked. "Why not Diggle?"

"Because the place we're going to is nearer this end, thirty minutes by boat, a good hour from the other end."

It had already been decided that Sarah and Kylie would not go into the tunnel. They would stay at the entrance, keeping vigil. Mrs C had made it clear from the outset that she would not go in without the protection of Father Joseph and at least four of the other spiritualists. So she had been left out. Not that she minded. It was a dangerous mission that she advised against though no one had listened to her.

She had, however, given Martyn a drawstring bag embroidered with depictions of the Holy Mother. Inside were sacred amulets, a small white pocket Bible and four Christian crosses. There was also a small vial of holy water.

"Just in case," she had said as she had leaned over and kissed him on the forehead, adding, "you know where I am if you need me."

"We'll light a fire, just over there on the bank," said Kylie, "and keep it going until you come out."

Gaynor nodded her approval before turning to two men standing at her side. "This is Paul, and his assistant Steve, they'll be in the second boat filming everything that happens. Martyn, Kev and Stuart, you'll be in the boat at the front with me. Martyn, can you be in charge of the outboard motor please?

Kill it when I tell you? Kev, you've brought the EVP recorder and the spirit box?"

Kevin nodded and held up the equipment so they could all see.

"Right," Gaynor continued. "You don't need me to tell you this is mega. Nothing like this has ever been captured on film before. This is an intrusion from another level of existence, another dimension if you like. It is real but it is only dangerous if we allow it to be. These effigies," she pulled the doll out of the bag she was carrying, "are its way of communicating and entering our sphere of existence. I say 'these' because there is another one in the tunnels. This entity is a sentient being and we must either send it back to its own dimension or bind it here so it can never again manifest. It was bound inside these hills by our remote ancestors and released when the tunnels were being dug. It latched onto Joseph Bradshaw whilst he was still a child and has continued to move from person to person ever since, wreaking havoc. It's last permanent home was McKenzie but, as I think you all know, it has the ability to come and go at will. I believe Frank Waite was in these tunnels the night you four came here. He was looking for the other effigy. He's told police that he believed if he destroyed them both, the thing he had identified as a demon would be destroyed. But he was wrong. Destroy these and the entity will be beyond any control. We must find the second effigy and bury both somewhere they will never be found. Without human contact, they will lose their potency and he will diminish.

"I've been in touch with Jayden and studied the plans for these tunnels. Approximately thirty minutes into the tunnel, there's a landing stage where we can access connecting passages. We'll tie up the boats there and disembark. In a connecting passage we'll find steps going to an upper level, into the disused railway tunnels. I believe we'll find the other effigy in there somewhere. It's not going to be easy guys and I warn you, it might take us a while to find it. We need to keep our nerve.

"Once we've found it, we'll cross into another passage, which will take us into an unfinished section, only partly excavated. Where that tunnel ends, there should be a deep construction shaft that by-passes the canal and acts as a drainage pit. That's where we drop both effigies. The entity will have no option but to follow. I fully expect it to try and stop us, so be prepared. Everybody clear?"

"Thanks for not including me," an angry voice came out of the darkness, accompanied by bouncing torchlight. It was Jayden Haskin.

"This is no place for kids, Haskin," shouted Stuart. "Go home."

"Don't think so, sir," he said as he stepped into a pool of light from Gaynor's head torch. "I'm part of this outfit, you said so yourself."

"It's fine," said Gaynor. "Jayden's been helping me understand the tunnel system. He's been here before, haven't you Jayden?"

"Been here loads of times, mapping the tunnels and the connecting shafts. Quite a few of them weren't on the original plan that I showed you all before. I'm the one that found the other thing, that doll. I know exactly where it is."

"Good lad." Gaynor sounded pleased to have him turn up. "Paul...is Jayden okay coming with you? Just to warn you all, it's pretty dark in there and it will take us at least half an hour to reach the landing stage. I don't want anybody freaking out. Right. Are we all ready? Everybody know what they're doing? Keep calm. Keep strong and you'll all stay safe."

60

There was only the sound of lapping water and the slow chug chug of the engines as the two boats made their way into the tunnel, staying close together. A thick mist was making the journey feel surreal. The atmosphere was still and lifeless.

Jayden commented that it was like a scene from the Stephen King movie 'It'. Despite conjuring up images of a malevolent clown in everyone's mind, he was showing no sign of fear, not even apprehension. Stuart, on the other hand, was terrified and told Jayden he didn't appreciate the simile. Perhaps he had more to lose than Haskin. Surely they were all aware that the entity could use him to disrupt their plans. He sincerely hoped Gaynor had taken that into account. She seemed so

307

cock sure of herself and confident that she could handle everything that might be thrown at them. But perhaps he had been blind to her potential when they'd been an item. He didn't remember her being so eager to lead from the front then.

"How did you manage to come here on your own, Jayden. You haven't even got a boat." It was a question Stuart had been thinking to ask ever since Jayden told him he'd mapped the tunnels.

"I got into the disused 1848 tunnel through the emergency escape route but where we're going is a long way from there, and much more dangerous, parts of the old tunnels have collapsed. This way's quicker, safer."

"Temperature increase from zero to two degrees," announced Kevin when they were about two hundred yards inside the tunnel. The faint flicker of Sarah and Kylie's fire could still be seen behind them at the entrance.

"Four degrees."

Ten minutes in and the thick still air was suddenly dispersed by a great rush of wind blowing from deep within the tunnel. It caused the air pressure to drop. It almost seemed as if they were being sucked into a vortex.

"Just means we're approaching a connecting passageway," shouted Gaynor. "All completely normal so far."

Stuart glanced round at the others in the boat and the ghostly shape of the second boat following, with the three shadowy figures, perfectly still, lifeless. He thought of the River Styx, carrying the dead to the underworld, and he shuddered. He was blanketed in a feeling so heavy and doom-filled that he could hardly draw breath.

Despite his apprehension, he was fascinated to see how the tunnel had been constructed. One minute perfectly arched and lined with brick and the next minute bare stone where it had been tunnelled through solid rock. In one section, the overhead rock appeared to be bulging so far down it hardly looked passable. Small stalactites dangled down like dirty icicles.

Every so often there appeared strange symbols daubed in white paint on the walls and ceiling. Circles with central dots, triangles and weird squiggles that reminded Stuart of shapes he had seen in ancient burial chambers.

"What are those?" he asked, addressing his question to Gaynor.

It was Jayden who answered. "Nobody knows but I read somewhere that they're magic symbols."

"Do we know who put them there?"

"They were done when the tunnel was being built," Gaynor added. "They're symbols of protection. Whatever this is, it's been a threat for a long time."

After what seemed an interminable length of time, though was only fifteen minutes or so, the sound of falling water echoed through the darkness. The noise became deafening the closer they got.

"If you've got a hood, I suggest you put it up now." Gaynor advised.

Suddenly they were under a waterfall, pouring down on them through a ceiling of ill-fitted wooden beams.

"We'll be going through a few of these I'm afraid." Gaynor said, shaking the water from her jacket.

Fifteen minutes of oppressive darkness and falling water followed, serving only to feed Stuart's uneasiness. Another five minutes and an overhead bridge loomed into view, which Jayden explained was the main Leeds to Manchester railway line. It was somehow comforting to know that they weren't as far from civilisation as it seemed.

Ten minutes later, the landing stage that was their destination appeared out of the mist. Its white handrail reflected the torchlight with dazzling brilliance, turning the modern support into a welcoming beacon.

"Cut the engines." Gaynor instructed. "Film crew first, don't forget to secure the boats. You'll find hooks in the wall."

Just as Gaynor had said, at the end of the passageway were a flight of steps going up to another tunnel. This one was dry and smelled of mould and rats. In the distance they could hear the sound of gushing water coming from deep within the hillside. Turning left under Jayden's direction, they walked on through the disused tunnel, with the sound of water getting louder.

"We're approaching a motion sensor," Jayden's voice sounded reassuring in the unfamiliar darkness. "There'll be lights and a man's voice warning us to get out. Don't worry, it's just the railway...they don't want people wandering round in here, it's too dangerous."

"That's comforting," Martyn said with a hint of humour in his voice that wasn't doing a very good job of hiding his anxiety.

Sure enough as they slipped into another connecting passage, a high intensity light illuminated the whole area and a voice boomed out. "This is a restricted area. To avoid prosecution please leave immediately by the same way you entered."

Even though they'd been warned to expect it, everyone except Jayden and Gaynor were startled and unnerved.

"Are there cameras here?" asked Paul.

"No," Jayden shouted back, his face illuminated in the golden glare of the lamps. It'll go off in a minute. When it does make sure you don't move until your eyes get used to the dark again."

Sure enough, after only a matter of a few minutes they were plunged back into darkness with only the torches to light their way. Continuing on, they reached a series of large props, placed so as to hold up an area between the tunnel they were in and the one above. Water was cascading over the props and plummeting down into the depths of a deep pit.

A little further on, the floor had been patched up with heavy wooden planks. They could see the dark water of the canal glistening in the torchlight below. An adit, high up on the ceiling, brought a surprising and welcome breath of fresh night air but was soon left far behind.

"Watch where you put your feet," Jayden shouted. "There's a plug hole into the canal somewhere round here."

On reaching it, Stuart shone his torch down. It appeared to be bottomless, a black hole into Hell. He shivered at the thought of anyone or anything falling into it.

As they walked on through the deepening blackness, they passed more construction shafts and connecting tunnels, with drainage systems running in all directions.

"What are all these connecting tunnels for?" asked Stuart. "There's so many."

"Some are escape tunnels in case of emergency," explained Jayden. "But most are just connecting tunnels used in the construction. Don't forget, there's four tunnels here, but two of the railway tunnels aren't used."

The irony of being lectured by one of his students wasn't lost on Stuart. It made him smile even though every nerve in his body was tingling with fear and primed for flight. Still, he was wishing Jayden wasn't here. If anything happened to the lad, his job would definitely be for the chop. No second chances after this.

At last, Jayden stopped. "It's here," he announced, shining his torch on an alcove high up on the wall.

"Oh my," gasped Martyn. "That's fuckin' scary."

Cast in the shadow of the torchlight, the figure looked to be about eight inches tall, the same as the one Gaynor had in the bag, but this one had the demeanour of a warrior with a bulging torso that seemed to be rippling with muscle though was undoubtedly from the effects of its macabre stuffing. There were strange markings painted on its face and chest and it was wearing some sort of headdress. There was a large knife in its right hand.

Kevin had had the forethought to bring along a telescopic trekking pole and he reached up to hook the figure down. Just then there sounded a deep rumbling noise that seemed to shake the foundations of the hill itself. A strong wind began to blow out of nowhere and the ground under their feet began to shake. The noise was getting louder with every passing second and debris was falling from the walls and the roof.

Stuart fell to his knees, pulling Martyn down with him.

"It's only a train," yelled Jayden. "It's the Trans-Pennine forcing air along the tunnel above us. The wind is escaping into all the shafts. It'll stop in a minute."

The noise continued to increase until, at last, a train roared past in the live tunnel above them. The noise of it was almost unbearable and the amount of debris falling on their heads made Stuart wonder if the whole tunnel might collapse at any moment. The silence that followed was palpable and even more menacing than it had been before.

"Everybody okay?" Gaynor asked. The assurances she got in reply were drowned out by a noise coming from further along the tunnel. A deafening banging noise coming towards them, shaking the ground.

"Paul. Camera," yelled Gaynor. "This is it folks, brace yourselves."

Everyone's torch was directed down the tunnel in the direction they were travelling and what was illuminated was shocking to them all, even Gaynor who had seemed to know what to expect. The entity appeared to be flying up the tunnel towards them. The only thing visible was the huge head and bearded face, wearing a murderous expression. Gaynor, being at the front of the little group, would be in line for the first blast.

"Temperature drop to minus five," yelled Steve.

Stuart tried to push his way through the others, feeling the need to protect Gaynor, but Kevin held him back.

"Abaddon!" screamed Gaynor, arms outstretched, blocking its passage. "You will stop. NOW."

The demon began to laugh, the threatening scorn searing into them.

"Abaddon, Lord of perdition and destruction," Gaynor's voice could barely be heard over the monstrous laughter. "Your time here is at an end.

You have served this world well, you have worked hard and done many things but now it is time for you to rest. We send you all our love and compassion. We pass no judgement on you for we are all sinners."

The laughter stopped as abruptly as it had started but the rumbling voice that followed was worse, permeating every cell in their bodies, like swamp gas, seeping in and smothering them.

"You have no power over me. Your delusion makes you weak. You think your words of false love will banish me? You think I am bound by those things you carry?"

As the demon spoke, the full body materialised before them, filling the tunnel and blocking their passage. The mouth, with yellowed teeth, was cruel and monstrous, the bottom lip full and protruding underneath a large, crooked nose that seemed to be breathing out fire. The eyes were as black as the dark tunnel, with no spark of light there, not even a faint reflection of the torchlight.

"We must press on," Gaynor yelled. "If he does not move, we will walk through him. But all stay together, hold onto the person in front of you and keep right behind me."

And so they moved forward, as one body. Gaynor at the front, followed by Kevin and Martyn. Stuart was behind, holding onto Martyn's jacket with one hand and Jayden's arm with the other. Steve and Paul were bringing up the rear, camera still rolling.

The feel of the demon was icy cold as they passed through him, causing the torches to flicker and die, one by one. It was like walking through a threshold from life into death. Stuart felt his heart racing and his breath coming in short, sharp rasps that were painful in his chest. He felt like he was going to faint. The air seemed to have taken on a heaviness that was still and stale. He began to feel dizzy. There was no oxygen. They were all going to die down here and no one would ever find them.

"We need to go back," he gasped, letting go of Martyn's jacket and turning round only to blunder into the cameraman. His knees were giving way, his legs had turned to jelly.

"No, Mr Ryder. It's the demon," Jayden was holding him up and dragging him forwards with the strength of a man. When did he become so strong? Even in his pain, Stuart was rationalising the fact that great panic confers great strength. Jayden must be more terrified than him. He was just a kid after all. Stuart tried to focus his eyes. Everything was blurred, the darkness, the black of the crumbling tunnel walls, the shadowy figures all around him but there was something else, something casting a faint glow, it was coming from around Jayden—a light, an aura of gold, sparkling with flashes of silver.

"Jayden, Jayden..." as Stuart whispered his name, the light brightened.

"Don't worry, sir," Jayden said in a voice that betrayed no sign of panic. "I'll protect you."

In the all consuming blackness, Gaynor's torch spluttered back to life. The other torches followed.

"Is the camera still rolling, Paul?"

"Affirmative."

"Kevin, what about the spirit box? How's that doing?"

"We're suddenly picking up a multitude. They appear to be coming out of the walls. EVPs coming thick and fast as well. Names, cries for help. And what seem to be warnings."

"Okay, make sure it's all being recorded. We're going to press on. There will be another attack. It's not going to go without a fight but remember, keep strong, keep a clear head and, most importantly, whatever happens, don't show fear."

Her words struck terror in Stuart's heart. He was the weak link here. He seemed to be the only one who was frightened half to death. And he was the one the demon could fuse with. He was the one who would let them down. As that last thought came into his head, there was an almighty crash behind them, followed by the sound of falling earth. Steve shone his torch down the tunnel where they had just been standing. The tunnel was nothing but a pile of rubble. The roof had caved in. They were trapped.

"Okay, keep calm." Gaynor's voice didn't waiver. "We're not trapped. There are still escape tunnels along this section. Come on, we have a job to do."

With that she strode forward into the darkness, her footsteps crunching on the loose pebbles that now covered the floor.

She was plucky, he would give her that. Yet he knew it was the promise of fame that was driving her. She wanted to nail this, wanted to be remembered. Whatever the cost to herself or them. For the first time, Stuart realised that could be a lethal mix. He knew she would do whatever it took to prove the reality of life beyond the grave.

"You okay, sir?"

Jayden's concern made Stuart feel stupid, humiliated. Here he was, a grown man, being looked after by a kid.

"Get your hands off me," he yelled, pulling himself away.

He felt his face burning, his eyes were smarting from the heat. He reached out behind him, grabbing Paul's camera, intending to throw it to the ground. Kevin was on him immediately, pulling him down. He felt a knee in his neck, his arms were yanked behind his back.

"Get a rope, a tie, anything," Gaynor was yelling. "Bind him for God's sake or we're finished."

Stuart was confused. What the hell was happening. Why were they hurting him. He felt his wrists being bound together, then his ankles, and then they rolled him over onto his back. The world looked strange from down here. There was a golden glow in the shape of a man looking down at him, surrounded by hundreds of shining orbs, dancing around, colliding into each other. He felt like he was on fire, burning up from the inside. He opened his mouth to speak but all that came out was a deafening, angry roar—a wounded animal caught in a trap.

A face drew close to his, coming down from above. It was Martyn, his friend.

"Almighty and most merciful God, we thy servants approach with fear and trembling before thee, and in all humility do beseech thee to pardon our blind transgressions. Grant oh most merciful Father, for His sake who died upon the cross, that our minds may be enlightened with the divine radiance of thy holy wisdom."

Another face drew close, this one holding up a cross before it. It was a child, an angelic being with hair of gold and plump, firm cheeks that shone with light.

The full horror of what was happening shot through Stuart like a bolt of lightning. He had been taken over. He was the demon. He must fight it. Evict it. He had to make it let go. He prayed in silence to a God he had never before believed in. He felt it loosen but then as soon as his resolve weakened it was back with more force than before.

"Open, O blessed spirit, the spiritual eye of his soul, that he may be released from this darkness that is spreading over him by the delusions of the outward senses." Stuart recognised Martyn's voice but his words were hurting him, like salt rubbed into raw flesh. "We pray thee, O Lord, above all to strengthen our souls and bodies against our spiritual enemies, by the blood and righteousness of our blessed redeemer, they son, Jesus Christ; and through him, and in his name, we beseech thee to save us from this enemy that lies before us."

Stuart was filled with rage. This was the one who had tried to banish him before. This was the one who had to be ripped from this place.

"Give us the strength to stand firm and unshaken against this evil spirit with whom we desire no communication."

Stuart's body was being torn apart from the inside. Organs tearing, blood gushing out of broken arteries. Stuart could feel it all, the stabs of pain were everywhere. He tried to scream but the only sound he could hear was the rush of his blood as it coursed along the tunnels of his life to leave his body. He felt his energy draining away, sinking into the dirt floor. He was tired, so tired.

"For God's sake, Stuart, fight it."

Was that Gaynor? No, that was Sarah's voice. Sarah. The woman who had killed his child. He roared again with every ounce of strength he could muster. The ties that were binding him broke asunder. Rising up into the shadows, he roared his intention.

"I am Abaddon. I am come from the seventh mansion where the furies possess and are given breath. I shall destroy and waste with war and evil discord. You cannot bind me. I am eternal."

They looked so small, those little beings who thought to banish him. But there was one, the smallest yet with the brightest light. That one was to be feared. That was the powerful one. The one who could harm.

"Abaddon! Abaddon! Come, I have something for you."

The head, feeling like a boulder on his shoulders, swung round to see who had called him.

The woman who had befriended him was standing, holding the two waxen figures that were binding him in these dark tunnels. He needed to destroy them. Only then would he be truly free.

"Give," he commanded.

"Come and get them," the woman cried and set off running away from him, running towards the deep pit.

He set off after her, a part of him was running and yet a part of him felt like he was floating. He was fragmented, split like an apple cleaved in two. He thought again of Sarah. Sweet Sarah. He had treated her so callously. As that thought seeped into the deepest part of his brain, he fell to the ground, feeling like he had run into a brick wall. Martyn's face was next to his immediately. It sounded like he was reciting another one of his mother's prayers.

"Oh mighty and most merciful God, please send your son to us in this our dire need. Please Lord, deliver us from this evil."

And then a gentle hand reached down and touched Stuart's arm. "You okay, sir?"

321

Was that Jayden? His face was illuminated by torchlight and his eyes were shining with a strange inner light. How come Stuart had never noticed that before?

"You're safe now, sir. I'll stay with you."

"We need to go after Gaynor." It was Kevin who spoke, his face ashen in the white light of Paul's head torch.

"You need to be careful," Jayden warned. "The pit we were going to throw those dolls in isn't far from here."

A piercing scream followed by an almighty roar shook the tunnels. The four men set off running, torches flickering, lighting up the darkness ahead.

62

The fire spluttered and crackled as dry leaves fell into the flames, blown to their fate by an icy breeze that was starting to blow. It had been three hours since the others had gone into the tunnel and Sarah and Kylie were becoming more anxious with every measured minute that passed.

The yellow light from the fire was casting a comforting glow but the flames were spitting like angry sprites demanding more food. Dancing shadows played hide and seek on their faces, distorting their features into macabre parodies of themselves. The small campfire had already consumed most of the stockpile of old branches and twigs and they would soon have to brave the cold and darkness to go and collect more.

Sarah looked at her watch.

"Why's it taking so long? They should be back by now."

"Try not to worry," Kylie assured her. "If anything was wrong, I'm sure Ron would have let me know."

What Kylie didn't say was that Ron had been unusually silent for days, ever since their talk of going into the tunnel as it happened. Was that coincidence? Kylie didn't think so. Having warned her about the tunnel once, and been ignored, perhaps he had given up on her and left.

If that was true, she wasn't sure how she felt about it. She'd grown quite used to having a spiritual companion, though she had to admit she had become weary of his whistling and the thought of him being an intrusion had unnerved her so much that she had started having nightmares again.

An owl screeched from a tree high on the banking, making her jump. She thought of a screaming banshee and shuffled a little closer to the fire.

"What do you make of everything that's happened, Kylie?" Sarah asked. "Have you found it as hard as I have to separate reality from the paranormal."

Kylie shrugged. "I think there's been a lot of stuff going on that we didn't know about."

"You mean Gaynor?"

"Not just her. Jayden too."

"Why? What's he been up to?"

"I don't quite know. All I know is that Gaynor referred to him as the Magician in the tarot. He'd appeared in a reading she'd done."

"Gaynor and her tarot cards!" Sarah exclaimed with more sarcasm than usual. "You'll believe anything."

"You should try and be a bit more open-minded, Sarah," Kylie said, feeling more affronted then usual by Sarah's denial of things she didn't understand. "Gaynor told me that he would be important in getting us through this but that we wouldn't recognise his worth. She said he was special."

Sarah laughed. "In what way?"

"She didn't say, but there is something unusual about him. I can see that. I just can't quite figure him out. Don't tell me you haven't noticed."

"I suppose. I know when we swapped stories about what had happened to us both, it was him comforting me, not the other way round."

"Old beyond his years. And fearless."

Sarah threw the last of the twigs onto the fire.

"Foolhardy more like. Fancy a lad his age going into those tunnels on his own."

Just then the sound of an outboard motor cut through the night.

"They're back. Come on." Both women ran down to the water's edge, blankets pulled tight around them.

The first boat to emerge from the tunnel was carrying the cameraman and his assistant, with Kevin at the tiller, clutching the spirit box to his chest.

Kylie helped them onto the bank. "What happened? Where are the others? Did you see it?"

None of them answered.

Steve slumped down onto the frozen ground, head in hands. Kevin remained by the mooring, eyes fixed on the tunnel entrance. The cold night air was vaporising his breath, making a ghostly shadow of smoke around his head. Paul had run up the banking. They could hear him retching.

"Where's Stuart?" Sarah yelled, breaking the silence. Kylie grabbed her arm, pulling her away from the water's edge.

Just then the faint chug chug of the second boat filled the night. As the dark hull appeared from the black void of the tunnel, they could see Stuart and Martyn sitting opposite each other, crouched over and looking small. Jayden was standing at the helm, steering the boat alongside the banking.

"Where's Gaynor?" shouted Kylie. "For God's sake, where is she?"

Ignoring her, Stuart stumbled from the boat, almost missing his footing on the slippery bank. Sarah grabbed him, pulling him to safety.

"I'm so sorry," he said, his voice little more than a whisper. "It's my fault. I wasn't strong enough."

Kevin was at his side immediately, pulling him away from Sarah's arms.

"Haven't you sussed it yet?" he yelled. "You were the bait. It was bound to follow with you there. Gaynor knew what she was doing. She had it all worked out. We saw what happened."

"What did happen?" demanded Sarah.

"She jumped...with those wax dolls in her hands...and it followed."

"She'll get her wish," Paul announced as he made his way back down the bank, holding out his camera. His voice was as cold as the night air. "This is what she wanted."

"No," cried Stuart. "She wouldn't have sacrificed her life for a story that no one's going to believe."

"Oh, they'll believe alright," Paul rebuked. "She's made sure of it. I got it all on camera, every minute, all of it."

Martyn, who had been silent so far, was standing at the side of the canal, looking over at Jayden who hadn't yet stepped off the boat. The black hull, almost invisible against the dark water, gave the impression that there was no boat beneath him.

"Are you okay, Martyn?" Kylie asked, removing the blanket from her shoulders and wrapping it around him.

He nodded in the direction of the water. "What do you see?"

Kylie looked. "It's Jayden."

"Look closer."

She screwed up her eyes to see better in the dim light. "That's weird. There seems to be a faint glow around him."

"You should have seen it in the tunnel," Martyn said. "Gaynor was convinced that we're all made from the same stuff. Not good, not bad; just a mix of everything. But she was wrong."

"What do you mean?"

Martyn took hold of Kylie's hand and placed it on the pocket Bible that his mother had insisted he carry.

"What we battled in there was pure evil. And wherever it's gone, Gaynor has gone with it."

"It was her choice."

"She didn't realise what it was."

"No one knows what it was, not for sure. Gaynor set out to prove to the world that other life forms exist and she's done that. We'll never know if it was a demon or not."

"I know," Martyn said, turning his gaze back to Jayden. "And I want everyone else to know. Because if demons exist, then so do angels."

THE END

Afterword

- being the last entry in Gaynor's research diary.

The expedition to send Abaddon back where he came from may well be the last thing I do.

Whether I return or not, I will be remembered as the woman who proved to the world that sentient beings are able to cross over from other dimensions and that they, like us, are manifestations of the conscious universe.

I have no doubt that individual consciousness persists, no matter where we are in this vast, cosmic landscape. I do believe we are immortal.

There is an immense force at work that is neither good nor bad, it just is. It is the creative spark that began as a singularity in the deep, black void of nothingness. It is omnipresent and omniscient, and every one of its manifestations possesses those same qualities. We do not see it because we are hypnotised by the heavy vibrations of this planet.

Sometimes, as it is with Abaddon, the energy of a manifestation has harmful consequences in its expression. In such cases, if it is returned to the source, the energy it holds can be transmuted.

I have been called to act as a psychopomp.

I cannot refuse. It is my destiny.

Note from the author

The idea for this book came from a ghost hunting evening at Standedge Tunnel in West Yorkshire.

To be honest, the evening was a little disappointing as we were expecting to be taken into the tunnel where surely there would be a multitude of ghostly goings on. Sadly, we were confined to the visitor centre and the grounds outside.

Nevertheless, I did capture one or two orbs on camera and we were given the opportunity to use some of the equipment brought by the psychic investigators leading the expedition.

Also, while there, we were advised to download the recommended ghost detecting App, which I have used to great effect during the writing of this book.

Be assured, there are certainly more things twixt Heaven and Earth than this world dreams of.

Which brings me to Abaddon; the demon in my story. Early on in the writing of this book I decided that my demon, with the imposing black beard, should have a name. I selected 'Abaddon' at random from a list of demons mentioned in the Hebrew Bible. I chose it because the harsh sounds of the consonants intimidated me and, besides, I thought it a very apt name for 'a bad one'.

On finishing the book, I accidentally stumbled on an 1801 publication by Francis Barrett, described as 'A complete system of occult philosophy, alchemy and magic lore.' To my horror, or joy depending on how you view demons, I was shocked to see that the illustration of Abaddon was uncannily similar to how I had described him.

I must now ask myself, 'Did Abaddon come uninvited and write himself into my story, or did I summon him?'

And more importantly, 'Is he still here?'

I'll let you, the reader, answer those questions for I would rather not know.

After reading this book, if you choose to believe that demons are not real, I hope you are strong enough to defend yourself against them. For it is well documented that such psychic intruders are all around us, seeking out every opportunity to haunt our imagination and our dreams.

And remember, it's not always easy to separate reality from the supernatural. My advice to you is that you say your prayers before you go to sleep tonight.

Illustration of the demon Abaddon from *The Magus
- A complete system of occult philosophy, alchemy
and magic lore.* by Francis Barrett (1801)

Printed in Great Britain
by Amazon